SOMETHING TERRIBLE,
SOMETHING LOVELY

By the same author

FIREMAN FLOWER
THREE
THE BODY
SOUTH
THE FACE OF INNOCENCE
THE PASSIONATE NORTH
A BED OF ROSES

C. 2

WILLIAM SANSOM

Something Terrible, Something Lovely

NEW YORK

Harcourt, Brace and Company

For
RUTH SHERADSKI

NOTE

Acknowledgements are made to the editors of the following publications, in which these stories first appeared: *Horizon, Penguin New Writing, Polemic, New Writing and Daylight, Orion, The Cornhill Magazine, English Story, Choice, Life and Letters, The Wind and the Rain, At Close of Eve, A Map of Hearts, The First Eighteen, Writing To-day.*

CONTENTS

Readers who are delighted by tales of horrifying revelation will welcome *Something Terrible, Something Lovely*. It describes those emotional crises when a slight, subtle shift of reality compels us to see everything afresh — with wonder, with fascination, or with horror. Mr. Sansom explores these crises with a fresh and untainted understanding — and the result is a power to shock which is surpassed by none of his contemporaries. It is rare indeed to find the gifts of an artful storyteller so strongly reinforced by an illuminating and sensuous intelligence.

Something Terrible, Something Lovely

THE day slate-dark, the air still, the cindertrack by the cottages empty and without life in a watered middle-day light—and young Nita came running, running home from school. Her satchel swung behind her, the blue exercise book fluttered its white leaves in her windmill hand, thin long legs and young-boned knees pranced before her like the separate legs of a pony careering the rest of her along. High on the brow of the slope that led down to the cottages she was already singing it out: "Dody! Dody!" so that her young voice shrill with life and so excited echoed round the black cindered emptiness of that path, sang in and out of the bricked cottage yards, rained against blind windows, rose and died with the tops of the green elms above the grey roofs, above the smoke that seemed to smell of cooked meat and coal.

Dody, her younger cousin, was squatting in the yard winding a little gramophone. The gramophone disc rotated at a wild speed, hurrying round ever faster to tin out a shrill voice that pranced up and down, as though its very bladder were bursting among the blazers and the pier-stage somewhere down the dark tin horn, screaming among the old jazz instruments to get off the stage and out of the box: 'Swanee, Swanee, How I love you, *How* I love you . . .' When Nita banged through the wooden yard gate and clustered herself feverishly down, all in one piece, satchel, hat, skirts, curls, like a bird alighting with wings askew by Dody's ear, the gramophone went on singing. She put her arm round Dody's neck and breathlessly whispered into her ear. Dody's eyes went round and fascinated, her mouth pressed itself small as though she would cry: the voice kept whispering, Nita's eyes opened and shut and rolled with every terrible word, her head waved from side to side, retreated, then back came those lips, wet and hot with breath close to the ear. 'I saw it . . . there, right in front it was, plain as day . . . I don't know how long, since yesterday I'm sure . . . anyone could see . . .' In short, dreadful gasps the whispers came out, the chattering secret. A silence, long and wise, as the two girls squatted and gazed at each other. Then from Dody a deep, heart-blown sigh. From Nita a nod, then emphatic quickening nods, one after the other, racing up to get breath to tell it all again, the lovely terrible thing.

For nothing like this had ever happened before—that was plain from the start. There had been terrible things before, as when the sweetshop woman fell on the line two summers ago, on a hot afternoon, and the train had run right over her. That was terrible, especially as it had been a picnic afternoon, hot and all the flowers out—but it was funny, too, when they made jokes afterwards about strawberry jam. And there was the time when the Leadbetters had suddenly gone: one day there were all the Leadbetters, seven of them from Granny Lead- better to little Angela, living in the cottage one door from the end—and then the next day they'd gone, there were no Lead- betters! A van had called, people said, in the night. Not a stick of a table or a chair was left in the cottage. The cottage was there still, Number Six still, but no Leadbetters! And no- body would say why or how. People knew, but there was something awful that they would never tell. They frowned, they pressed their lips into ruler-lines. 'Don't ask no questions,' they said, 'and you know what you won't be told none of.' Nita and Dody had asked for weeks, they had stood outside Number Six and peered into the windows. They had rattled the back door and kicked the empty bottles. The newspaper man had even left the Sunday paper sticking in the letterbox, the dead letterbox. Since then, no Leadbetter had ever been seen. They had gone in a hush. There was something nasty about the Leadbetters.

Those events were memorable but they were memories only, misted and vague as the uncley sort of God one heard stories about in Sunday School. But here—here was something new, alive, overwhelming, something that was happening now, at

2

the very minute, as the clock ticked, as the church bell tolled!
The church bell just then tolled suddenly, like some great
celestial dustbin-lid beaten against the grey sky, and then
started its measured echoing march through the September
Wednesday noon. The children whispered frantically. The
gramophone whirred round grating and clicking; the singing
had stopped. All about that little yard, with its washing hanging abandoned, its pramwheels and cans and its derelict
wooden hutch—all this stayed empty and desolate as the
cinderpath. But the children felt none of it. They saw none of
the lowering green leaves against that slatey sky with its white-
bottomed clouds, nor the vegetable green of the little leaves
climbing the elm-trunks, nor the old tin shelters with the weeds
in them and the jars of dried paintbrushes, nor the allotment
beyond, nor the blanched grey of the walls of the seven
cottages—a scene of only grey and heavy green and cinder-
black.

"What shall we do? What shall we do . . .?" chattered Dody
to Nita and Nita to Dody, making backwards and forwards
glances wise and sophisticated, lunatic and tender. At eight
and nine years of age their faces were old in gesture, their ex-
pressions poised into magical replicas of feelings that they
seemed to expect rather than experience. And suddenly Nita
was saying over for the twentieth time, "*Who* could have done
it? Who *could* have done it?" Dody jumped up and clapped her
hands and began dancing. "Dody knows, Dody knows what
we'll do . . ." she sang, chanted, repeated hopping round the
yard with her eyes brilliant and mad. She suddenly ran back
to Nita and said what was very simple, but to these two an idea
of impossible daring, a breath-taking stroke. "It was the boys
done it," Dody said. "We'll do it back on the boys!"

They both gasped. Nita's hand was up at her mouth. She
was going to cry or to laugh, something was bursting in her.
But all she did was to say in a little voice, not exactly her own:
"What'll we do then?"·

Dody laughed and screamed delightedly: 'We'll do it back
on the boys . . .'

"What? What though?" whispered Nita, who knew.

3

"The same, the same!" screamed Dody, then clapped her hand over her mouth.

Nita nestled close up to her, took her arm, ran over to the corner of the yard, then whispered more slowly but with her eyes bright with appetite for the words she knew would come but only wanted to hear over and over again: "Tell, tell! Tell me what we'll do, Dody . . ."

Dody bent her head and whispered it again.

Their hot dinner never seemed to be going to end, though that in itself was delicious. Nita's Mum, in her apron still, gave them their mutton boiled juicy grey and the white wet potatoes. And all through Nita and Dody kept tittering, staring at each other across the cruet with fearful eyes, then looking down at their plates and spooning round the barley in that gluey pale gravy. Nita's Mum kept asking them what was the matter. Then they hung their heads, continuing on a lower plane and with slanted eyes the same exchange of secret glances and held giggles. Once Nita sang out, "Oh dear, what can the matter be?"—but Dody, crammed with barley, nearly choked herself, and at this Nita's Mum lost patience and told them to go straight up to their bedroom without any pudding. And that was just what they wanted, to slide out on the linoleum, with the blessed door closed behind them, to leap up the stairs away from the white table-cloth and its bread-crumbs, up to the bedspread where they just burst themselves laughing and where Nita suddenly stopped and said confidentially: "Tell, tell."

Half an hour later Dody said, "Where's your box? We'll need the you-know-what . . ."

Nita's face fell, suddenly blank, as though now there was something to hide. She fidgeted. Then she looked up tearfully. "I forgot, I haven't got any."

Dody jumped up appalled. "Where is it? Where is it?" And when Nita pointed miserably to the washstand where, between the soap-dish and the white water-jug a pencil-box jutted out woodenly—she ran across the room and fingered it open in a second. Inside there were ink-stains, a green Koh-i-noor, a stub of pink rubber stabbed with black pencil-marks, two paper-clip-hair-pins. Dody turned round wailing, "There isn't any. There isn't any . . ."

At which Nita sat bolt upright and said, thoughtfully, tragically, slowly: "At any rate, I've still got my penny."

"Your penny!"

"My penny."

"PENNY!"

In a moment they were chattering again, the penny was out, they were fingering it with love, and Dody said again and again: "We can get lots of it now."

"Lots of what?"

"Lots of you-know-what!"

"When?"

"Oh, now, now, now now now . . ."

Nita rose then to her feet, a dreadful pallor straining her face with age and sickness. "Oh," she said, "it's Wednesday!"

"*Wednesday!*" Dody mouthed after her, as though she were munching something she would never swallow. "Shop's shut!"

That night they knew they would do it to-morrow. That night was as long as one of the nights sometime before Christmas, when Christmas is near yet still will never hurry nearer, as long too as the nights of early bed in the summer when the windows were open and the music of the fair came so clearly across the common. That night the windows were open too, but outside it was dark, dark and warm, telling about the winter in the wrong way, without any cold, and thus in a queer way threatening; like some Monday nights in the kitchen with the washing about, when nobody could be bothered with you, when the minutes stopped altogether and no treats lay ahead. To-night though, there was something ahead, but still there was the waiting, and so the room lay deadly and the electric light beaming out at the back dull and unmoving.

They were told off for bed early, as soon as that September

dark came down, and when they had washed nestled near on the big pillow, sucking the stringy ends of the white coverlet, making caves in the pillow and telling, over and over again, telling. Word for word Dody knew and Nita knew exactly what was to happen, but the words themselves had to be repeated, and each time marvellously they brought the picture succulently clear.

"When'll we go to the shop?" Nita whispered.

"In breaktime."

"What'll we ask for?"

"Chalk."

"A ha'penny-worth?"

"Pennyworth! A whole pennyworth!"

Then there was a giggling, and suddenly Nita stopped. Her voice sounded terrified, and as though it wanted to be terrified. "And what if someone sees? What if one of the boys comes round the corner, just then, and *sees*?"

Dody mouthed fiercely, idiotically with her tongue stuck out in the dark: "We'll run and run and run and *run!*"

But the telling could only last minutes at a time. In between they lay in silence, thinking hard, the thoughts racing, but far too fast for the minutes, or for the long-drawn-out darkness marked only by faint noises from downstairs, from Nita's mum's cough, from Dad's rustling paper. The light from the stairs came through the door and made a patch like a clown's hat on the ceiling. There was a soapy smell.

Once, much later, as they were at last nearly asleep, Dody pushed her head nearer and whispered, much nearer than before, and as though she had been thinking of this all the time: "I say Nita . . ."

Nita whispered: "Yes?"

"I say you don't . . . do you?"

A pause, fearful and long. "Don't what, Dody?"

Dody breathed quickly. "Love Stan?"

The pillow heaved up, it was Nita turning and pressing her face hard into the pillow, gritting her teeth, stopping herself from saying anything, from crying, from laughing, from screaming, from showing any of herself even in the dark. The dark whirled round her like a blush. But then her head was up again and she laughed: "Who, me? What you take *me* for?"

The next day was dull and low-clouded as before, the pale smoke from the cottage chimneys pencilled up paler than the sky, almost white against the dying green of the beeches above: pencilled, then blew suddenly down untidily on to the roofs, as though some huge invisible bird had swooped past. There were the beginnings of small winds, but the day was too heavy for them; the grey roofs seemed to shine against such a weight of dullness.

Though Dody and Nita had awoken early, breakfast was a scramble—and they went off to school much earlier than usual. But outside the school gates and in the playground there lay a vast emptiness, as though nothing were ever to happen again—nobody there, the doors open, and the clock outside resting its gold hands at half-past-eight. That clock seemed to have stopped. And when at last the other children came first drifting then running hot-faced in, and school was assembled, the other clock in the inky oak classroom seemed also to keep stopping. So the morning dawdled, stopping and dragging, towards eleven.

At half-past ten their excitement returned, they began to feel the eyes of the others, their secret grew huge and vulnerable again. Earlier, Nita had stared blushing at the book, sure that the others knew and were looking and laughing at her: but soon, when she had looked round, it had been disappointing to see that no one at all was taking any notice of her. Now, at twenty-five to eleven, the feeling came back: soon they were to do this thing and so it seemed that everyone knew about it. By five to eleven they were looking at each other and at the clock, it seemed an endless time—when a miracle happened! The Mistress suddenly shut the book from which she had been reading and herself looked up at the clock. Just then the clock jumped a minute forward, and this must have decided her, for she smiled and said: "All right. Off you go—*quietly*, children."

7

They walked to the door and then bolted down the steps and out onto the asphalt, out through the gate and never stopped until they were at the shop. Nita handed over her penny clasped hot and stayed outside while Dody went in. The shop-door bell rang loud and crisp like a tram-bell, much too loud, startling, so that Nita looked fearfully up and down the street. If the boys heard, they would know—for sure, for sure! But there was only a soldier in washed blue sitting on a bench, two old ladies with shopping baskets looking at a cat. The cat rubbed itself up against their black skirts and the ladies laughed, one stroked it with her stick. The street had an empty look, no cars, no bicycles, and thus it seemed all the more empty for the ringing and echoing chattering cries of all the children hidden away in the playground round the corner. The bell clanged again and Dody crashed out holding something small hard against her breast, and nodding with her chin right in, and holding out urgently one hand to drag Nita in the direction her legs seemed already to be running. They ran together, away from the school, and Dody whispered: "Yellow and white pieces she gave me—lots—come on . . ."

Up the road, up the steep road, higher and higher up to the asylum! The asylum tower, purple and green, stood out above them, very near, but the asylum wall was really much further away when you were down in the streets. And the streets suddenly ended, the common began. They raced along, hurrying against the minutes, the fifteen minutes of Break, and came to where the may-bushes started and the ground rose to meet the beginning of the tall asylum wall.

Here a chalky, scrap-grass path led in between the may-bushes. Along this they ran, along by the rainy smell from under the bushes. The wall came suddenly, and then the path continued straighter between the wall, high and purple and iron-spiked on the top, and the dark underneath of the straggling may-bush wood. The may stopped, and the other bushes withering dark-green with their dusty crimson berries —and Nita stopped too. Dody stopped. They could peer out now at the huge asylum wall curling out into the open, standing high and commanding over the open common. Deep purple and darker glazed bricks, severe and authoritative, glowered at the open grass that fanned away on all sides down from it. This wall was the summit point of the common, the place to which everyone eventually walked—and now Nita pointed in its direction and whispered: "Look! Look! *There!*"

They looked round then fearfully. No one in sight. Only the bare common, gorse, chalk-patches, dying grass. They left the may-bushes and raced off up towards the wall, two small figures growing smaller up the slope, growing murky like half-seen flies in all that dull, dead common-land.

Later, when they had gone, the wall still stood glowering out over the empty common. Once a watery sunlight opened up and for a moment chalk boulders and something metal like a can winked weakly, the pale copper-green asylum cupola glittered into transient life. Then it was as dark, darker than before. A single cyclist was drawn slowly as on a string across some distant intersecting path. The leaves of the few straggling trees hung still, dark green and hardened, shrunk to the last point before they would turn colour. And on the wall, intimately lonely among the greater lonelinesses of the weather and that wide vacant space, there could be read two messages written in chalk, white on the purple brick, spidery and scrawled straight capital letters, words that looked bare and cold out there in the open:

NITA HOBBS LOVES STAN CHUTER .

A long chalk line had been drawn through this, and underneath was written, emphatically, with yellow first letters to each word:

THE PERSON WHO WROTE THIS IS DAFT.

The Cliff

PODEVIN had finally parted from a love of many years, and guided by some sort of desperate wish for new horizons, for a breath of air, for detachment in fact—he had taken a journey to the sea-coast.

It might be argued that now he was more attached than ever, for now he had memories to contend with; but to Podevin walking high up a cliff path it seemed that at last he could taste the feeling of freedom. If only during these moments of his walk indeed, for afterwards—he knew enough of life—he might well be enclosed in a great loneliness and then all his energies would be expended in the search among people and among things for a way out. But during these instants of echoing sea air and sweet-smelling brambles, of wide breezes and the coastline lying mapped far ahead—he felt the sense of freedom.

Dark clouds moved at a flying speed across the sky ahead—astonishing, for only a light breeze blew on the path—but such a thunderous pace and such dark riders suited the rockbound coast, they shadowed the sea so that it lay bleak and hard as slate, they drew from the silent cliffs some of the venom latent in that primeval stone. Then, far along the coastline, the sun shone, illuminating like a searchlight a distant headland of yellow corn. This startling projection of yellow nosed right out into the slate-dark sea. The searchlight travelled and lighted on two gull-rocks, bringing from them a similar yellow gleam, so that for a moment of comedy they became two female haystacks drawing shyly away to sea, away from the nosing of the yellow corn-mouse. But this happened in a land remote from the barren cliffs upon which Podevin walked. Such cliffs as these could never smile, they were huge and desolate, precipitous to the sea, cragged, bouldered, with steep walls touched by no live thing but weeds and the ghostly gulls.

At frequent points the sea had bitten into these stone giants, small pebbled coves had formed, the cliffs had subsided—but ungraciously, clawing instantly round each erosion with sharp and predatory pincers of rock. Now Podevin arrived above one of these coves. He looked down. The path divided into two, one continuing along the top of the cliff, the other zig-zagging dizzily down the almost vertical descent to a small circular beach quite enclosed. His eyes focused on something white lying on the grey pebbles far beneath. Although it lay still, as still as the rocks themselves, his eye fixed upon it immediately, instantly alert—for it was a human body. Far below imprisoned at the bottom of this deep grey cylinder lay the little figure of a human being, a woman; she lay motionless, in a white bathing costume, asleep or waiting for the sun.

Podevin stood still. Just then the sun broke through again—but this time it cast its searchlight into the cove. The sea flashed blue, the grey stone boulders grew shadows and lived, and round the rocks below the shallow water gleamed with translucent green and purple. The girl's legs shone whitely as gulls' wings. Podevin took a step towards the path down into the cove.

No act is ever performed for one reason alone. One reason may predominate—but this is too easily annotated as the unique agent by minds that of their nature crave for simplification. But men and men's minds are not so simple as the creeds they evolve, men are much more cautious than this. Before any real decision is taken, every concomitant ingredient of the moment, every possibility of profit and loss is weighed and measured instantaneously by the mechanism of past influence and future desire; man moves only according to the answer he records, adjusted or maladjusted, right or wrong. And just so in Podevin's walk many influences were at work— the cove appeared, the girl, the fortuitous sunlight. The sea air had freshened his lungs. The smell of wild flowers, simple and erotic, was blown at him and mixed itself with the virility of the salt air. He was free; he felt therefore capable. Momentarily a sense of guilt came to repress him, and then was lifted, adding thus by its released check to the impetus of freedom. Quite by chance, and despite the fact that he travelled alone, he had been given a double room in his lodging house—this he now remembered vividly. And perhaps he was moved most of all—here is the influence that must be presumed dominant— by the recession of what had only some hours before seemed the deepest sorrow of his life.

In the train his throat had been choked, he had kept his eyes strained on his book fearful that someone might talk to him. Only once throughout the long journey he had risen—to give his seat to a nurse, whose thanks he had then been unable to receive with grace, so that he had turned to stand in the corridor, never daring throughout the journey to look back into the carriage again. Later he had strolled hopelessly out on to the harbour quay; he found it barren, but knew how much beauty they together would have found. He wished, how he wished for her! He saw only her image as he most admired her—all the uglinesses that had frustrated him were unexpectedly forgotten. His regret had grown unbearable. He had even returned to the station and had bought a ticket, intending suddenly to return. But there had been no train. He had decided to climb out of this village of blank faces, to walk alone on the cliff.

Self-pity overwhelmed him, overwhelmed poor Poddy as he suddenly saw himself, as he imagined old friends might talk of him, poor Poddy the lonely ego of his mother's choice, Poddy he had seen in mirrors, long-nosed Poddy who seemed never more than a passenger, his only anchors certain intimate habits—Poddy never wearing a vest winter or summer, Poddy who liked very much the crisp knuckle at the end of the joint. Poddy of certain past achievements, too, standing out from the past as though he had been photographed—Poddy who had worn a white suit once at a regatta somewhere, Poddy who had played a shuffling game with his woman shussss-ing the autumn leaves over a gravel path. Poddy secretive and smelling of chlorine in the locked cubicle of a swimming bath.

Now—magically it seemed—this 'poor Poddy' could scarcely be recollected. Podevin had grown strong again, over-strong. He took the first step towards the path, then paused a moment longer, assessing quickly whether his intrusion upon the girl's solitude might not appear too obvious—and then this last diffidence was rejected and he was clambering fast down the path to the cove. His momentum increased, he felt that nothing now was beyond his power. The exhilaration of a swift descent to level land gripped him—the dangerous heights were left behind, the ground approached where men's feet trod securely. Podevin felt the stretch of his diaphragm and the alert poise of his whole able body as he leapt running down the path. . . .

At the bottom the beach was shielded by a high ridge of rocks. There the grass straggled on to a preliminary drift of white and grey pebbles; but to arrive at the beach proper it was necessary to circumvent the rock-screen and pass through a narrow alley close against the perpendicular cliff itself; otherwise out by the sea, over wet and slippery rocks, pools and brown weed left bare by the low tide. Podevin hesitated. The girl was hidden from him. What would he say?

But he was beyond policy, he was breathing hard and only thought: 'Say anything, and be damned.' He kicked the twisted white raffia of a dried-up root and sent it circling like a spider down the pebbles. 'And damn that, too. Damn the whole damned world.' He looked round at the rocks with contempt.

Then, as he started towards the alley between the rocks and the cliff wall, he looked up. For the first time he noticed the full weight of the cliff looming over him. Above its dizzying skyline the clouds raced, driving inland, so for a moment it seemed that the cliff moved, gradually pivoting over its huge mass on to the beach and on to Podevin in particular. At once he felt that he was threatened. He said upwards to the cliff, aloud: "And damn you, too."

He regretted this instantly. He stepped on towards the cliff, further beneath it. Now his foot trod tenderly, as though it wished to tread in silence, and his eyes were still raised to the cliff-top—he was forced to keep a watch on it. He stopped, carefully took a step backwards. His mind repeated thunderously: 'I didn't mean that. I didn't mean to say it . . . you knew that all the time, you did really?'

He stared up at the cliff, fascinated by a sudden obtrusion of all its detail, each layer of slate, each projecting ledge, each clump of weed. His eyes travelled slowly up the giant primeval ruin, from its slate-packed base up the mass of wall to the sky-line with huge boulders frozen into dangerous miniature—and all this time his mind repeatedly addressed some shapeless omniscient power, something vaguely personable, for he called it 'you'. It might have been a personality implicit in the cliff itself, something asleep since the beginning; or perhaps the shapeless god-creation always in control of him and now ready to use the cliff as an immediate weapon against even so slight a hint of presumption on Podevin's part; or it might have been the personification of his own guilt. He wondered, secretly—and while he welcomed with an almost joyful sense of sacrifice the first two possibilities, he grew angry at the suggestion of his own guilt. For a moment his bravado rose and he cursed again. But a little bird, a little black swift, flew from some-where and darted with perilous decision to a point half-way up the cliff-face. This bird, so small yet so sure of its flight, assumed the half-truth of an echo. It became giddying, too quick for the human grasp. It darted like a fly about the im-mense cliff-side, drifting and swooping anywhere, drawing a vanishing black line about the high dangers, describing the height and in its rise and fall bearing Podevin with it. His fear took hold of him again—the bird had drawn his attention to the integral danger, to the centre of the cliff. For there in the centre height and weight lay above and below without retreat. There the greatest weight was massed, there Podevin imag-ined himself clinging in despair, unable to climb higher, dread-ing to take a step down. The sensation of climbing against this monster could not be separated from a fear of being crushed by it.

Podevin suddenly began to tremble, he grew acutely afraid. Perhaps this was even a desirous fear, perhaps he wished in some spirit of love for his own destruction to give himself to the resident above; or perhaps in the presence of such ele-mental power his normal values of measurement were un-steadied, he was giddied, his human perspectives had been suddenly dispersed—so that he seemed to leave the earth for the rock yet remained small on the earth, he was carried up on the fleshless echo yet shuddered still in his vulnerable flesh beneath, with small eyes overwhelmed by such vast surfaces and his brain stripped of its defences by the old ominiscience high over him.

Yet in another and secret compartment of his mind there ticked over the knowledge of the girl lying beyond the rock, of the bulge in his pocket of a packet of everyday cigarettes, of the normal lapping of the sea behind. This background of reality mixed with his stronger fear despised such fear for a foolish fancy. But nothing just then could decide whether the fancy was really no less real than what had always seemed his real body.

Nevertheless—as the sharp little bird darted high up, as the wind blew on the cliff-face, as the small waves rustled behind, as a few flies buzzed in the sunlight about the carcass of a crab —nevertheless Podevin again advanced, still with great care, still holding with his brain a wild conversation in which repeatedly the same questions were posed and the same answers given, ceaselessly as a noiseless singing that echoed louder within his ears at each step forward, as his ears stretched alertly for sounds of danger. He kept telling himself that the cliff had never fallen in hundreds of years, he produced for himself proof of this in the sea-washed smoothness of each boulder on the beach—their sharpness had long been washed away. His brain pointed out to him that there were no sharp stones. . . .

'But,' came the answer instantly, 'this might yet be the one moment, the one moment in a thousand years!' . . . Ridiculous! It's a risk that anyone must take—really, Podevin! . . .

'But haven't you read of rock falls, just as may happen here, a line in a paper, no more, no tale of tragedy and awe, just a line about a death?'   .

Instantly he answered himself. . . . Yes, but how often do such lines occur? Seldom, seldom, once in so many years and then to a millionth part of a people. Not to me . . .

'What was that?'

. . . Not to me . . .

'Not to you, eh? Who on earth are you, then, to put yourself outside the management of fate? Who are you to presume in this kind of way—answer, go on, say——'

. . . Well, perhaps . . .

'Go on, go on?——'

. . . Well, perhaps I didn't quite mean that—the way you put it—not that at all . . .

Whatever lay above had plainly heard him! He knew it had heard him! But—how could he be sure that it might not have understood, that it might not have taken his tentative argument for some more deliberate self-assertion? If the power thought itself flaunted—it would be tempted to act! But then again he bit his tongue and apologised within himself immediately for attributing to the ominiscience such a weakness of temptation.

And all the while the ringing in his ears grew louder. Yet still he walked forward. He felt now the flesh all over his body to be transparent, stripped and sensitive. He wanted to run, but feared to disturb the stones, feared to make provocative sounds, any sound that might be misconstrued as forceful and presumptuous. Outwardly walking, yet running inside himself, with veins alert and peppering, Podevin came beneath the shadow of the cliff and into the narrow passage.

The rock exhaled a chill dampness. A salty bush grew a few feet above his head and from this there dripped water from a slow spring. The water ran along a ledge, formed into drops, then dripped ceaselessly, colouring the slate with wet red iron. The ledge was moulded above his head, hanging over with a cave-like moisture. But the opposite wall of the alley was of smooth sea-washed stone, basined inwards by the wash of clean high tides, immaculate as the hide of a grey fish. Such an erosion emphasised the years; it told Podevin plainly that all the years were no more than a minute to the rock. The pebbles rolled under his shoes, ringing hollow and too loud. He walked faster. He wanted fearfully to run. He had to grip himself hard. The passage seemed to grow dark. Or his eyes were closing? . . . And then he felt the cliff move.

He threw himself into a run. He could hear already the rumbling thunder of rock descending. The force within the cliff had woken. Angrily, feeling Podevin's passing, resenting his immodest assertions. Now it breathed once a dreadful silent breath before subsiding hard on him.

Podevin panicked out into the sunlight. He stumbled out on to dazzling white pebbles. He stood panting in the round day-lit safety of the cove.

The girl lay ahead of him. He saw that she was naked. A long tentacle of brown oiled seawrack had caught its frills in her hair. She was dead, washed up by the tide.

He stared, desperately trying to realise this fact of death, trying to translate the reality lying to sun before him. But he could only see the body as part of the cliff's design, part of some ancient conspiracy of the sea and its rock. The sea was not blue then—but dark, green, deep and monstrous as stone. The white body had been cast down as a bait for him, a cold lure deposited by the coastline—for Poddy who had broken with the demands of the past, for Poddy in his high-blown independence jaunting with the freedom of the cliff.

He began to run down the beach. He ran past the body not daring to touch it. The pebbles ran with him, following him, echoing up the cove. He ran towards the sea, to a range of rocks not yet submerged that offered a path out and round into somewhere else. He leapt on to these rocks, slithering on the thick weed that grew over them, losing his foothold, falling, stumbling into deep pools, cutting his ankles in sharp pockets, bruising his hands as he clutched for support. His brain pounded with hate for the sea. The blue sea! The devouring shapeless sea with its evil swell, its monstrous depth, its wintry breakage of wooden boats, its cruel rocks, its drawing of bodies in such cold and nerveless draught, its vertiginous flatness sparkling and deceiving, its roots of oil and the furred and shelled beasts that preyed slowly on its bed, all of its wrack and wreck and rotting cold embrace and the tides that day after day, age after age, crawled up the beaches and then left them, desiring all but never needing, breaking uselessly and cease-lessly at the earth and at man.

There this account of Podevin's afternoon might have ended, but for what seemed to be a chance event. Had this never happened, Podevin might well have rounded the rocks into the neighbouring cove and climbed the next path to the cliff-top, bearing with him his terror, his guilt, and a memory that would perhaps have shadowed the rest of his years.

But instead, a dead fish barred his path over the rocks. A dead fish with its gullet torn open and a red salivary tread trailing on to the rock. The sight shocked his mind back to the intimacy of blood. He stumbled, caught his foot in a rock hole and suddenly felt the pain—a moment before he had cut the same ankle and felt nothing.

He paused, looking at the fish, while the day around him seemed to grow lighter. Distance occurred to either side. A moment before the world had been wrapped tightly over him, as if he had been running in a tight sphere of daylight compressed by a terrible weight of shadowed fears. Like a headache lifting, the weight of fear lightened, he could feel himself again standing on ground, in boots that he knew, with space and smells around him. Whether the fish was the cause of this return to earth, or whether in any case he was due to return and the fish merely provided the most immediate agency—that cannot exactly be known. But in effect the return was made and Podevin bent down to rub his bruised ankle.

Instantly he remembered the girl in the cove. Perhaps she had not been quite dead! Perhaps he could have done something to save her! A few turns of some respiratory exercise. . . . Podevin turned and clambered back towards the cove.

The girl had gone. He looked quickly at the wet marks of the incoming tide, but these still ringed the beach low down. And the strand of brown frilled weed lay alone high up on the pebbles. Then he caught sight of an arm moving. It seemed to wave from behind one of the boulders, and then disappeared. A silk vest was thrown momentarily into the air. This too disappeared.

Displaced Persons

HAVE you watched Time eating at a place? The bearded jaws tearing unseen at the air of a still room, the stiller for so many silent people, the stiller for a drying-off of thought and of those motions of building that alone can compensate for the wolfish mouthfuls of living every minute hugely lost? The voracious bearded jaws, biting off the air, always up somewhere near the ceiling, between the frieze and the quiet electric cord?

The Indian House stood furnaced in melancholy red by a September sunset; such a light was brassy, spacious, and seemed to glow up from below, underlining thus the shadows and the tall empty windows of that immense Indian-built warehouse in such a way that a sense of desolation and black-veiled sorrowers, of a Second Coming made a funeral of the Indian part, of the brownish plastered façade of an already mournful London evening. But there were no black-bowed figures, no figures at all, the pillared and domed warehouse stood irrevocably empty, consumed within by its own void and on the outside, reflecting on mogulish plaster screens and friezes, by the faraway funeral red. Such a dead design was of course accentuated by the business in its forecourt, where there were piled and strewn huge chunks of grey granite and rough white marble, material for the grinding of tombstones. Strange wooden hoisting devices stood about, lashed and poised, like derelict siege catapults. But the tombstone industry was silent, it was past six o'clock, the only movement was to be sensed across the road, across the tramlines and under the overhead wires, where the doors of the Admiral's Discretion stood open.

Inside, in the wan electric light, between walls of faded orange, they were drinking. Little noise: they talked, worriedly, in whispers, leaning slightly towards each other. When the bell of the cash-till rang, one of them started, looked up for a moment bewildered; he shook his head and then, as though there was nothing else to be done, slowly as though the whole world and the rest of time were empty and could provide no further move, slowly the hand reached to his waistcoat pocket and from there drew out a small silvery machine. With this, without looking, sinking back, he rolled a cigarette. He had the face of a pale pike, grey all over and greyer where the stubble grew; on his head was pulled down hard a fawn-coloured homburg with a greased silk brim.

This man was sitting in that untidy corner improvised by the door bolted open. Along from him, on the same polished pine bench perforated by so many holes, a small straight-necked woman in navy-blue serge sat alone; her hair jet-black, her cheeks flushed with rouge, the very white skin at the back of her neck grained with black ticks where she had been shaved for her shingle, her eyes hardly visible under the felt of a pale blue hat. She was looking at a picture hanging on the wall above, a military scene framed in fumed oak. When this woman with the straight neck and the blinding hat looked up, her whole body had to swing back so that she could see at all. Now, at such a tortured angle, she watched a grey Cardigan charging his Light Brigade into the fly-blown Russian cannon at Balaclava. After a while, a long while, as the electric clock pounced on, as the September sunset through the frosted glass burned darker, as the beer slowly sank in the glasses all around, as this beer then tasted round the teeth and the palates of those mouths and sank again to wash pooling behind waistcoats and the grimed elastic of corsets—after a while, the woman pursed her lips, swung herself vertical, took a peck at the stout-glass, and then with a slight brown froth on her upper lip re-elevated herself towards Cardigan. She remained in this position, strained; but more as if she were waiting for something to happen there in the bar than for Cardigan to make a move.

Indeed this same sensation of waiting hung over all those others who stood singly or in groups round the semi-circular bar. They all faced inwards, as though the expected and long-awaited happening might only occur at the pivot of their

yellow pine semicircle, the central point where the cast-metal
cash-till stood beneath its awning of draped Union Jacks and
cards into which were stitched little bottles of aspirin tablets.
To either side of the till stood and leant the two bar-tenders,
sallow women of uncertain age, one spectacled and frizz-
haired, the other taller and sleeker and provided with a jaw
so enormous that it was weak—but both pale and slightly
moist of skin.   They also were waiting. Leaning with their
backs to the bottles they stared vacantly just above the heads
of the people who circled them. When one or other of the
drinkers motioned for his glass to be refilled, one of these
attendants would walk over the intervening space—and what
a fine, round space, with the drinkers hemmed so close against
their pale wood railing!—and inquire the nature of the request
still with her eyes raised just so slightly above the drinker's
head. And these drinkers would receive their new glasses
mournfully and remain staring inwards towards the till.
    But some talked. There was a naval captain accompanied
by two ladies and an elderly man wearing a cap, a stiff white
collar and a tweed coat. This elderly man carried the rough
walking stick of the retired. And the ladies! One had dyed
her hair blonde, so that from behind she looked quite like a
young girl; but that the bobbed hair hung straggled over a
neck that shrunk away from it—and, of course, when she
turned her head, one saw the face of disaster, painted in bright
American colours, lifted, stitched up, the new-born virgin of
fifty with thin fallen-in lips and every line pouched to a fever-
pitch of anxiety: anxiety, but for the eyes, pale, filmed,
popping out but not caring. Her sister wore the unmistakeable
marks of the tropics, the ancient tan, the melancholy wasted
skin and the iron-grey hair, the seedy sportswoman and
bridge-queen into whose attire there always crept the touch
of silk that once had brought an *hauteur* to the far-flung club
of stranded values where, for so many long and now finished
years, her honeymoon had slowly set. The naval captain had
eyes with a furtive, trustless twinkle. He stood drowned in a
dark naval raincoat. The four of them drank long watery
whiskies—and often nodded. Yet, however much they nodded,

however many times they reasserted the rightness of the world, they too seemed to be waiting: the woman with the blonde hair often looked up at that pouncing clock, the elderly gentleman coughed and turned away and turned back again, the naval captain and his sportswoman stood opposite each other and jigged from toe to heel, like automatic toys, without ever stopping.

Two white-faced boys then lurched in, giggling. But when they faced up to the bar, the realisation of some manly inheritance turned their cheeks suddenly red, as though a neon gas was momentarily infused into them, and then as quickly the new colour faded, so that their faces were white again, faintly greyed with oil—and they ordered ginger beer and bowed their heads over a black bicycle bell. Youth was to have its watery fling! Two others, older, idler, with strapping padded shoulders and about them a sprinkling of brassy gold, on their fingers, their ties, in their teeth—these two with their flat pints leant eagerly over the little balls in the pin-table machine. Eager, and thin-lipped. But between such feverish pulls and pokes at the machine, these two also lounged back and looked up at the clock, at the door, at the fading light; they were waiting, like the others, for the something that would never happen.

But, surprisingly, it did. Suddenly into this hushed air, with its whispers, its shufflings of feet, its dead chinking, and above all and over everything its pervading, soundless whirring of the small yellow electric light bulb, that constant thing, unshaded, throwing its wan unmoving light straight at the top corners where the ceiling met those orange walls—now into this hush there broke a sudden huge sound. It exploded in from the street, with no warning—the deafening metal burst of a barrel organ.

What happened then was ubiquitous, the same small movement jerked all that drinking room, all the faces of the drinkers—each face moved slowly round towards the door and there hung, for a second as if out of joint, pressed forward slightly off the equilibrium of the neck; mouths opened for breath, more breath; eyes blank but in their fixature intent upon peering through the fog of shock. Everybody looked at the door. Nobody saw anything.

The barrel organ must have been placed just beyond the upright jambs, probably on the pavement neatly squared with the wall so that the room formed an extra sounding box; indeed, something new and dark was flushed against the frosted glass. The pike-faced man was staring straight into the bolted door, some six inches from his stony bewildered snout. The naval officer and those others had stopped talking, the bar-girls had each lowered their eyes so that now they peered through the drinkers instead of above them. The bicycle bell lay abandoned in the oily boy's hand, slackly extended forward, as if it were offered to the door as a warm wet present. The pin-table youths had struck subtly the attitude of boxers, toes preened, shoulders high and heads forward—while behind them their last little silver balls went hurrying round the garish presentation of a painted, modern city, flashing on lights in the urgent accumulation of silver, red, green, yellow and pale-blue skyscrapers, among meteor planes and overhead railways, among the short skirts of citizens dressed in rubbery romanish-mediaeval toguettes of the twenty-first century. These lights, in fact, provided now the only movement, they snowballed on and off, faster and faster like a gale warning. And the gale, the metal-belling wind churning through the door rushed straight about that room, entering it and filling it immediately like a flood-wind, grasping round the crevices among the bottles, under the bar, up to the corners at the very ceiling, down underneath the serge-skirted woman's ankles, round and about Lord Cardigan and everyone who was there, filling, filling the void absolutely. And when this in that thunderous second was done and the place was a block of sound—so other small movements hesitated and began. Smiles! Nods! Shufflings of feet! For at last the explosion was recognised to be music, and well-loved music, a tune of warmth and reminiscence, a war-time tune:

> 'Bless 'em all, bless 'em all,
> The long and the short and the tall——'

This music rang round the bar, again and again, a circling tune that came back every few seconds to where it had started and then went off again, round and round, waltzing and merry despite its metal fibre.

But merry to no applause. For one by one, like the lights on the pin-table, the smiles cut out. The faces dropped. The heads turned back towards the bar. The shufflings of feet, the beginning of a dance, stopped. The morose emptiness returned; and with it, unceasing, whirling round the room, the giddy music continued. There was no echo. The sound was hard, bright, filling the empty room with metal rods that clashed for breath; only that sound, exact, reporting without echo.

The drinkers drank without flinching. It was suddenly plain—they were beyond flinching, just as they had been beyond keeping up the first smile that had for a moment seemed to warm them. It was just not worth it.

I was reminded then of two things, both strangely to do with big dogs—perhaps dogs with faces so heavy and eyes as mournful as those that now gazed in again at the cash-till. One of these dogs was the bloodhound once seen at the bottom of an escalator in a Tube station. This dog sat like a rock on the platform at the very edge of the immense progression of upward moving empty stairs. His master tried to urge him on, patting, whispering, purring, whistling, and once even kicking. But move the dog would not. He sat absolutely. He sat and stared sadly at the ceaseless stairs emerging from the ground and travelling emptily upwards to Heaven. He seemed to be nodding and saying to himself: 'There, that's another thing they've done . . .'

The other dog is to be found in a quotation from *Henri De Montherlant*. He writes: ' . . And for a long time the baron, sitting in his chair, kept that beautiful gravity of face that men get—it almost gives them the illusion of thoughtfulness—when they lose money. Then he sighed. Newfoundland dogs often have a little humidity at the commissure of the eyes, falling like tears. Why do Newfoundland dogs cry? Because they have been tricked.'

24

The Vertical Ladder

AS he felt the first watery eggs of sweat moistening the palms of his hands, as with every rung higher his body seemed to weigh more heavily, this young man Flegg regretted in sudden desperation, but still in vain, the irresponsible events that had thrust him up into his present precarious climb. Here he was, isolated on a vertical iron ladder flat to the side of a gasometer and bound to climb higher and higher until he should reach the vertiginous skyward summit.

How could he ever have wished this on himself? How easy it had been to laugh away his cautionary fears on the firm ground . . . now he would give the very hands that clung to the ladder for a safe conduct to solid earth.

It has been a strong spring day, abruptly as warm as midsummer. The sun flooded the parks and streets with sudden heat—Flegg and his friends had felt stifled in their thick winter clothes. The green glare of the new leaves everywhere struck the eye too fiercely, the air seemed almost sticky from the exhalations of buds and swelling resins. Cold winter senses were overcome—the girls had complained of headaches— and their thoughts had grown confused and uncomfortable as the wool underneath against their skins. They had wandered out from the park by a back gate, into an area of back streets.

The houses there were small and old, some of them already falling into disrepair; short streets, cobbles, narrow pavements, and the only shops a tobacconist or a desolate corner oil-shop to colour the grey—it was the outcrop of some industrial undertaking beyond. At first these quiet, almost deserted streets had seemed more restful than the park; but soon a dusty air of peeling plaster and powdering brick, the dark windows and the dry stone steps, the very dryness altogether had proved more wearying than before, so that when suddenly the houses ended and the ground opened to reveal the yards of a disused gasworks, Flegg and his friends had welcomed the green of nettles and milkwort that grew among the scrap-iron and broken brick.

They walked out into the wasteland, the two girls and Flegg and the other two boys, and stood presently before the old gasometer itself. Among the ruined sheds this was the only erection still whole, it still predominated over the yards, towering high above other buildings for hundreds of feet around. So they threw bricks against its rusted sides.

The rust flew off in flakes and the iron rang dully. Flegg, who wished to excel in the eyes of the dark-haired girl, began throwing his bricks higher than the others, at the same time lobbing them, to suggest that he knew something of grenade-throwing, claiming for himself vicariously the glamour of a uniform. He felt the girl's eyes follow his shoulders, his shoulders broadened. She had black eyes, unshadowed beneath short wide-awake lids, as bright as a boy's eyes; her lips pouted with difficulty over a scramble of irregular teeth, so that it often looked as if she were laughing; she always frowned —and Flegg liked her earnest, purposeful expression. Altogether she seemed a wide-awake girl who would be the first to appreciate an active sort of a man. Now she frowned and shouted: "Bet you can't climb as high as you can throw!"

Then there began one of those uneasy jokes, innocent at first, that taken seriously can accumulate an hysterical accumulation of spite. Everyone recognises this underlying unpleasantness, it is plainly felt; but just because of this the joke must at all costs be pressed forward, one becomes frightened, one laughs all the louder, pressing to drown the embarrassments of danger and guilt. The third boy had instantly shouted: " 'Course he can't, he can't climb no higher than himself."

Flegg turned round scoffing, so that the girl had quickly shouted again, laughing shrilly and pointing upwards. Already all five of them felt uneasy, Then in quick succession, all in a few seconds, the third boy had repeated: " 'Course he bloody can't." Flegg had said: "Climb to the top of anything." The other boy had said: "Climb to the top of my aunt Fanny." The girl had said: "Climb to the top of the gasworks then."

Flegg had said: "That's nothing." And the girl, pressing on then as she had to, suddenly introduced the inevitable detail that made these suppositions into fact: "Go on then, climb it. Here—tie my hanky on the top. Tie my flag to the top."

Even then Flegg had a second's chance. It occurred to him instantly that he could laugh it off; but an hysterical emphasis now possessed the girl's face—she was dancing up and down and clapping her hands insistently—and this confused Flegg. He began stuttering after the right words. But the words refused to come. At all costs he had to cover his stuttering. So: "Off we go then!" he had said. And he had turned to the gasometer.

It was not, after all, so very high. It was hardly a full-size gasometer, its trellised iron top-rail would have stood level with the roof-coping of a five or six story tenement. Until then Flegg had only seen the gasometer as a rough mass of iron, but now every detail sprang into abrupt definition. He studied it intently, alertly considering its size and every feature of stability, the brown rusted iron sheeting smeared here and there with red lead, a curious buckling that sometimes deflated its curved bulk as though a vacuum were collapsing it from within, and the ladders scaling the sides flush with the sheeting. The grid of girders, a complexity of struts, the bolting.

There were two ladders, one Jacob's ladder clamped fast to the side, another that was more of a staircase, zigzagging up the belly of the gasometer in easy gradients and provided with a safety rail. This must have been erected later as a substitute for the Jacob's ladder, which demanded an unnecessarily stringent climb and was now in fact in disuse, for some twenty feet of its lower rungs had been torn away; however, there was apparently some painting in progress, for a wooden painter's ladder had been propped beneath with its head reaching to the undamaged bottom of the vertical ladder— the ascent was thus serviceable again. Flegg looked quickly at the foot of the wooden ladder—was it well grounded?—and then at the head farther up—was this secure?—and then up to the top, screwing his eyes to note any fault in the iron rungs reaching innumerably and indistinctly, like the dizzying strata of a zip, to the summit platform.

Flegg, rapidly assessing these structures, never stopped sauntering forward. He was committed, and so while deliberately sauntering to appear thus the more at ease, he knew that he must never hesitate. The two boys and his own girl kept up a chorus of encouraging abuse. "How I climbed Mount Everest," they shouted. "He'll come down quicker'n he went up." "Mind you don't bang your head on a harp, Sir Galahad." But the second girl had remained quiet throughout; she was already frightened, sensing instantly that the guilt for some tragedy was hers alone—although she had never in fact opened her mouth. Now she chewed passionately on gum that kept her jaws firm and circling.

Suddenly the chorus rose shriller. Flegg had veered slightly towards the safer staircase. His eyes had naturally questioned this along with the rest of the gasometer, and almost unconsciously his footsteps had veered in the direction of his eyes; then this instinct had emerged into full consciousness—perhaps he could use the staircase, no one had actually instanced the Jacob's ladder, there might yet be a chance? But the quick eyes behind him had seen, and immediately the chorus rose: "No you don't!" "Not up those sissy stairs!" Flegg switched his course by only the fraction that turned him again to the perpendicular ladder. "Who's talking about stairs?" he shouted back.

Behind him they still kept up a din, still kept him up to pitch, worrying at him viciously. "Look at him, he doesn't know which way to go—he's like a ruddy duck's uncle without an aunt."

So that Flegg realised finally that there was no alternative. He had to climb the gasometer by the vertical ladder. And as soon as this was finally settled, the doubt cleared from his mind. He braced his shoulders and suddenly found himself really making light of the job. After all, he thought, it isn't so high? Why should I worry? Hundreds of men climb such ladders each day, no one falls, the ladders are clamped as safe as houses? He began to smile within himself at his earlier perturbations. Added to this, the girl now ran up to him and handed him her handkerchief. As her black eyes frowned a smile at him, he saw that her expression no longer held its vicious laughing scorn, but now instead had grown softer, with a look of real encouragement and even admiration. "Here's your flag," she said. And then she even added: "Tell you what—you don't really have to go! I'll believe you!" But this came too late. Flegg had accepted the climb, it was fact, and already he felt something of an exhilarating glow of glory. He took the handkerchief, blew the girl a dramatic kiss, and started up the lowest rungs of the ladder at a run.

This painter's ladder was placed at a comfortable slant. But nevertheless Flegg had only climbed some ten feet—what might have corresponded to the top of a first-floor window— when he began to slow up, he stopped running and gripped harder at the rungs above and placed his feet more firmly on the unseen bars below. Although he had not yet measured his distance from the ground, somehow he sensed distinctly that he was already unnaturally high, with nothing but air and a precarious skeleton of wooden bars between him and the receding ground. He felt independent of solid support; yet, according to his eyes, which stared straight forward at the iron sheeting beyond, he might have been still standing on the lowest rungs by the ground. The sensation of height infected him strongly, it had become an urgent necessity to maintain a balance, each muscle of his body became unnaturally alert. This was not an unpleasant feeling, he almost enjoyed a new athletic command of every precarious movement. He climbed them methodically until he reached the ladderhead and the first of the perpendicular iron rungs.

Here for a moment Flegg had paused. He had rested his knees up against the last three steps of the safely-slanting wooden ladder, he had grasped the two side supports of the rusted iron that led so straightly upwards. His knees then clung to the motherly wood, his hands felt the iron cold and gritty. The rust powdered off and smeared him with its red dust; one large scrap flaked off and fell on to his face as he looked upwards. He wanted to brush this away from his eye, but the impulse was, to his surprise, much less powerful than the vice-like will that clutched his hands to the iron support. His hand remained firmly gripping the iron, he had to shake off the rust-flake with a jerk of his head. Even then this sharp movement nearly unbalanced him, and his stomach gulped coldly with sudden shock. He settled his knees more firmly against the wood, and though he forced himself to laugh at this sudden fear, so that in some measure his poise did really return, nevertheless he did not alter the awkward knock-kneed position of his legs patently clinging for safety. With all this he had scarcely paused. Now he pulled at the staunch-ions of the iron ladder, they were as firm as if they had been driven into rock.

He looked up, following the dizzying rise of the rungs to the skyline. From this angle flat against the iron sheeting, the gasometer appeared higher than before. The blue sky seemed to descend and almost touch it. The redness of the rust dissolved into a deepening grey shadow, the distant curved summit loomed over black and high. Although it was immensely stable, as seen in rounded perspective from a few yards away, there against the side it appeared top heavy, so that this huge segment of sheet iron seemed to have lost the support of its invisible complement behind, the support that was now unseen and therefore unfelt, and Flegg imagined despite himself that the entire erection had become unsteady, that quite possibly the gasometer might suddenly blow over like a gigantic top-heavy sail. He lowered his eyes quickly and concentrated on the hands before him. He began to climb.

From beneath there still rose a few cries from the boys. But the girl had stopped shouting—probably she was following Flegg's every step with admiring eyes. He imagined again her frown and her peculiarly pouting mouth, and from this image drew new strength with which he clutched the rungs more eagerly. But now he noticed that the cries had begun to ring with an unpleasant new echo, as though they were already far off. And Flegg could not so easily distinguish their words. Even at this height he seemed to have penetrated into a distinct strata of separate air, for it was certainly cooler, and for the first time that day he felt the light fanning of a wind. He looked down. His friends appeared shockingly small. Their bodies had disappeared and he saw only their upturned faces. He wanted to wave, to demonstrate in some way a carefree attitude; but then instantly he felt frustrated as his hands refused to unlock their grip. He turned to the rungs again with the smile dying on his lips.

He swallowed uneasily and continued to tread slowly upwards, hand after hand, foot after foot. He had climbed ten rungs of the iron ladder when his hands first began to feel moist, when suddenly, as though a catastrophe had overtaken him not gradually but in one overpowering second, he realised that he was afraid; incontrovertibly. He could cover it no longer, he admitted it all over his body. His hands gripped with pitiable eagerness, they were now alert to a point of shivering, as though the nerves inside them had been forced taut for so long that now they had burst beyond their strained tegument; his feet no longer trod firmly on the rungs beneath, but first stepped for their place timorously, then glued themselves to the iron. In this way his body lost much of its poise; these nerves and muscles in his two legs and two arms seemed to work independently, no longer integrated with the rhythm of his body, but moving with the dangerous unwilled jerk of crippled limbs.

His body hung slack away from the ladder, with nothing beneath it but a thirty foot drop to the ground; only his hands and feet were fed with the security of an attachment, most of him lay off the ladder, hanging in space; his arms revolted at the strain of their familiar angle, as though they were flies' feet denying all natural laws. For the first time, as the fear took hold of him, he felt that what he had attempted was impossible. He could never achieve the top. If at this height of only thirty feet, as it were three storeys of a building, he felt afraid—what would he feel at sixty feet? Yet... he trod heavily up. He was afraid, but not desperate. He dreaded each step, yet forced himself to believe that at some time it would be over, it could not take long.

A memory crossed his mind. It occurred to him vividly, then flashed away, for his eyes and mind were continually concentrated on the rusted iron bars and the white knuckles of his hands. But for an instant he remembered waking up long ago in the nursery and seeing that the windows were light, as if they reflected a coldness of moonlight. Only they were not so much lit by light as by a sensation of space. The windows seemed to echo with space. He had crawled out of bed and climbed on to a chair that stood beneath the window. It was as he had thought. Outside there was space, nothing else, a limitless area of space; yet this was not unnatural, for soon his logical eyes had supplied for what had at first appeared an impossible infinity the later image of a perfectly reasonable flood. A vast plain of still water continued as far as his eyes could see. The tennis courts and the houses beyond had disappeared; they were quite submerged, flat motionless water spread out immeasurably to the distant arced horizon all around. It lapped silently at the sides of the house, and in the light of an unseen moon winked and washed darkly, concealing great beasts of mystery beneath its black calm surface. This water attracted him, he wished to jump into it from the window and immerse himself in it and allow his head to sink slowly under. However he was perched up too high. He felt, alone at the window, infinitely high, so that the flood seemed to lie in miniature at a great distance below, as later in life when he was ill he had seen the objects of his bedroom grow small and infinitely remote in the fevered reflection behind his eyes. Isolated at the little window he had been frightened by the emptiness surrounding him, only the sky and the water and the marooned stone wall of the house; he had been terrified yet drawn down by dread and desire.

Then a battleship had sailed by. He had woken up, saved by the appearance of the battleship. And now on the ladder he had a sudden hope that something as large and stable would intervene again to help him.

But ten rungs farther up he began to sweat more violently than ever. His hands streamed with wet rust, the flesh inside his thighs blenched. Another flake of rust fell on his forehead;

this time it stuck in the wetness. He felt physically exhausted. Fear was draining his strength and the precarious position of his body demanded an awkward physical effort. From his out-stretched arms suspended most of the weight of his body. Each stressed muscle ached. His body weighed more heavily at each step upwards, it sagged beneath his arms like a leaden sack. His legs no longer provided their adequate support; it seemed as though they needed every pull of their muscle to force themselves, as independent limbs, close to the ladder. The wind blew faster. It dragged now at his coat, it blew its space about him, it echoed silently a lonely spaciousness. "Don't look down," the blood whispered in his temples, "Don't look down, for God's sake, DON'T LOOK DOWN."

Three-quarters up the gasometer, and fifty feet from the ground, Flegg grew desperate. Every other consideration suddenly left him. He wanted only to reach the ground as quickly as possible, only that. Nothing else mattered. He stopped climbing and clung to the ladder panting. Very slowly, lowering his eyes carefully so that he could raise them instantly if he saw too much, he looked down a rung, and another past his armpit, past his waist—and focused them on the ground beneath. He looked quickly up again.

He pressed himself to the ladder. Tears started in his eyes. For a moment they reeled red with giddiness. He closed them, shutting out everything. Then instantly opened them, afraid that something might happen. He must watch his hands, watch the bars, watch the rusted iron sheeting itself; no movement should escape him; the struts might come creaking loose, the whole edifice might sway over; although a fading reason told him that the gasometer had remained firm for years and was still as steady as a cliff, his horrified senses suspected that this was the one moment in the building's life when a wind would blow that was too strong for it, some defective strut would snap, the whole edifice would heel over and go crashing to the ground. This image became so clear that he could see the sheets of iron buckling and folding like cloth as the huge weight sank to the earth.

The ground had receded horribly, the drop now appeared

terrifying, out of all proportion to this height he had reached. From the ground such a height would have appeared unnoteworthy. But now looking down the distance seemed to have doubled. Each object familiar to his everyday eyes—his friends, the lamp-posts, a brick wall, the kerb, a drain—all these had grown infinitely small. His senses demanded that these objects should be of a certain accustomed size. Alternatively, the world of chimneys and attic windows and roofcoping would grow unpleasantly giant as his pavement-bred eyes approached. Even now the iron sheeting that stretched to either side and above and below seemed to have grown, he was lost among such huge smooth dimensions, grown smaller himself and clinging now like a child lost on some monstrous desert of red rust.

These unfamiliarities shocked his nerves more than the danger of falling. The sense of isolation was overpowering. All things were suddenly alien. Yet exposed on the iron spaces, with the unending winds blowing aerially round him, among such free things—he felt shut in! Trembling and panting so that he stifled himself with the shortness of his own breath, he took the first step downwards. . . .

A commotion began below. A confusion of cries came drifting up to him. Above all he could hear the single voice of the girl who had so far kept quiet. She was screaming high, a shrill scream that rose in the air incisively like a gull's shriek. "Put it back, put it back, put it back!" the scream seemed to say. So that Flegg, thinking that these cries were to warn him of some new danger apparent only from the ground—Flegg gripped himself into the ladder and looked down again. He glanced down only for a fractional second—but in that time saw enough. He saw that the quiet girl was screaming and pointing to the base of the iron ladder. He saw the others crowding round her, gesticulating. He saw that she really had been crying, "Put it back!" And he realised now what the words meant—someone had removed the painter's ladder.

It lay clearly on the ground, outlined white like a child's drawing of a ladder. The boys must have seen his first step downwards, and then, from fun or from spite they had removed his only means of retreat. He remembered that from the base of the iron ladder to the ground the drop fell twenty feet. He considered quickly descending and appealing from the bottom of the ladder; but foresaw that for precious minutes they would jeer and argue, refusing to replace the ladder, and he felt then that he could never risk these minutes, unnerved, with his strength failing. Besides, he had already noticed that the whole group of them were wandering off. The boys were driving the quiet girl away, now more concerned with her than with Flegg. The quiet girl's sense of guilt had been brought to a head by the removal of the ladder. Now she was hysterically terrified. She was yelling to them to put the ladder back. She—only she, the passive one—sensed the terror that awaited them all. But her screams defeated their own purpose. They had altogether distracted the attention of the others; now it was fun to provoke more screams, to encourage this new distraction—and they forgot about Flegg far up and beyond them. They were wandering away. They were abandoning him, casually unconcerned that he was alone and helpless up in his wide prison of rust. His heart cried out for them to stay. He forgot their scorn in new and terrible torments of self-pity. An uneasy feeling lumped his throat, his eyes smarted with dry tears.

But they were wandering away. There was no retreat. They did not even know he was in difficulties. So Flegg had no option but to climb higher. Desperately he tried to shake off his fear, he actually shook his head. Then he stared hard at the rungs immediately facing his eyes, and tried to imagine that he was not high up at all. He lifted himself tentatively by one rung, then by another, and in this way dragged himself higher and higher . . . until he must have been some ten rungs from the top, over the fifth story of a house, with now perhaps only one more story to climb. He imagined that he might then be approaching the summit platform, and to measure this last distance he looked up.

He looked up and heaved. He felt for the first time panicked beyond desperation, wildly violently loose. He almost let go. His senses screamed to let go, yet his hands refused to open.

He was stretched on a rack made by these hands that would not unlock their grip and by the panic desire to drop. The nerves left his hands, so that they might have been dried bones of fingers gripped round the rungs, hooks of bone fixed perhaps strongly enough to cling on, or perhaps ready at some moment of pressure to uncurl their vertebrae and straighten to a drop. His insteps pricked with cold cramp. The sweat sickened him. His loins seemed to empty themselves. His trousers ran wet. He shivered, grew giddy, and flung himself froglike on to the ladder.

The sight of the top of the gasometer had proved endemically more frightful than the appearance of the drop beneath. There lay about it a sense not of material danger, not of the risk of falling, but of something removed and unhuman—a sense of appalling isolation. It echoed its elemental iron aloofness, a wind blew round it that had never known the warmth of flesh nor the softness of green fibres. Its blind eyes were raised above the world. It might have been the eyeless iron vizor of an ancient God. It touched against the sky, having risen in awful perpendicular to this isolation, solitary as the grey gannet cliffs that mark the end of the northern world. It was immeasurably old, outside the connotation of time; it was nothing human, only washed by the high weather, echoing with wind, visited never and silently alone.

And in this summit Flegg measured clearly the full distance of his climb. This close skyline emphasised the whirling space beneath him. He clearly saw a man fall through this space, spread-eagling to smash with the sickening force of a locomotive on the stone beneath. The man turned slowly in the air, yet his thoughts raced faster than he fell.

Flegg, clutching his body close to the rust, made small weeping sounds through his mouth. Shivering, shuddering, he began to tread up again, working his knees and elbows outwards like a frog, so that his stomach could feel the firm rungs. Were they firm? His ears filled with a hot roaring, he hurried himself, he began to scramble up, wrenching at his last strength, whispering urgent meaningless words to himself like the swift whispers that close in on a nightmare. A huge weight pulled at him, dragging him to drop. He climbed higher. He reached the top rung—and found his face staring still at a wall of red rust. He looked, wild with terror. It was the top rung! The ladder had ended! Yet—no platform . . . the real top rungs were missing . . . the platform jutted five impassable feet above . . . Flegg stared dumbly, circling his head like a lost animal . . . then he jammed his legs in the lower rungs and his arms past the elbows to the armpits in through the top rungs and there he hung shivering and past knowing what more he could ever do . . .

The Little Fears

IT was one day when I visited the coffee bar that such a
strange thing occurred. I was sitting at one of the little rose-
topped tables on the left side of the room, the gas-jet burnt
slowly through the trellis beneath the urn, the Madame in her
tranquil casework of bosom and black silk stood watching the
cups and not moving: we were waiting, in the morning quiet,
for my coffee to make itself. The café—an exiled French place
of rose-tiled tables, cream walls, polished mahogany—was not
otherwise empty. A business man sat near the door reading a
page of accounts spread before him on the table; another man
sat at the back end of the café, by the bar, tented by his out-
stretched newspaper and lost in the shadow angled beneath a
high window; the small waitress stood on a chair and polished
some brass spikes on a coatstand. All were thus engaged quietly
with themselves, all waited in divisions of their own absorbed
silence. Perhaps it was such a remoteness among people
grouped intimately in what was quite a small café that made
me suddenly aware of a presence invested in the silence, a
presence as intimate as the human presence was remote. It
seemed a silence more of pause than of tranquillity.

Of course, it is more difficult to sit at ease among such a small
group of individuals than in some indeterminate crowd. At
any moment the business man might have raised his glass, the
man in the shadows might have lowered his paper—and I
would have found myself addressed. So that, silence or no
silence, it was necessary for me to keep my head a little bowed,
to trace with my fingernail the pattern of the rose tiles. In this
way I felt that I, too, appeared absorbed, armoured: though I
longed for the complete armour of a newspaper. Soon I would
be re-reading a letter, then examining those well-known
contents of my wallet.

Sometimes I looked up and around me; but then again, in
the clearer lighter air freed from those darknesses that press

down upon a head bowed in apprehension, that distinct and uneasy sense of pause remained. The windows—at the front these were curtained with cool cream curtains, they diffused dully the daylight from the street that passed opaquely outside. And at the back of the café one small window only was set high up in the wall: this window looked out upon a well in the buildings about, a grimed place of service lifts and tiles, and the only light that filtered through was reflected from these tiles; except for a line of white sky, thin as escape, elusive as holiday, that was just visible above the buildings opposite. Inset in the wall just below this window a circular iron ventilator revolved, its fan wheeling very slowly. Thus the coffee-room lay only in a diffused light, bare and without colour, so that there was much soft shadow casting altogether a recessive, sleeping atmosphere over each fitment and furniture. The mahogany frames of the wall mirrors gave off a melancholy lustre, the cream panels no more than whispered the design of their dust-embossed floral festoons. The coat-spikes shone with a yellow and faded glint of brass. There was light enough for Madame, the waitress and her customers easily to be recognized; yet each one of them seemed to throw out a veil of darkness, as if their own shadows groped to possess them, like the darkness that suddenly overtakes a face moving away against the window's light, like the shadows obscuring with premonitory gloom the figures in a steel engraving. Wall mirrors, on which still stared the remnants in white lettering of a word '. . . ocolat', reflected with greater emphasis these shadows and dull lights: yet these old mirrors also sparkled with the only brightness in the room—jagged points of quicksilver flashed and winked back the light of a gas fire glowing quietly in its hearth of rose tiles. Over all there was bound this resident silence. The room just breathed. The Madame watched the coffee.

Then that man sitting back in the darkest part suddenly rustled his newspaper. The noise fluttered with abrupt violence —at the same time his chair or his shoe grated shrilly on the floor. It made the shuddering sound of steel scraping glass. I looked down at my table, instantly, senses shrivelling in like snails' horns. The noise had come violently—now it ceased as abruptly, the silence returned with greater violence. Now, too, this silence was reinforced by a soft and continuous sound—a hissing, rubbery noise—Madame must have turned up the gas-jet beneath the urn. I looked up and saw that this was true, she was still fidgeting with a rubber tube that supplied the brass jet like the tube of a bunsen burner. Half-fearfully, half-boldly shaking these fears away, I looked over towards the man who had rustled his paper.

He was still hidden. The newspaper seemed not to have moved. His two hands were crushing the paper they grasped. I could just make out the nature of those two hands. Short, square-ended fingers, like the flat heads of hammer-headed fish, fatter and thicker each head than the finger-bodies them-selves: bloodless, but thick and yellow with strength. I looked away from them, down, and saw then with a shock that be-neath the table, like the engine of some varnished leathern torture, there rested a large club-footed boot. The rubbered end of a cane leant against it. I looked away and saw with relief that the small waitress was carrying across from the bar a tray, and my coffee.

I asked her for a bill and a glass of water, wishing now only to escape as quickly as possible. I poured some of the water into my coffee glass and began drinking this cooler coffee as quickly as I could. I poured in more water. It was ridiculous, I knew then that I was panicked simply by little fears, by distastes emanating from earlier years, chiefly by the appearance of that club-foot, and by an undefined nausea towards the chocolate colour of the polished wood, the evocation of this and the rose tiles calling out a forbidden image of chocolates with pink 'insides'. The pale cream curtains like a dull bedroom in the endless lilac afternoons. The shadows, the brass, the mirrors, the ventilator, the bunsen all re-created the setting of some forgotten misdeed.

Again . . . the crushing of paper from that dark corner be-neath the ventilator! Almost with the sound itself I rose, I had decided instantly this time to leave—easier than waiting, lowering the eyes, entering again into the dark little circle of nerves. As I achieved my height I felt a certainty of escape. But can such escape be so easily achieved? As I rose, so the paper was thrown angrily aside, the man behind it jumped to his feet. The street bell clanged, people began to enter through that door behind me, the café seemed instantly to be filled with people, crowding in, choking the café full. Their chattering thickened the air, they seemed to be pushing me forward—and forward lay only the man with the paper, and the bar; from whence now issued the Madame flanked by her small waitress.

The Madame stood quite still, regarding me with an air of inquiry, as though she wished to put to me a question, yet dared not in view of certain unstated circumstances: but with the waitress at her side she barred effectively the alley-way behind the bar, a way of escape; and indeed perhaps there was in her bearing a knowledge even of this, she was aware that she barred this escape and leant forward not in a mood of inquiry but rather in explanation of her action. But there was no time to think of her, no time at all—the man with the club-foot had already taken a pace forward, away from his table and nearer to me. His large body lowered against the light and now, with that overwhelming certainty of danger that stabs the crisis of a nightmare, when all hopes are suddenly chilled, hopes that perhaps the danger was all the time imagined, that the suspense would suddenly be proved false and subside then into a kindly reality, even that all the time the whole dreamed episode was itself a dream—such hopes died and I found that this man had raised his stick and was thrashing it at me.

(How like a nightmare indeed. I was unable to move. That spectral perception of a 'myself', thought to resemble me yet never quite seen, who had feared this very eventuality, who had wished to escape, and who until now had been invested, even while I was believing the scene into being, with a para-doxical power of incredulity that could dispel these un-pleasantnesses with a single cunning wink. Yet now the crea-tion had expanded beyond control, in place of the wink there remained now only a sudden certitude of something unendur-able. And the presence of so many people, chattering shadows behind and on all sides, who seemed to be pressing yet never once touched me. And the sudden appearance of that man, sprung so suddenly from behind his secretive paper, sprung abruptly into the full panoply of presence, even in the first instance of perception into an horrible abrupt detail, clear as the instant of terror.)

His face blackbearded, his shoulders square and pegging up some flowing frockish coat. Bearded, like a huge frock-coated grandfather, a grandfather of no figure but only of immense and flowing shape, and blundering heavily on his engined foot, big enough to crush heavily—and a grandfather with a stick. He was beating forward with his stick, thrashing round me in a short-breathed temper of fury. Yet he never seemed quite to strike me.

I remember—I felt immediately at fault. I was to blame. I had done wrong. I was surprised, perhaps, and wanted to know what was my wrong—but the thought of protesting never entered me. He gave me no time to stutter even a first word of apology—not that as much time as it takes to say a word could yet have elapsed, the episode was still in its first instant—he hobbled a step forward and struck closer with his stick, but prodding now more than thrashing, so that the rubbered cap at the end of the stick once touched my trouser-knees. I could hear a mutter, but no words, hissing and bubbling from his beard, a blathering sound of wet lips and bad teeth. (He would have had small teeth, small teeth look bad, as if their bulk has already decayed and been dissolved.) Then, suddenly, a dog barked behind me! Of course . . . he had been poking at some little dog of his! Only that, after all, a little dog playing hide and seek among so many startling legs!

But the bark repeated itself, and this time it was no bark but the rasp of a chair-leg on the tiles, now repeated more shrilly. There was no dog . . . the man was really hitting at me. And it seemed now that we two were isolated in the empty café, this dark halo of rage looming with the light behind, this patriarchal figure—and the lesser me, into whose spinning head there entered now a further and final conviction more terrible than any other. (An empty café, yet the consciousness of a

42

crowd remained; it was plain that many people were still about, and that in particular Madame and her waitress still stood propped like sewn dolls in their grooves . . . but for all their presence, for all the chatter of the crowd that echoed now distantly in my etherised ears, nevertheless these people had all receded, they were now unseen, for that small fear had compressed the vision of my eyes, I could see neither to right nor left, never beyond the dark walls of guilt that seemed to be projected from temples and brow forced huge by the little burden, so that finally only the man, the window and its light were plainly—and how plainly!—visible in a telescoped circle of vision. In this way I was alone with him.) The conviction came, suddenly and unmistakably sure, that this was no idle rage—there was intention and malice and pursual of the moment. I was being murdered. There was no question—then, just then, I was being murdered.

People are always afraid that others are going to attack them. Watch them in the street, watch the eyes of two people passing! From a distance, each sizes the other up. So much is safe, preparations can be made. But the gulf of safety is quickly decreasing, not by familiar paces but by leaps, for this gulf is shortened by the forward paces of not one but two approachers multiplying to a swift and dangerous speed. There is little time —the eyes look away! Then like quicksilver the glance of one pair returns, searching anxiously to know the other yet eager to be off, unobserved, at the very moment when these other averted eyes will surely return . . . and return they do, with a jolt, with passion—stony with pride and fear. Who will attack whom? Who is the stronger? As the two glide together over another of these deceptive paces, the two pairs of eyes hold each other, attracted snakily, watching for the glint of attack— or of scorn, of ridicule, of recognition? Four eyes of stone, defence-bound, glittering behind their lapidary glaze with all the bright lights of fear, these four eyes search each other for the worst . . . and the worst, you may be sure, is that one pair of eyes does indeed glint, diverts its path, halts, swings, approaches and addresses the other! The other freezes! How incredible is this new frozen stone, a thousandfold stonier than before! And the head and body bearing the eyes recoil, moving back and away and around by a full pace, circling away in pure defence! . . . And this, all this, because one wishes to ask the other the time.

What then are they afraid of? There is finally one answer—murder. They are afraid, finally, of physical attack. But with all the streets and all the people passing on them, day after day, year after year, the process is not always as pure as murder, it has its inversions: so that you may well find, and one cannot tell how often, and this in turn is an additional danger—you may well find that one who fears such attacks has already decided to strike first, at anyone, anywhere, with the result that this fierce-eyed monster of fear traverses whole streets slaying mercilessly all adversaries, looking only for trouble, seeking to produce exactly that situation he has always feared, and somehow, in a strange way, feeling afterwards comforted. And perhaps later—exhausted. The only ones exempt from these battles are street-vendors and policemen, smooth-nerved slayers by principle of their calling.

Murdering, then . . . this was now in the café the realization of all probable fears, of all previous passings—this what I had always instinctively feared had come at last true. It was happening, my murderer was operating upon me, with a stick, ever more violently in the thrashing of a second, glossing over with dreaded speeds all the passages of warning and suspense for which experience had prepared me. This man attacked directly. In all this time, until now his stick came at last prodding full into my chest, perhaps he had not waved, thrashed or pushed his stick more than five times—single moments of such activity last longer than five hundred thrashes. God, his figure was tall, taller than me, dark against the high window shining beyond and above. I had to raise my chin, raise it and expose my neck beneath to see into his eyes, to find his eyes and see perhaps through their angry windows into the dangerous source . . . but there were no eyes, no face, only a featureless mask ringed round with black beard, and the beard glossed alive with white fire from that high blinding daylight behind. The light above shone like pale milk, and I saw the old black ventilator revolving. I saw, too, the cream ceiling with its corners shadowed falsely with dust, and as I raised my chin further, as my face went back, as the rubber prodded on my bare throat's flesh, I saw the ceiling upside down, as though it were a floor, and the walls reversed growing from down upwards, so that in this bare room, such as I had many times created from the nursery ceiling lying in bed for the endless hours of summer evenings long ago, there grew in the centre a nobbed growth of white ivy, and from this, dizzily straight, rose like a hatefully ruled line the black iron stem of the lamp chain, gauzed with the dead leaves of cobwebs, and bearing only one flower, a single circular flower formed of one insatiable marble petal, in whose centre glittered acutely the light. It was across this funeral flower that the black dots swam like massing flies, like diamond fireflecks willing me down, until, choking, I forgot.

Much later, it seemed, the air cleared and I felt as though people were picking me up. I was, in fact, picking myself up—I must have fallen—and Madame and her maid were in some way helping me, they leaned over and smiled and chattered their solicitudes, and perhaps they rested lightly their hands on my shoulders, giving above all their presence and the colour of familiarity. As if this were echoed in other things, the café seemed to fill again with real people and not shadows. Voices came plainly, a saner light had dispelled the vertiginous murmuring and made of it blessed sentences and human tones. Of my murderer—as my eyes gradually brought into focus the realities about me—of my murderer there was no sign. He had gone. His paper lay on the floor, dead. And nothing more remained but a nervous ache about my throat. I heard people talking: "It shouldn't be allowed—they shouldn't allow him to be out. . . ." (Was it of me they were speaking, or of him?) And: "Good heavens, a thing like that! All over in a moment, too—I've never seen anything like it." (Had I committed the crime?) And: "Why doesn't somebody fetch the police?"

I had risen. Quickly I thanked Madame, picked up my hat —and by God I was out of that place. As my hand felt the lady-like handle of the door, and as the cream-curtained glass door clicked behind me, I heard a last voice say: "Picked up his hat and left! Just left!" (Was it of me, or of him?)

Was it me, was it him? Again and again I achieve certainty, only to find it reversed, incontrovertibly reversed by a simple, unseen readjustment of first premises! Incontrovertible— rather, controversive, for even the reversal itself becomes then insecure, the reversal may be reversed in the fawning of a new perspective. Permutations then extend without horizon . . . error, error, error. All ideas, however sure, seem to germinate within their true seed the other seed of their destruction, and it is this suicide germ that produces the mirror, the sly alternative distorting and damning them: often such an alternative proves to be its exact opposite.

I know nothing. Knowledge has become an apparition— insubstantive and only of ephemeral wonder. It is a sensation. An unnerving experience. Take a simple example—one may live until one's middle age, one may read and live and to- gether achieve a critical poise superior to the platitude. During that time one has heard, let us say, such a suspicious phrase as this spoken by men to women: "I feel so lonely." Examine the phrase. It has meaning, it has a direct clarity. Yet it is said too often, its undertones are suspect, its meaning is lost. However . . . wait until suddenly, somewhere in the middle of your life, you wake up to hear those same five words ringing dangerously near your own ears! Ringing in your ears from your own lips. And admit then the certainty that the words sound no longer like a phrase, you yourself mean them, you are yourself at last living the loneliness that first created them, so that now each word stands again in its own right, and with all your void heart you mean the pathetic string of them! This living sense tells you that perhaps before you have never truly lived. Or— and this is the worst—that all these people, these multitudes whom you from your booktop once considered only half aware, that these have been all the time more sensitive than you, that day after day in repeating these simplicities they have suc- ceeded in living them, that life itself consists of a repetition of a limited number of simple experiences, again and again, repeated and repeated—so that only to the critical and the ill do these experiences sound dull, for they have lost the keen sense to savour them, for they themselves are the true insensitives.

This kind of atrophy lies at the root of my distrust of myself, of such as my conclusions after the café episode. First,I concluded that my little fears were drawn from some traditional unease laid in my childhood. Set among circumstances of the chocolate and the pink, shaded by silken cream curtains and lit only by the weary afternoon light, I believed that my mind had been lulled into a melancholy of the past, a mood receptive to the incursion of the strange tyrant. And such a villain! Bearded, dressed in black, club-footed! A stick! He was the epitome of all I was first taught to fear. He was—I must have been certain—wigged. Had the light revealed his features, then there would have been no nose; some dreadful naevus would have cut across the eyes. He was the solitary limping maniac I sometimes connect now with barbers' saloons, with gas-lit railway corridors, with the dark dripping of laurel . . . and someone who, even without these adult inferences, had the stature of an angry patriarch and an infirmity of the cursed! If my killer had been of a contempoarary kind, slim-waisted and high-shouldered, Sicilian, slug-eyed, a sinuous dummy of the dance halls and the boxing ring—then I would never have been afraid: or, if afraid, my fear would have been simple, and I too might have attacked. No, it was certainly the sudden evocation of the past, this figure that my memory could never escape, this apparition that had un-nerved me.

Yet—a few days later I was proved wrong. My fears again rose . . . this time for different reasons. This time there could be imagined no reflections of my childhood, this time, a contemporary ghost assailed me. I should have known, it had happened before, at least a terror as similarly and as plainly divorced from anything of the past had touched me before . . . a different fear again, yet interwoven with the others. Let me tell you about it first, quickly, before I come to this more extraordinary affair of the moment. I can tell it quickly. It was as simple as this . . . during the time of national trouble I used to walk, perhaps through a small park in the city, perhaps along an avenue, and suddenly I would become aware of a certain tree or a certain house that lay in my path: it was forced upon me that the tree or the house held a secret of tremendous value, a secret fatal to me, but of inevitable necessity to the whole world. Say, in the park—it was a tree. Then, by the tree, or perhaps some yards off, there would be standing a man. This man would be watching: though perhaps I never saw his eyes see me, he would be watching— indeed, sometimes the man himself would not even appear, sometimes he would remain invisible, mixed with a crowd somewhere up on the higher level of the park. Yet even so he would be studying through his binoculars, he would be watching, and his presence would be felt just as strongly as if he had in fact been standing by the tree. And here is the reason for his vigilance—up in a cleft of the tree, hidden from the casual eye, yet just visible to such inquisitives as myself, there would be a hole, or perhaps a sudden round ball of diseased bark, a growth like an oaken hock: in this hock, unseen, yet carelessly available to the passerby who might conceive a sudden interest in the hock, inside lay the most vital military secret. A weapon of unimagined ferocity that would finally decide the issue—but now still secret, fragile and secret, held in reserve. Rather than hide such a weapon—of whose existence all the warring nations were aware—in the obvious vaults, impregnable though they were judged, yet by this very negation 'impregnable' inviting of attack—rather than this the authority had devised the plan of the oak-hock and its watcher. The innocence of the tree, the presence of the crowds were the protection of this vital secret. But—every now and then it was conceivable that an inquisitive passer, some botanist or irresponsible casuist, would take it into his head to ascend the tree and examine the hock! Innocent, yet from that moment irremediably guilty! . . . And it was the moment for the watcher to act! Before the guilty one had taken his first step, before he had touched the tree, when only his searching eye had fixed on the hock and proclaimed its purpose—then the watcher would approach, tap his victim on his shoulder, produce a card asserting his authority, and request the passer to accompany him to the park-keepers' hut. In through the laurel hedge they would go. The blind ivy-grown windows of the hut would announce no intention, yet the door would open, they would enter. With a little rattle of gravel and earth the door would close.

Later, the watcher would emerge. Without the passer-by. The passer-by would never be heard of again. He would, in fact, have been liquidated, quietly with cords and lime, one life to preserve a million.

It was sensible, it was true. At first I fancied the whole affair to be an illusion; but then its very reasonableness was forced upon me, I knew it was exactly the truth. And, of course, whenever this feeling came to me, whenever I suspected the presence of the watcher and his cache, I took care to hurry, eyes lowered to my boots, trembling, my shoulders bowed against the watcher's tap, the gravel path a bright and detailed road running swiftly through the world curtained off above and to either side. Sometimes, choked with guilt, I would watch this bright stream, fearful that the smooth flow of clayed pebbles should be disturbed by an iron grating, some innocent drain-cap, the vagrant cache itself beneath my very boots! So that's how I used to feel. . . . And it must be plain that this obsession could never have arisen from any recollection of the dark and early days—there was no special scene for it, no smell, no reminiscent angle of the light. A park, an avenue, a shipyard—the feeling and the fear might occur anywhere.

And now what of this latest danger! This dread that threatens me now, as I write this . . . it happened early in the summer, this summer, and again, as chance has it, it happened in a park. But it was a different park, one filled with flowers, gracious and lovely, a place where one could walk in peace and savour at once the flowering growth and man's orderly arrangement of it, a fine architecture of desire and discipline, balanced superbly, serene and breathing at least some illusions of a perfection that is said to be found in peace.

In this park I used to walk and enjoy the quietudes. I came to know each path, each bed of flowers, each tree. Yet, however well one knows such configurations of tree and flower, there remain always new and startling surprises, fresh beauties to be observed. The outline against the sky of this clump of birch and hazel, of that long-fingered ashtree will change with the season and the year: different patterns are formed, reminiscent, familiar yet subtly, breathlessly changed. And beside the broad lawns the flowers rise in banks, each growth ticketed, so that one may imagine each bloom to have its personal supervisor who has watched it, trained it, watered it with every skilful tutelage to produce from the maiden its most perfect flowerhood. Gardeners, indeed, were to be seen everywhere. Dwarfed and isolated by the huge beds, they could be seen picking away in some corner, or hoeing among the long lanes of the parterre, or standing against the watery haze of their hose-fountains on the hottest summer mornings. Then, when this water softly sprouted and showered, one could drink with one's eyes the coolness, one saw the gravel itself darken to a deeper yellow and exude, a moisture it seemed, of its own making. The roses sparkled heavily with their drink, the rose-branches glistened. It was usually in this rose-garden, quite close to the road, that I heard the distant approach of my new visitor.

At this point the road runs level with the flat area of the rose garden. Inwards, the park rises in small hills decorated with acacias, magnolias, other feathery and luxurious growths: these form a screen to the rest of the park, so that in the rose-garden one stands in a shallow arena enclosed by these hills and the road. This road runs in a circle round the entire park. It is kept away by tall iron railings, but it may be seen flickering past through these, the broad stone-black road, and in the rose-garden one is nearer to this road than at any other point. The rose-trees are cropped short, they form a rose-red carpet not more than a foot from the ground. One stands, then, isolated in this carpet, with no trees near, no projection but oneself rising from the acre of roses.

It is often when I stand thus, now fearful of the roses, which have assumed, despite their beauty, a quality of poison, but to which, nevertheless, I am inevitably drawn—it is then that

far away in the distance I hear the threatening purr of my
assailant. It is hardly a sound, yet my ears are ready, they
deduce it skilfully from the still, perfumed air. At such a time I
know him to be far out somewhere on the circular road;
possibly, ingeniously, at its farthest diametric distance from the
rose-garden. Ingeniously, for he knows that thus the sound of
his approach and the suspense of his growing threat will be
given the greatest play.

I divine the purr, the sound like silence—and then the first
whispering of an engine: it is a high-pitched engine, angry and
chattering, battling and spitting, it makes the sound of a
'contraption' more than of a machine, as though it were propelled by some brittle fusillade of thin steel sticks ceaselessly
inter-exploded, rather than by the oiled pistons that were
really its motor. For this stranger rode a motor-bicycle.

Gradually, as I stood rooted among the roses, the anger of
this machinist rode towards me, spitting its fanlike warning,
cracking, muttering, droning, roaring louder and louder. Until
at last, blurred through the iron palisade like a shadow behind
a screen, his small black presence came into view, smudged
and flying fast. With the speed of the shadow of a bird's wing
he came, flying and growing every second greater—until
through the nearer and more separate iron railings, I saw his
real shape, huddled and black over the angry black machine.
He came flickering like a kine-film, ever more apparent as the
interstices broadened—until he was flying past the open gates
themselves, full in view, the sunlight glinting on his rubbery
coat, his amber goggles flashing, legs braced in a predatory
spring, head and shoulders hunched forward against the wall
of air. A small, white pennant raised on the handlebars flew
straight back, without quivering.

I stood among the roses, my head only moved, perhaps only
my eyes as they followed the slow parabola of his race . . . and
at last the moment came when he drew opposite me, when the
railings seemed to vanish, when I saw him plainly, near, and
suddenly, for the first time, he raised his eyes from the road and
turned their amber circles straight upon me. He stared and then
momentarily laughed. His jaw opened and the teeth set in a

grin, as the half of an airman's face grins from the cockpit—masked above with leather and dark glass; only the bony teeth and the jaw-bone smiling, the eyes retreated and dangerous with inward thought.

He stared, laughed, turned his head again to the road and was gone, leaving the air charged and busy with an invisible smell as blue as burnt ethyl, with a strange emptiness, as though his impression against the trees beyond had been violently torn away, taking with it a cubic cut of the atmosphere shaped and sized precisely as he was. The spitting engine sound grew smaller as he retreated—yet I knew that really this recession was an advance, once again he was on the circle, instantly beginning again with ravenous speed the scissoring of his intent circuitous attack. While I stood still among those roses, not moving to listen the better, never making a gesture of recognition so that in fact, this stranger knew he was recognized the more clearly—while I stood thus like the statue of a shadow among those alive, perfumed petals, the machinist raced round and round the circular road. Sometimes he laughed, sometimes just turned his head and stared. Once his engines fired into a single air-shattering explosive crack; and again once it seemed that, heard through the summer air, his distant sound had turned off into a side-alley—but only a second later to come vibrating back into the stillness with redoubled strength.

Later, both he and I seemed to tire of the game—for it seemed that I turned away just at the time when, once and for all, the sound of the machine vanished. But how could I be sure that the sound had not vanished first, and that this was only a release that at last permitted me to turn away? Or, if the opposite were true, and my turning away caused the sound to be dispersed—then indeed a worse suspicion arose, the suggestion that my own will itself attracted the attack! Could I, myself, be inviting these assailants? Was I, somehow, in love with my murder? I, the real seducer, drawing upon myself these agents of my destruction who would at some time, drawn close enough, really destroy me . . .?

Roses mean death, nothing more. Their petals, immobile

and curled into a pose of innocence, appearing to unfurl graciously, yet unfurling only to give off a perfume of evil essence—these petals are poison, breathing a sin of grace, a pot-pourri heavy with dews of the monotony that kills. In the dark, against black-green bushes they shine red: they stay stained red in the silver moonlight: when the clouds are heavy, their red burns in the slatey air. But this red is never the red of blood—it is a purple red of venom, a red of hidden violet, the red of a doomed and ancient velvet gown. Incandescent, nameless, timeless, venomous—but always? They were chosen as the emblem of love—for their red hymn that desire kills, that love kills.

I hear him sometimes in the streets, sometimes from behind blocks of brick buildings: his throttle echoes along unseen, he rides parallel to me and invisible. Sometimes, swiftly, he roars across the road behind me, gone by the time I have turned, silenced and swallowed up instantly in tall canals of concrete that as instantly reveal him. A sudden visitant, and always now, always about to appear . . .

The other day I crossed a street in front of a dray-horse munching into its bag of straw. The huge dray and the munching horse lent the street an air of good, healthsome quiet—one smelt the large odour of the horse and the brisk straw, one sensed a protection in the solid size of the great wooden dray. But—even there, just as I passed the horse's head . . . this machinist was upon me! This time, he grazed my side with his mudguard! He came quietly—he was free-wheeling his black machine. He saw me and slewed round straight at my body. Even at that pace—the purulent vapour still issued from behind, the squat pipes still shivered eagerly—even as he weaved the walking machine at me on slow-swimming crab's legs, the mudguard hit me hard. He was looking straight at me through the amber goggles, from the black knight's rubbery armour. From behind his leathern wind-mask he apologized, curtly, and then swerved away. He gave me no sensation that the episode was closed.

The Kiss

AS Rolfe began to lean over her, knowing the moment had come, he understood for the first time the meaning of isolation. On the very brink of it he was separated from her suddenly by a grim and cold distance along whose way could be detected the chill of reality. Perhaps all he had dreamed of had been stripped naked, suddenly, casually, by fact.

She lay back in the cushions, her hair loose on the taffeta, her lips parted in a smile of invitation. The pink tip of her tongue lingered between her teeth. In that hot weather there were night-flies, and away by the lamp one of these hummed through the stillness of an apprehensive room. Only once was this silence, the silence of the dynamo, disturbed—when the girl raised her arms towards his, when the taffeta cushions rustled and the starched crinkle of her silken dress livened the air with whispers that seemed to mould musically the shape of her own delighted motion.

Why should he have felt at that time so separate, more separated from her than ever before, more even than at their first strange meeting? In the wisp of time when his lips approached hers—even then!—he sought wildly for the reason. Perhaps he had flung himself back the better to leap forward, recoiling instinctively for the assault? Perhaps he was afraid of refusal, so that in his wounded pride the hate had already begun to crystallize? Perhaps he was certain of acceptance; and thus with the knowledge of conquest saturating his hope, he was already reaching out for another star, belittling the planet whose illusory brilliance had faded in the shadow of his near approach. All these three emotions had a part in him then, but the last predominated.

Yet—whatever the mind said, the lips and the instincts were already on the move. Wherever hope had flown, desire was gathering momentum; desire must be consuaged. Now it seemed to free-wheel—like the gilded mountain train that has

54

strained so desperately towards the summit, with pistons boiling, with each socket shuddering in a cloud of steam and smoke and noise, only to reach the top, pause and then run coolly into its descent, freewheeling with relief, sure of its rails and its effortless glide down to an inevitable destination below. How simple it seemed! Yet that was only the beginning.

For as his head bent lower the idea of conquest became an idea of possession. Still from a distance, but nearer, so much nearer, he saw his love as he wished her to be. He saw the curve of her bare shoulder shining whitely even in the pink glow of the shaded gaslight. He saw how the shoulder was thrust towards him, so that her cheek nestled against it, her head a little to one side, not coquettish, but thoughtful, as though she were considering carefully and with deep satisfaction the beloved moment and the fulfilment that lay at its end. Her eyes half-closed, so that under dark brows their blue gleamed cloudily between lids heavy with the night's honey. And one strand of her hair blew free across her cheek, touching the corner of her mouth. She smiled lazily, with teeth so slightly parted, the smile of one awakening from the warmth of sleep. At the collar of her dress an ivory locket breathed quickly and lightly. He repeated and repeated to himself: 'This is mine! This is all mine to kiss! This is the property of that stranger I call myself, whom I have watched growing, whom I have applauded and despised, whom once I saw as a little boy breaking his nails on a walnut shell, running to his mother, carrying a prize off the school platform with violent self-satisfaction; and as a young man miserable in the first secrecies of love, walking cleverly to the office, always seeing himself as a different person much older; and now as a man whose ambitions are outlined, who has failed often, but who has known small successes too, and feels them rising into a tide of achievement. And now—once more a moment of success, the greatest yet! The stranger has achieved the ability to kiss this lovely and fabulous creature, so recently held to be far beyond his feeble reach! The stranger has exerted his charms and he has won, so that now the treasure lies at his feet, and he himself stands above that which was once considered too high for him.

Shall the stranger now brush this treasure aside with his boot?

Not on his life! For the momentum of desire is piling up its swift descent, Rolfe's head is bending lower, the lips are forming themselves into the framework of a kiss. Besides, vanity is not the only emotion that stirs the stranger's heart; he begins as well to appreciate purely and profoundly the loveliness that lies before him.

As Rolfe bends forward, the room around departs, his eyes focus only on the figure in the light beneath, and then softly over this vision creeps a sentimental mist that suffuses the hair, the eyes, the lips, the face with a lustre of even great beauty, as though a halo has been thrown round it and over it, as though it were a face seen through tears. A wishful sob mounts in his throat. Her hands touch his shoulders.

But—even then he is distracted! At one side of the halo a golden tassel shines in the light. Somehow, although he is looking directly down into her face, the corner of his eye manages to digest the fact of this golden tassel. In an instant his mind has travelled all the way to a theatre curtain, a stage, a particular play, and a tired quarrel afterwards in a drawing-room where there was no fire and the sandwiches were bent and stale.

Then his eyes advance, so that the tassel is lost in the grey mists that circle his vision, departing as suddenly as it had arrived, leaving no impression at all.

His eyes are so near to her face that suddenly he can see everything! He can see clearly, as though through an optical glass, the lowered lids with their rim of blue mascara, the pubic tenderness of the hairs at her brow, the mineral lustre of the greasepaint that makes a black beauty spot of the brown mole on her cheek. Her lips are filmed with wetness through which he can see the dry rouge. There is a tiny bubble of saliva between two teeth. He notices that there are larger pores on the sides of her nostrils, and that the powder has caked beneath them. She has a moustache! But how fine, how sweet, a mirage of the softest down!

And now truly love sweeps over him. For he loves all these things, their nearness, their revelation their innocent nudity offered without care. He loves it that beneath the perfect vision there lie these pathetic and human strugglings. The vision has become a person. He has at last penetrated beneath the cloak of the perfume and smells at last the salt that breathes closest to her skin. This is a magic moment when ambitions are more than realized, even before they are tasted! For now the moment of fulfilment is so very close that the urgency of desire's speed seems to vanish. There is a second of leisure, a last fondling of the object soon to be grasped—that will never recur. Perhaps the only real moment of possession is this, the moment just before possession, when desire knows that there is not longer even the necessity to freewheel! Can there be such a pause in the great momentum? It must be so. Just as the mountain train having completed the swift gradient runs for the last lap once more on level rails, slowing without effort its speed, but never doubting that it will glide surely to its final rest at the buffers.

Their eyes closed. With parted lips they kissed. He opened his eyes, so slightly, to look once more at the face he loved. An agony clutched his spine! He saw with terror that her eyes were wide open, wide and blue, staring at the ceiling! Heavens—had they ever closed? Had they opened at the very moment that their lips had touched? Had she remained unkissed? Had she never kissed him? Would he ever know? How could he trust her answer—perhaps that her dress had caught, or that her eyes were open in a dream? Were these eyes blind with the distances of passion, or were they alert with thought? And what thought? How could he ever know? Even as he tried to solve them her eyes turned from above and stared straight into his.

Various Temptations

HIS name unknown he had been strangling girls in the
Victoria district. After talking no one knew what to them
by the gleam of brass bedsteads; after lonely hours standing
on pavements with people passing; after perhaps in those hot
July streets, with blue sky blinding high above and hazed
with burnt petrol, a dazzled head-aching hatred of some
broad scarlet cinema poster and the black leather taxis; after
sudden hopeless ecstasies at some rounded girl's figure passing
in rubber and silk, after the hours of slow crumbs in the empty
milk-bar and the balneal reek of grim-tiled lavatories? After
all the day-town's faceless hours, the evening town might have
whirled quicker on him with the death of the day, the yellow-
painted lights of the night have caused the minutes to accel-
erate and his fears to recede and a cold courage then to arm
itself—until the wink, the terrible assent of some soft girl
smiling towards the night . . . the beer, the port, the meat-
pies, the bedsteads?

Each of the four found had been throttled with coarse
thread. This, dry and the colour of hemp, had in each case
been drawn from the frayed ends of the small carpet squares
in those linoleum bedrooms. 'A man,' said the papers, 'has
been asked by the police to come forward in connection with
the murders,' etc., etc., . . . Ronald Raikes—five-foot-nine,
grey eyes, thin brown hair, brown tweed coat, grey flannel
trousers. Black soft-brim hat.'

A girl called Clara, a plain girl and by profession an invisible mender, lay in her large white comfortable bed with
its polished wood headpiece and its rose quilt. Faded blue
curtains draped down their long soft cylinders, their dark
recesses—and sometimes these columns moved, for the
balcony windows were open for the hot July night. The night

58

was still, airless; yet sometimes these queer causeless breezes, like the turning breath of a sleeper, came to rustle the curtains —and then as suddenly left them graven again in the stifling air like curtains that had never moved. And this girl Clara lay reading lazily the evening paper.

She wore an old wool bed-jacket, faded yet rich against her pale and bloodless skin; she was alone, expecting no one. It was a night of restitution, of early supper and washing under-clothes and stockings, an early night for a read and a long sleep. Two or three magazines nestled in the eiderdowned bend of her knees. But saving for last the glossy, luxurious magazines, she lay now glancing through the paper—half reading, half tasting the quiet, sensing how secluded she was though the street was only one floor below, in her own bed-room yet with the heads of unsuspecting people passing only a few feet beneath. Unknown footsteps approached and re-treated on the pavement beneath—footsteps that even on this still summer night sounded muffled, like footsteps heard on the pavement of a fog.

She lay listening for a while, then turned again to the paper, read again a bullying black headline relating the deaths of some hundreds of demonstrators somewhere in another hemisphere, and again let her eyes trail away from the weary greyish block of words beneath. The corner of the paper and its newsprint struck a harsh note of offices and tube-trains against the soft texture of the rose quilt—she frowned and was thus just about to reach for one of the more lustrous magazines when her eyes noted across the page a short, squat headline above a blackly-typed column about the Victoria murders. She shuffled more comfortably into the bed and con-centrated hard to scramble up the delicious paragraphs.

But they had found nothing. No new murder, nowhere nearer to making an arrest. Yet after an official preamble, there occurred one of those theoretic dissertations, such as is often inserted to colour the progress of apprehension when no facts provide themselves. It appeared, it was *thought*, that the Victoria strangler suffered from a mania similar to that which had possessed the infamous Ripper; that is, the victims were mostly of a 'certain profession'; it might be thus concluded that the Victoria murderer bore the same maniacal grudge against such women.

At this Clara put the paper down—thinking, well for one thing she never did herself up like those sort, in fact she never did herself up at all, and what would be the use? Instinctively then she turned to look across to the mirror on the dressing-table, saw there her worn pale face and sack-coloured hair, and felt instantly neglected; down in her plain-feeling body there stirred again that familiar envy, the impotent grudge that still came to her at least once every day of her life—that nobody had ever bothered to think deeply for her, neither loving, nor hating, nor in any way caring. For a moment then the thought came that whatever had happened in those bed-rooms, however horrible, that murderer had at least felt deeply for his subject, the subject girl was charged with positive attractions that had forced him to act. There could hardly be such a thing, in those circumstances at least, as a disinterested murder. Hate and love were often held to be variations of the same obsessed emotion—when it came to murder, to the high impassioned pitch of murder, to such an intense concentration of one person on another, then it seemed that a divine paralysis, something very much like love, possessed the murderer.

Clara put the paper aside with finality, for whenever the question of her looks occurred then she forced herself to think immediately of something else, to ignore what had for some years groaned into an obsession leading only to hours wasted with self-pity and idle depression. So that now she picked up the first magazine, and scrutinized with a false intensity the large and laughing figure in several colours and few clothes of a motion-picture queen. However, rather than pointing her momentary depression, the picture comforted her. Had it been a real girl in the room, she might have been further saddened; but these pictures of fabulous people separated by the convention of the page and the distance of their world of celluloid fantasy instead represented the image of earlier personal dreams, comforting dreams of what then she hoped one day she might become, when that hope which is youth's unique asset outweighed the material attribute of what she in fact was.

(In the quiet air fogging the room with such palpable stillness the turning of the brittle magazine page made its own decisive crackle.)Somewhere outside in the summer night a car slurred past, changed its gear, rounded the corner and sped off on a petulant note of acceleration to nowhere.)The girl changed her position in the bed, easing herself deeper into the security of the bedclothes) Gradually she became absorbed, so that soon her mind was again ready to wander, but this time within her own imagining, outside the plane of that bedroom. She was idly thus transported into a wished-for situation between herself and the owner of the shop where she worked: in fact, she spoke aloud her decision to take the following Saturday off. This her employer instantly refused. Then still speaking aloud she presented her reasons, insisted—and at last, the blood beginning to throb in her forehead, handed in her notice! . . . This must have suddenly frightened her, bringing her back abruptly to the room—and she stopped talking. She laid the magazine down, looked round the room. (Still that feeling of invisible fog—perhaps there was indeed mist; the furniture looked more than usually stationary. She tapped with her finger on the magazine. It sounded loud, too loud. Her mind returned to the murderer, she ceased tapping and looked quickly at the shut door.) The memory of those murders must have lain at the back of her mind throughout the past minutes, gently elevating her with the compounding unconscious excitement that news sometimes brings, the sensation that somewhere something has happened, revitalising life. But now she suddenly shivered(Those murders had happened in Victoria, the neighbouring district, only in fact—she counted—five, six streets away.)

The curtains began to move. Her eyes were round and at them in the first flickering moment. This time they not only shuddered, but seemed to eddy, and then to belly out.(A coldness grasped and held the ventricles of her heart. And the curtains, the whole length of the rounded blue curtains moved towards her across the carpet. Something was pushing them. They travelled out towards her, then the ends rose sailing, sailed wide, opened to reveal nothing but the night, the empty balcony—then as suddenly collapsed and receded back to where they had hung motionless before. She let out the deep breath that whitening she had held all that time. Only, then, a breath of wind again; a curious swell on the compressed summer air. And now again the curtains hung still. She gulped sickly, crumpled and decided to shut the window—better not to risk that sort of fright again, one never knew what one's heart might do. But, just then, she hardly liked to approach those curtains. As the atmosphere of a nightmare cannot be shaken off for some minutes after waking, so those curtains held for a while their ambience of dread. Clara lay still. In a few minutes those fears quietened, but now forgetting the sense of fright she made no attempt to leave the bed, it was too comfortable, she would read again for a little. She turned over and picked up her magazine. Then a short while later, stretching, she half-turned to the curtains again. They were wide open. A man was standing exactly in the centre, outlined against the night outside, holding the curtains apart with his two hands.

Ron Raikes, five-foot-nine, grey eyes, thin brown hair, brown sports jacket, black hat, stood on the balcony holding the curtains aside looking in at this girl twisted round in her white-sheeted bed. He held the curtains slightly behind him, he knew the street to be dark, he felt safe. He wanted to breathe deeply after the short climb of the painter's ladder—but instead held it, above all kept quite still. The girl was staring straight at him, terrified, stuck in the pose of an actress suddenly revealed on her bedroom stage in its flood of light; in a moment she would scream. But something here was unusual, some quality lacking from the scene he had expected —and he concentrated, even in that moment when he knew himself to be in danger, letting some self-assured side of his mind wander and wonder what could be wrong.

He thought hard, screwing up his eyes to concentrate against the other unsteady excitements aching in his head— he knew how he had got here, he remembered the dull disconsolate hours waiting round the station, following two girls without result, then walking away from the lighted crowds into these darker streets and suddenly seeing a glimpse of this girl through the lighted window. Then that curious, unreasoned idea had crept over him. He had seen the ladder, measured the distance, then scoffed at himself for risking such an escapade. Anyone might have seen him . . . and then what, arrest for house-breaking, burglary? He had turned, walked away. Then walked back. That extraordinary excitement rose and held him. He had gritted his teeth, told himself not to be such a fool, to go home. To-morrow would be fresh, a fine day to spend. But then the next hours of the restless night exhibited themselves, sounding their emptiness—so that it had seemed too early to give in and admit the day worthless. A sensation then of ability, of dexterous clever power had taken him—he had loitered nearer the ladder, looking up and down the street. The lamps were dull, the street empty. Once a car came slurring past, changed gear, accelerated off petulantly into the night, away to nowhere. The sound emphasized the quiet, the protection of that deserted hour. He had put a hand on the ladder. It was then the same as any simple choice— taking a drink or not taking a drink. The one action might lead to some detrimental end—to more drinks, a night out, a headache in the morning—and would thus be best avoided; but the other, that action of taking, was pleasant and easy and the moral forehead argued that after all it could do no harm? So, quickly, telling himself he would climb down again in a second, this man Raikes had prised himself above the lashed night-plank and had run up the ladder. On the balcony he had paused by the curtains, breathless, now exhilarated in his ability, agile and alert as an animal—and had heard the sound of the girl turning in bed and the flick of her magazine page. A moment later the curtains had moved, nimbly he had stepped aside. A wind. He had looked down at the street— the wind populated the kerbs with dangerous movement. He parted the curtains, saw the girl lying there alone, and silently stepped onto the threshold.

Now when at last she screamed—a hoarse diminutive sob— he knew he must move, and so soundlessly on the carpet went towards her. As he moved he spoke : "I don't want to hurt you" —and then knowing that he must say something more than that, which she could hardly have believed, and knowing also that above all he must keep talking all the time with no pause to let her attention scream—"Really I don't want to hurt you, you mustn't scream, let me explain—but don't you see if you scream I shall have to stop you. . . ." Even with a smile, as soft a gesture as his soft quick-speaking voice, he pushed forward his coat pocket, his hand inside, so that this girl might recognise what she must have seen in detective stories, and even believe it to be his hand and perhaps a pipe, yet not be sure: ". . . but I won't shoot and you'll promise won't you to be good and not scream—while I tell you why I'm here. You think I'm a burglar, that's not true. It's right I need a little money, only a little cash, ten bob even, be- cause I'm in trouble, not dangerous trouble, but let me tell you, please, *please* listen to me, Miss." His voice con- tinued softly talking, talking all the time quietly and never stuttering nor hesitating nor leaving a pause. Gradually, though her body remained alert and rigid, the girl's face relaxed.

He stood at the foot of the bed, in the full light of the bed- side lamp, leaning awkwardly on one leg, the cheap material of his coat ruffled and papery. Still talking, always talking, he took off his hat, lowered himself gently to sit on the end of the bed—rather to put her at her ease than to encroach further for himself. As he sat, he apologised. Then never pausing he told her a story, which was nearly true, about his escape from a detention camp, the cruelty of his long sentence for a trivial theft, the days thereafter of evasion, the furtive search for casual employment, and then worst of all the long hours of time on his hands, the vacuum of time wandering, time wast- ing on the café clocks, lamp-posts of time waiting on blind corners, time walking quickly away from uniforms, time of the headaching clocks loitering at the slow pace of death towards his sole refuge—sleep.) And this was nearly true—only that he omitted that his original crime had been one of sexual assault; he omitted those other dark occasions during the past three weeks; but he omitted these events because in fact he had forgotten them, they could only be recollected with difficulty, as episodes of vague elation, dark and blurred as an undeveloped photograph of which the image should be known yet puzzles with its indeterminate shape, its hints of light in the darkness and always the feeling that it should be known, that it once surely existed. This was also like anyone trying to remember exactly what had been done between any two specific hours on some date of a previous month, two hours framed by known engagements yet themselves blurred into an exasperating and hungry screen of dots, dark, almost appearing, convolving, receding.

So gradually as he offered himself to the girl's pity, that bedclothed hump of figure relaxed. Once her lips flexed their corners in the beginning of a smile. Into her eyes once crept that strange coquettish look, pained and immeasurably tender, with which a woman takes into her arms a strange child. The moment of danger was past, there would be no scream. And since now on her part she seemed to feel no danger from him, then it became very possible that the predicament might even appeal to her, to any girl nourished by the kind of drama that filled the magazines littering her bed. As well, he might look strained and ill—so he let his shoulders droop for the soft extraction of her last sympathy.

Yet as he talked on, as twice he instilled into the endless story a compliment to her and as twice her face seemed to shine for a moment with sudden life—nevertheless he sensed that all was not right with this apparently well-contrived affair. For this, he knew, should be near the time when he would be edging nearer to her, dropping his hat, picking it up and shifting thus unostensibly his position. It was near the time when he would be near enough to attempt, in one movement, the risk that could never fail, either way, accepted or rejected. But . . . he was neither moving forward nor wishing to move. Still he talked, but now more slowly, with less purpose; he found that he was looking at her detachedly, no longer mixing her image with his words—and thus losing the words their energy; looking now not at the conceived image of something painted by the desiring brain—but as at something unexpected, not entirely known; as if instead of peering forward his head was leant back, surveying, listening, as a dog perhaps leans its head to one side listening for the whistled sign to regulate the bewildering moment. But—no such sign came. And through his words, straining at the diamond cunning that maintained him, he tried to reason out this perplexity, he annotated carefully what he saw. (A white face, ill white, reddened faintly round the nostrils, pink and dry at the mouth; and a small fat mouth, puckered and fixed under its long upper lip: and eyes also small, yet full-irised and thus like brown pellets under eyebrows low and thick: and hair that colour of lustreless hemp, now tied with a bow so that it fell down either side of her cheeks as lank as string: and round her thin neck, a thin gold chain just glittering above the dull blue wool of that bed-jacket, blue brittle wool against the ill white skin: and behind, a white pillow and the dark wooden head of the bed curved like an inverted shield. Unattractive . . . not attractive as expected, not exciting . . . yet where? Where before had he remembered something like this, something impelling, strangely sympathetic and—there was no doubt—earnestly wanted?

Later, in contrast, there flashed across his memory the colour of other faces—a momentary reflection from the scarlet-lipped face on one of the magazine covers—and he remembered that these indeed troubled him, but in a different and accustomed way; these pricked at him in their busy way, lanced him hot, ached into his head so that it grew light, as in strong sunlight. And then, much later, long after this girl too had nervously begun to talk, after they had talked together, they made a cup of tea in her kitchen. And then, since the July dawn showed through the curtains, she made a bed for him on the sofa in the sitting-room, a bed of blankets and a silk cushion for his head.

66

(Two weeks later the girl Clara came home at five o'clock in the afternoon carrying three parcels. They contained two coloured ties, six yards of white material for her wedding dress, and a box of thin red candles.)

As she walked towards her front door she looked up at the windows and saw that they were shut. As it should have been —Ron was out as he had promised. It was his birthday. Thirty-two. For a few hours Clara was to concentrate on giving him a birthday tea, forgetting for one evening the fabulous question of that wedding dress. Now she ran up the stairs, opened the second door and saw there in an instant that the flat had been left especially clean, tidied into a straight, unfamiliar rigour. She smiled (how thoughtful he was, despite his 'strangeness') and threw her parcels down on the sofa, disarranging the cushions, in her tolerant happiness delighting in this. Then she was up again and arranging things. First the lights—silk handkerchiefs wound over the tops of the shades, for they shone too brightly. Next the tablecloth, white and fresh, soon decorated with small tinsels left over from Christmas, red crackers with feathered paper ends, globes gleaming like crimson quicksilver, silver and copper snowflakes.

(He'll like this, a dash of colour. It's his birthday, perhaps we could have gone out, but in a way it's nicer in. Anyway, it must be in with him on the run. I wonder where he is now. I hope he went straight to the pictures. In the dark it's safe. We did have fun doing him up different—a nice blue suit, distinguished—and the moustache is nice. Funny how you get used to that, he looks just the same as that first night. Quite, a quiet one. Says he likes to be quiet too, a plain life and a peaceful one. But a spot of colour—oh, it'll do him good.)

Moving efficiently she hurried to the kitchen and fetched the hidden cake, placed it exactly in the centre of the table, wound a length of gold veiling round the bottom, undid the candle-parcel and expertly set the candles—one to thirty-one—round the white-iced circle. She wanted to light them, but instead put down the matches and picked off the cake one

67

silver pellet and placed this on the tip of her tongue: then impatiently went for the knives and forks. All these actions were performed with that economy and swiftness of movement peculiar to women who arrange their own houses, a movement so sure that it seems to suggest dislike, so that it brings with each adjustment a grimace of disapproval, though nothing by anyone could be more approved.

(Thirty-one candles—I won't put the other one, it's nicer for him to think he's still thirty-one. Or I suppose men don't mind—still, do it. You never know what he really likes. A quiet one—but ever so thoughtful. And tender. And that's a funny thing, you'd think he might have tried something, the way he is, on the loose. A regular Mr. Proper. Doesn't like this, doesn't like that, doesn't like dancing, doesn't like the way the girls go about, doesn't like lipstick, nor the way some of them dress . . . of course he's right, they make themselves up plain silly, but you'd think a man . . .?))

Now over to the sideboard, and from that polished oak cupboard take very carefully one, two, three, four fat quart bottles of black stout—and a half-bottle of port. Group them close together on the table, put the shining glasses just by, make it look like a real party. And the cigarettes, a coloured box of fifty. Crinkly paper serviettes. And last of all a long roll of paper, vivid green, on which she had traced, with a ruler and a pot of red paint: HAPPY BIRTHDAY RON!

This was now hung between two wall-lights, old gas-jets corded with electricity and shaded—and then she went to the door and switched on all the lights. The room warmed instantly, each light threw off a dark glow, as though it were part of its own shadow. Clara went to the curtains and half-drew them, cutting off some of the daylight. Then drew them altogether—and the table gleamed into sudden night-light, golden-white and warmly red, with the silver cake sparkling in the centre. She went into the other room to dress.

Sitting by the table with the mirror she took off her hat and shook her head; in the mirror the hair seemed to tumble about, not pinned severely as usual, but free and flopping—she had had it waved. The face, freckled with pin-points of the mirror's tarnish, looked pale and far away. She remembered she had much to do, and turned busily to a new silk blouse, hoping that Ron would still be in the pictures, beginning again to think of him.

She was not certain still that he might not be the man whom the police wanted in connection with those murders. She had thought it, of course, when he first appeared. Later his tender manner had dissipated such a first impression. He had come to supper the following night, and again had stayed; thus also for the next nights. It was understood that she was giving him sanctuary—and for his part, he insisted on paying her when he could again risk inquiring for work. It was an exciting predicament, of the utmost daring for anyone of Clara's way of life. Incredible—but the one important and over-riding fact had been that suddenly, even in this shocking way, there had appeared a strangely attractive man who had expressed immediately an interest in her. She knew that he was also interested in his safety. But there was much more to his manner than simply this—his tenderness and his extraordinary preoccupation with *her*, staring, listening, striving to please and addressing to her all the attentions of which through her declining youth she had been starved. She knew, moreover, that these attentions were real and not affected. Had they been false, nevertheless she would have been flattered. But as it was, the new horizons became dreamlike, drunken, impossible. To a normally frustrated, normally satisfied, normally hopeful woman—the immoral possibility that he might be that murderer would have frozen the relationship in its seed. But such was the waste and the want in lonely Clara that, despite every ingrained convention, the great boredom of her dull years had seemed to gather and move inside her, had heaved itself up like a monstrous sleeper turning, rearing and then subsiding on its other side with a flop of finality, a sigh of pleasure, welcoming now anything, anything but a return to the old dull days of nothing. There came the whisper: 'Now or never!' But there was no sense, as with other middle-aged escapists, of desperation; this chance had landed squarely on her dootstep, there was no striving, no doubt—it had simply happened. Then the instinctive knowledge of love—and finally to seal the atrophy of all hesitation, his proposal of marriage. So that now when she sometimes wondered whether he was the man the police wanted, her loyalty to him was so deeply assumed that it seemed she was really thinking of somebody else—or of him as another figure at a remove of time. The murders had certainly stopped—yet only two weeks ago? And anyway the man in the tweed coat was only wanted *in connection with* the murders . . . that in itself became indefinite . . . besides, there must be thousands of tweed coats and black hats . . . and besides there were thousands of coincidences of all kinds every day. . . .

So, shrugging her shoulders and smiling at herself for puzzling her mind so—when she knew there could be no answer—she returned to her dressing-table. Here her face grew serious, as again the lips pouted the down-drawn disapproval that meant she contemplated an act of which she approved. Her hand hesitated, then opened one of the dressing-table drawers. It disappeared inside, feeling to the very end of the drawer, searching there in the dark. Her lips parted, her eyes lost focus—as though she were scratching deliciously her back. At length the hand drew forth a small parcel.

Once more she hesitated, while the fingers itched at the knotted string. Suddenly they took hold of the knot and scrambled to untie it. The brown paper parted. Inside lay a lipstick and a box of powder.

(Just a little, a very little. I must look pretty, I *must* tonight.)

She pouted her lips and drew across them a thick scarlet smear, then frowned, exasperated by such extravagance. She started to wipe it off. But it left boldly impregnated already its mark. She shrugged her shoulders, looked fixedly into the mirror. What she saw pleased her, and she smiled.

As late as seven, when it was still light but the strength had left the day, when on trees and on the gardens of squares there extended a moist and cool shadow and even over the tram-torn streets a cooling sense of business past descended— Ronald Raikes left the cinema and hurried to get through the traffic and away into those quieter streets that led towards Clara's flat. After a day of gritted heat, the sky was clouding; a few shops and orange-painted snack-bars had turned on their electric lights. By these lights and the homing hurry of the traffic, Raikes felt the presence of the evening, and clenched his jaw against it. That restlessness, vague as the hot breath before a headache, lightly metallic as the taste of fever, must be avoided. He skirted the traffic dangerously, hurrying for the quieter streets away from that garish junction. Between the green and purple tiles of a public house and the red-framed window of a passport photographer's he entered at last into the duller, quieter perspective of a street of brown brick houses. Here was instant relief, as though a draught of wind had cooled physically his head. He thought of the girl, the calm flat, the safety, the rightness and the sanctuary there. Extraordinary, this sense of rightness and order that he felt with her; ease, relief, and constant need. Not at all like 'being in love.' Like being very young again, with a protective nurse. Looking down at the pavement cracks he felt pleasure in them, pleasure reflected from a sense of gratitude—and he started planning, to get a job next week, to end this hiding about, to do something for her in return. And then he remembered that even at that moment she was doing something more for him, arranging some sort of treat, a birth-day supper. And thus tenderly grateful he slipped open the front-door and climbed the stairs.

There were two rooms—the sitting-room and the bedroom. He tried the sitting-room door, which was regarded as his, but found it locked. But in the instant of rattling the knob Clara's voice came: "Ron? . . . Ron, go in the bedroom, put your hat there—don't come in till you're quite ready. Surprise!"

Out in the dark passage, looking down at the brownish bare linoleum he smiled again, nodded, called a greeting and went into the bedroom. He washed, combed his hair, glancing now and then towards the closed connecting door. A last look in the mirror, a nervous washing gesture of his hands, and he was over at the door and opening it.

Coming from the daylit bedroom, this other room appeared like a picture of night, like some dimly-lit tableau recessed in a waxwork-show. He was momentarily dazzled not by light but by a yellowed darkness, a promise of other unfocussed light, the murky bewilderment of a room entered from strong sunlight. But a voice sang out to help him: "Ron—HAPPY BIRTHDAY!" and, reassured, his eyes began to assemble the room—the table, crackers, shining cake, glasses and bottles, the green paper greeting, the glittering tinsel and those down-cast shaded lights. Round the cake burned the little upright knives of those thirty-one candles, each yellow blade winking. The ceiling disappeared in darkness, all the light was lowered down upon the table and the carpet. He stood for a moment still shocked, robbed still of the room he had expected, its cold and clockless daylight, its motionless smell of dust.

An uncertain figure that was Clara came forward from behind the table, her waist and legs in light, then upwards in shadow. Her hands stretched towards him, her voice laughed from the darkness. And thus with the affirmation of her presence, the feeling of shock mysteriously cleared, the room fell into a different perspective—and instantly he saw with gratitude how carefully she had arranged that festive table, indeed how prettily reminiscent it was of festivity, old Christ-mases and parties held long ago in some separate life. Happier, he was able to watch the glasses fill with rich black stout, saw the red wink of the port dropped in to sweeten it, raised his glass in a toast. Then they stood in the half-light of that upper shadow, drank, joked, talked themselves into the climate of celebration. They moved round that table with its bright low centre-light like figures about a shaded gambling board—so vivid the clarity of their lowered hands, the sheen of his suit and the gleam of her stockings, yet with their faces veiled and diffused. Then, when two of the bottles were already empty, they sat down.

Raikes blinked in the new light. Everything sparkled suddenly, all things round him seemed to wink. He laughed, abruptly too excited. Clara was bending away from him, stretching to cut the cake. As he raised his glass, he saw her back from the corner of his eye, over the crystal rim of his glass—and held it then undrunk. (He stared at the shining white blouse, the concisely corrugated folds of the knife-edge wave of her hair.) Clara (The strangeness of the room dropped its curtain round him again, heavily.) Clara, a slow voice mentioned in his mind, has merely bought herself a new blouse and waved her hair. He nodded, accepting this automatically. But the stout to which he was not used weighed inside his head, as though some heavy circular hat was being pressed down, wreathing leadenly where its brim circled, forcing a lightness within that seemed to balloon aerily upwards. Unconsciously his hand went to his forehead—and at that moment Clara turned her face towards him, setting it on one side in the full light, blowing out some of those little red candles, laughing as she blew. (The candle flames flickered and winked like jewels close to her cheek. She blew her cheeks out, so that they became full and rounded, then laughed so that her white teeth gleamed between oil-rich red lips.)

Thin candle-threads of black smoke needled curling by her hair. She saw something strange in his eyes. Her voice said: "Why Ron—you haven't a headache? Not yet anyway . . . eh, dear?"

Now he no longer laughed naturally, but felt the stretch of his lips as he tried to smile a denial of the headache. The worry was at his head, he felt no longer at ease in that familiar chair, but rather balanced on it alertly, so that under the table his calves were braced, so that he moved his hands carefully for fear of encroaching on what was not his, hands of a guest, hands uneasy at a strange table.

Clara sat round now facing him—their chairs were to the same side of that round table, and close. She kept smiling; those new things she wore were plainly stimulating her, she must have felt transformed and beautiful. Such a certainty together with the unaccustomed alcohol brought a vivacity to her eye, a definition to the movements of her mouth. Traces of faltering, of apology, of all the wounded humilities of a face

73

that apologizes for itself—all these were gone, wiped away beneath the white powder; now her face seemed to be charged with light, expressive, and in its new self-assurance predatory. It was a face bent on effect, on making its mischief. Instinctively it performed new tricks, attitudes learnt and stored but never before used, the intuitive mimicry of the female seducer. (She smiled now largely, as though her lips enjoyed the touch of her teeth; lowered her eyelids, then sprung them suddenly open; ended a laugh by tossing her head—only to shake the new curls in the light; raised her hand to her throat, to show the throat stretched back and soft, took a piece of butter-coloured marzipan and its marble-white icing between the tips of two fingers and laughing opened her mouth very wide, so that the tongue-tip came out to meet the icing, so that teeth and lips and mouth were wide and then suddenly shut in a coy gobble.) And all this time, while they ate and drank and talked and joked, Raikes sat watching her, smiling his lips, but eyes heavily bright and fixed like pewter as the trouble roasted his brain.

He knew now fully what he wanted to do. His hand, as if it were some other hand not connected to his body, reached away to where the parcel of ties lay open; and its fingers were playing with the string. They played with it over-willingly, like the fingers guiding a paintbrush to over-decorate a picture, like fingers that pour into a well-seasoned cook-pot. Against the knowledge of what he wanted, the mind still balanced its danger, calculated the result and its difficult aftermath. Once again this was gluttonous, like deciding to take more drink. Sense of the moment, imagination of the result; the moment's desire, the mind's warning. Twice he leant towards her, measuring the distance then drawing back. His mind told him that he was playing, he was allowed such play, nothing would come of it.

Then abruptly it happened(That playing, like a swing pushing higher and then somersaulting the circle, mounted on its own momentum, grew huge and boundless, swelled like fired gas. Those fingers tautened, snapped the string. He was up off the chair and over Clara. The string, sharp and hempen, bit into her neck. Her lips opened in a wide laugh, for she thought he was clowning up suddenly to kiss her, and then stretched themselves wider, then closed into a bluish cough and the last little sounds.)

A Small World

IT may have been only to the outsider of short acquaintance that Craven and his wife Dodo in their desuetude appeared more than usually destined for rapid extinction. Certainly they were so fated, certainly they were so extinguished—long before their time. But whether Craven or Dodo knew this as others might have guessed it—is questionable. Most probably they knew nothing of their danger, because of course they lived inside the scene they provided and so never saw it. In the same way anyone might look for years at, say, fashionable photographs of house parties on the terraces of huge mansions, and feel from them an immaculacy of manner, a tweeded brilliance fabled by the pilasters and tall windows of the great terrace . . . only to find at last when one arrives finally upon such a terrace that the magic is evanescent, the scene is narrower than was imagined, one is still absolutely oneself, one sees only parts of the scene through the binoculars of one's own too intimate eyes, one smells the tweed smell, sees the fluff and grit and flesh and powder of an ordinary day, tastes only the tobacco of usuality.

So in his very dissimilar environment Craven must have lived more with his tobacco pouch and the taste of his mutton than with the convolvulus, the dead chromographs of lupined gardens and past terriers, and the declining shares in obsolescent concerns which seemed to mark so surely his approaching disaster: and Dodo would have felt more closely the nine of diamonds fanned out in her hand of cards, and the seductive label of her library book—than again the convolvulus, the Eton crop and the short skirts, the declining gifts of housekeeping money that for her also seemed to mark an ambience of jolly shadow, of death before her time.

Their flat backed onto a canal in a lost suburb. The backwall of the garden was fenced high, and on this fence grew a thick screen of convolvulus. The small green leaves and their

76

spiralling stems twisted in and out of the trellis, forming a thick
curtain of several layers, which took by the chance of their
hunger a horizontal growth inwards towards the house. Somewhere buried beneath this tenting lay the black, rotting stumps
of a line of pollarded trees sucked dry and torn down years
before: and now over these digested remnants the creeper
awned down onto the lawn and was already far on its journey
towards the peeling stucco of the old grey house itself. Looking
out from the veranda, where Craven and his wife liked to sit
drinking their westering gin in the last light—from there the
creeper presented an astounding spectacle. In three horizontal
layers it stretched its heart-nailed fingers over the garden—
swiftly on the level of the lawn itself, more slowly yet with
ruthless agility over any small projection—a croquet hoop or
the low-brushing branches of several untrimmed limes—and
lastly topping with immaculate precision the side-walls, the
wall-high branches, the tops of two disused garden sheds. Thus
the convolvulus advanced horizontally, hanging its curtains
outwards into the garden on both sides, declining into the dip
of the lawn in the centre. On the lawn itself a lawn-mower
stood; this had been sculpted in its exact shape by the little
leaves, it stood like a soft green T casting a shadow over the
parent carpet beneath. The woodsheds were beginning to
crumble, weighted down by moisture and stifled from the sun.
And always with some speed the smallest and brightest leaves
at the advancing fringe lanced out a thousand tongues towards what was patently to be their last objective, the house.
They grew so quickly! They escaped the eye—yet perhaps if
one looked away for an hour or two, a sudden glance back
might distinguish amazingly that a small wormhill standing
once pryamidically so black had begun to disappear; the
convolvulus had bitten.

Inside, behind the veranda, that pale brown-painted lounge
waited in its own shade. The evening sun had wheeled away,
so that its melancholy gold, interwoven now with the sad echo
of a summer gramophone, had left the room to itself and the
slow night beginning. Shadow gathered over the last sad
gleaming of little chromium ornaments—an aeroplane, a fox

terrier, a Tudor lamp bracket—and about the gold-painted plasterine dancers engaged in the pallid swirl, now halted forever, of a slow hesitation-waltz. The gramophone needling round in the corner reflected their movement, monotonously circling just such a waltz, while a forgotten voice whispered from the dust in the shellac grooves that it was 'All Alone by the Telephone'. The music was in turn reflected in the glass of the pictures, the photographs on the pianola, the mauve and yellow and pink and blue vistas of bright herbaceous borders in their art-frames, the plucked flesh of a white rubbery dog drawn with a top hat and red nose and called 'One over the Eight'. These and the other relics gathered to themselves the evening gloom, and for the moment prepared to sleep —before Dodo would come in to switch on the sudden yellow light and bring into startling inaction again the bright colours jaded everywhere, the orange and black cushions, the pink and black party-dolls, the opaque glass bowl of mauve anemones with their president green and yellow parrot. Bright colours, but all of them dead, not faded so much as arrested, dead colours of their time, stored in that room and washed daily of the dust, only so that they should again stare out for one more false day, one more attestation of their time past and forever finished, one more grotesque jazz-play against the pale brown walls— and then another night of silent fixed inaction in the rigid yellow light. Electricity waxed them with the bright immobility of coloured effigies. That they were clean and dustless heightened this effect. They never spoke of regret. Conceived as sensation, as movement without artistry, these furnishings of the mid-nineteen-twenties only appeared stopped, braked, left forever in the moment of their moving. Or for as long as the Cravens lived, the two Cravens whose heads now lolled back in their deck chairs and appeared thus from their room like two black blobs against the golden last light and the midges clouding above the convolvulus that screened the quiet, unmoving canal.

Craven raised his gin glass to his lips, felt for one uneasy moment the first dampness in the twilight, then from the corner of his eye noticed the gleam of an orange-painted cock's tail on his glass—and felt instantly secure. Dodo patted her blonde cropped hair, flinched at the thought of the midges, looked down at her thinning legs in their haunch-short skirt, crossed them so that they looked fatter, inhaled a long smoke of relief from her amber holder. Neither spoke, they were listening to 'All Alone by the Telephone'.

So they might have sat, though declining, yet for years. The creeper made no sound. The sun tinged its green with a final fire. One never saw it move. However, far up in the sky the dying quiet was broken by a distant sound, faint at first then growing slowly to eminence, like a sound drawn by a pencil in a slow, straight line across the summit of the sky. An aeroplane, remote, driving high above in another world, a peaceful and unrelated sound. Both Craven and his wife, young in the young years of aviation, looked up. They could see nothing. Both thought of past air raids, of the two past wars whose bombardment had left miraculously the house unscathed. They warmed to their gifted security.

So the pencil line buzzed across the sky, growing louder, yet keeping to the sky. Its regularity kept it remote and maintained an absolute separation from the tiled suburban fields quiescent below. But what would Dodo have said, it may be wondered, if she had known that a man with red hair and a broad Cumbrian accent, and into whom two days before she had bumped in the street—that this man was in fact the overhaul mechanic of the aeroplane now drawing its line across the sky? Would she have remarked upon the coincidence? Would she have marvelled that the mechanic after a night in the metropolis had travelled halfway across the country to his home airfield to overhaul by chance the aeroplane that now had flown back to the sky just above *her*, Dodo Craven? She would have thought vaguely perhaps that the world was certainly getting smaller, that progress was a marvellous thing, that these days you hardly knew who you would run up against next. She would then have sipped her gin and forgotten the marvel. But would she have pondered longer, much longer perhaps, with perhaps a certain unease—so simply dismissed as superstition—had she known more? That the red-haired Cumbrian had in that second of their bodies meeting and their unsmiled apologies noted a quality in her face distasteful to himself, some configuration reminiscent generally to him, of no particular note but to his mazed associative brain? That possibly it was such a momentary distaste that put the seal for him on a troublesome day? And that he had then turned into the black-timbered Irish bar instead of into the teashop of innocuous fish, that the whisky and the liver-bitter beer had mixed badly in his veins, sending him drunk, missing for him his last train, catching him a shivering dark train in the hour before dawn, setting him down at his job with a shaking hand and little sleep, a boiling head and a carelessness that had thus left uncared for the tiny mechanism that even now in the aeroplane's engine was glowing hot and about to split? Would Dodo have wondered? Certain such telepathic probabilities had been envisaged, some proved, others still relegated to the provinces of superstition and coincidence . . . but who should yet say? . . . so in every way this too might have been no more than the curious incidence of two things together?

The regular line suddenly wavered, stuttered its pencil with helpless dashes, with stifled dots—then collapsed into pure silence, pure as the evening, pure as though the aeroplane had simply disappeared from the sky in the surprise of its first cough. But a second later the engine came droning on again, this time angrily, so that it zoomed down with an open throttle describing an ever-thickening, ever-curving line towards the ground. Such a sound thundered into the quiet air—a few heads poked from obsolescent windows everywhere. Then again abruptly it stopped, gathered itself, and resumed for a moment an even drone. But this in turn exploded again into the savage zoom—and these changes in fact took place time and time, so that all the people in all the houses felt that in the sky above them an aeroplane had run amok, or possibly that some young pilot was showing his tricks; eyes strained up against the blinding yellow sunset, watering cans paused, books were set aside, wirelesses turned down—Craven and Dodo's glasses of gin momentarily lowered.

Sometimes now they caught sight of the little bird high up, the sulphur glint of the sun on its wings: then, just as they fixed it, so the remote agony would seem to wheel it over, it would vanish, and only its sound sirening like a buzz-saw would go on, then zoom angrily louder, until the bird itself would abruptly reappear elsewhere, flying now low, spluttering, coughing, jerking and suddenly brushing its dark wing-shadow over a garden, a window. It came thus screaming its wind sometimes close over roof-tops. Then it rose again, ascending more like a moth than a bird, for now its rounded wing-tips and its fat body could be felt, the steel armour became an insect carapace. So up again, while people breathed relief—and once more it entered into its agonic circling and diving. Of an agony there was now no question. Such a flight was fugitive, rolling and wrestling to be free of a poison inside it. Those who scanned its course grew dreadfully certain of this, and began to see in its path an imagined course like the spiralled delirium of some giant racer at the fair. So, for those few seconds, it struggled about the mad air-skein.

Then the smoke came. And in the next moment the zoom fled straight down to earth, the shadow of its coming grew savagely huge, multiplying itself at a nightmare anæsthetic rate, huge the sound and huge the shadow in Craven and Dodo's ears, huge that this time their fascinated eyes saw suddenly at the last, final, splitting second that this time the roofs would not be skimmed, that the shape was theirs, the sound, the immense devouring shadow . . . they screamed, and had time even then to throw themselves one, but only one step in towards the shady veranda.

The aeroplane nosed a foot into the earth of the garden a yard from where they stood. It exploded instantaneously, veiling its flame out over everything, over the veranda, the lawn, the convolvulus, over Craven and Dodo. Those two were, of course, burnt up. Their story was finally a contemporary one, a story not of familiar passions and local forces, but of independent and possibly capricious movements and effects over the new great distances that have made the world so small. Possibly capricious—but possibly interwoven beyond the wildest dreams of prescience, possibly the first faint blue-printing of the system scorned as fate.

Days afterwards, when the firemen had long finished picking over the embers, when the water from the hoses had soaked deep into the soil—then the convolvulus that had been for a time singed took its deepest drink and reached forward. Profoundly, ruthlessly, as though it had been sure all along of such final masterplay, its green bulk clambered monstrously on, curling out thin tentacles, tonguing forward its angry green hearts. This red herring of appearance might have seemed after all to have won, to have completed the death by desuetude for Craven and Dodo that once it had seemed to promise. But that is all appearance. When at last it clambered up on top of the charred skeleton of the house that had survived two wars, when finally it rotted and pulled even those black ribs to the ground—then it had nothing to do with the narrow human conflict of the Cravens. The convolvulus was just pursuing its vegetable course, a vegetable on the move, eating, mopping up. It is never the cow that chews the cud, the cud it is that quietly champs the cow. In its own time. This vegetating ignores the single life. It goes for the larger fry of civilizations, races, genus. And as a vegetable, wins.

Crabfroth

MOVING in one vast stream, like a giant army liquidating, the nest of sandfleas came wriggling and leaping up the beach. The tide followed them, keeping its treacherous distance, but also keeping pace, disguising each approach with falsely receding waves. And how the sandfleas raced! With what a single energy they strove to evade the oncoming water! How devotedly they maintained the one direction of their allotted common course! An instinct must have warned them of the water's approach. Embedded dark in the sand they had been warned and instinctively the whole giant nest of them had emerged and flung itself into this urgent flight from the old sand soon to be drowned.

Was this a unique flight? Or was it a process recurrent with each tide? Neither of the watching sailors could answer this—they knew little of the habits of the beach. But lying with their heads close to the pebbles neither could fail to be impressed by the urgent purpose of this gallant little multitude moving across the small world beneath them. The sandfleas were uncountable, there were tens of thousands of them, they came wriggling and hopping and clambering forward over the pebbles in endless number, from far down the beach by the sand, from where the froth of the first shallow waves now searched. With their heads so close to the pebbles the sailors saw the fleas as giant white monsters clambering over mighty rocks. The landscape of pebbles magnified itself into a vast and desolate lunar scene; smooth boulders of tremendous height barred the approach of this upsurging phalanx of strange armoured beasts; the beasts waved forward their whitish feelers and leapt, legs racing like white fur beneath opaque armoured sides. No obstacle was too great for such indomitable instinct. They leapt, fell back, leapt again, hurtled over the precipitous fall beyond, curled themselves, righted themselves and wriggled hopping out of another gigantic abyss. Nothing distracted their will to move in the one direction. Each flea of the monstrous herd was prompted by an identical need. There was only one course for them to run. Perhaps deep in each others' eyes there might have appeared many familiar dissimilarities, but in the main they followed in the great common herd their general course upbeach. There were needs endemic in each that made this the one inexorable course.

The sailors were making tea. They had erected a brazier of large stones upon which rested a tin of water now nearly boiling. Little bubbles rose from the bottom of the tin and disappeared through the surface into their brother air. One of the sailors pointed to these bubbles and said: "The Chinese call them crabfroth. Little bubbles . . . crabfroth."

The other sailor nodded and settled to watch the bubbles rise. They rained upwards endlessly, forming magically at the bottom, jogging swiftly to the surface, disappearing into nowhere. The sailor eventually raised his head and resumed the long afternoon's discussion. "Give a man his necessities," he said, "and a man's got a chance. Give him a roof, give him the money, give him all that he wastes his energies striving for. Then he has a chance."

The older sailor said: "And then?"

"He can settle down to live as he wants, free from fear, free from pain—he can have a time for thinking then."

The old man said: "Do you see much evidence of that in those already provided for?"

"The rich? They're spoiled, they're riddled with old diseases. No—a new people, a new state of being."

The younger sailor's eyes narrowed into slits of enthusiasm. He peered into the sun. "Yes, with that evil thing washed away."

The old man lowered his eyes. "You're right," he said. "You're a man and men will always hope for that." He paused and looked out over the endless mineral sea. Then he whispered, perhaps to himself, perhaps to the sea, but in a low voice, as if he dared not identify his own lips with the words, but rather wished to sigh them impersonally on to the wind that would then drift them out to the great elements, the sky, the rocks, the sea, that stretched far out before him: "And what then? What when there is no pain?"

He gazed out to sea, then turned to his friend. "I'm an old man," he said. "I've travelled far, I've known many kinds. Yet I am still confused. But for the sake of that very confusion, let me tell you two tales of the men I know. One from the South, one from the North."

The young sailor nodded.

The old man continued: "Remember that I said from the South and from the North, from the extreme lands. I do not know any tales from in between—possibly there are none. The first story is about a man in the dark, the second of a man out in the broad day. But first the man in the dark. He was called Senate."

Senate returned home on an ordinary evening, washed, changed his coat, cut himself some bread and sausage and settled down for the evening in his big armchair by the fire.

The fire burned well, the room grew quiet. Curtains covered the window, so thick that they drowned the outside world and its weather like a wall. The one reading lamp was heavily shaded, its beam fell directly on Senate's bald head and on his book, then stretched out in a low dimming circle over the bare carpet. The walls had receded and hung in shadow. Senate's was a secluded room, soft and safe, draped with quiet. No sound from the passages outside—the room was situated at the end of its own corridor. Not even a draught blew in to tell that any other world existed outside this one room. Nothing disturbed the long quiet evenings when Senate sat reading. No one ever called.

After reading for perhaps an hour—an hour or two hours, there was no measurement of time—Senate put down his book and stared round him. Now he could taste the quiet. Straining his ears he could almost hear the dry dews of silence dropping. How this pure silence thrummed with unheard sound! Sometimes, Senate felt a tremendous pity for himself sitting alone and quiet in this room of his solitary making. Was he not missing something? Wasting his still fertile body, letting the time for laughter pass? A communion of people somewhere far outside—and he poor Senate committed to his solitude! . . . But not always. No, he went out and about. Two evenings ago he had dined with friends, a week ago he had nearly made a proposal of marriage. Yes, he went out and about but in between times he returned to these hours of solitude. Nevertheless, they still brought with them the same sense of martyrdom, a regret and a pity that he was wasting himself.

He read for perhaps an hour, perhaps two hours. Who knows what time it is at night? The sun has fallen, the meals are over, the clock becomes faceless for it is no longer needed. Time extends itself and dozing drifts out of shape. It can be any hour.

Presently from the depths of his book Senate became aware again of the silence. Perhaps it was the silence, he could not be sure . . . but for certain he found himself suddenly alert—whereas a moment before his mind had been sunk deep in the written thoughts. Now his ears strained feeling for the sound that must have disturbed him—but no sound came. He stared at the white vellum, momentarily bewildered, perplexed by something unperceived of which he felt he should be vitally aware. What had happened . . .? He waited and sensed no answer. Some subconscious association of the words he was reading? Some unfelt itch in the brain? He decided to dismiss it—it could hardly matter. He frowned then to recapture the words on the page, the words on the top right-hand line; and then as his eye concentrated again on the top of this page, it saw the top line and the number of the page and above the white angle of the page itself the dark curtains beyond. They were moving.

He held himself still. The curtains could never have moved. He must have been shaking the book, the background of curtains had just seemed to move in relation to the book. Then, thinking this, he looked again. The curtains were moving. Slowly without a sound Senate lowered the book. The page went down and the dark thick curtains revealed their length to the floor. They swayed all the way down their central join, as though something were tugging at them from the bottom, from close to the carpet. Senate stared and suddenly thought: 'A cat. A cat's got in.' And at the same time his mind prayed: 'Pray God it's a cat. Oh, let it be only a cat.'

Senate stared at the deep dark folds, praying, and then from beneath the intersecting bases of the curtains there crept out what appeared to be the head of a white worm. It poked itself out from the curtain, then paused, weaving its eyeless end in the air like a snout smelling for sight.

Senate lowered his eyes quickly at his book. His pulse throbbed in his wrists, somewhere by his ears. His ears stretched for a sound. But no sound came from the curtains—they were made from heavy plush. The coal in the fire was caked and glowing solid, so that now no lumps would fall to break the silence, no flames would flicker to move the light. Senate read over and over a single meaningless line of words, he still hoped hard that he had been mistaken. There was nothing there. There never had been. His eyes were tired with reading, they were playing him false tricks . . . and very slowly he raised them again, hoping and almost trusting that his wish would be realized.

But the worm stared back at him. He saw now that it was a finger. He noticed clearly the two joints, the gleam of a nail. He began to calculate the space between the curtain and the windows behind, knowing well that there was no space, for the curtains hung flatly against the window—but trying desperately to invent room enough for a body to lie behind. However disconcerting might have been the appearance of a body, in whatever state of illness or violation it lay, even so this would have been preferable to the dreadful suspicion that here was a hand alone, without a body—for where could the body lie?—and a hand that moved.

But there was no hand. Even as this final possibility occurred to Senate the finger disengaged itself from the curtain and began to move forward across the floor alone. No hand, no arm followed it. It moved alone, only a stumped finger, hunching up its joints into an arch, dragging its stump thus to meet the pad beneath the nail, then instantly shooting the nail forward over new ground. It arched and extended thus like a caterpillar. And in this way it travelled from the curtains to the centre of the lamp's circle on the carpet, sometimes deviating towards the door to the lefthand corner, but always then pausing and turning itself again towards Senate sitting in his chair. Once it seemed to have caught Senate's scent—for with a certain new decision it scuttled forward, quite sure of its route, and revealing a dangerous swiftness of movement. Then as suddenly it stopped absolutely still, its nail pointing at Senate, quiet as a beetle, its back half flexed in readiness for instant movement. It remained thus, still and deadly, in the very centre of the carpet.

Senate had lowered his book and moving soundlessly on the soft cushions had thrust himself half-kneeling off the chair. His hands gripped the leather arms—he too could lever himself and spring at his instant wish. But he moved no further than this. An instinctive alert had activated him so far, urging him towards the thing that fascinated his eyes, much as a nestgazer might move forward his head suddenly at the sight of some bird of transcendental worth, forward but no further, a movement only in reflex to the instinct, held instantly in check for fear of disturbing the watched. Senate held himself still, terrified to make a sound, terrified to make any abrupt movement, terrified to know himself watched. Any sharp movement might appear aggressive, might provoke the little creature to action. Now it was quiet. Senate allowed his eyes for an instant to glance away at the door. He knew it was locked. The key was in his pocket. But he dared not move his hand to search for it. Not only a single movement for Senate to leap free from the room—but two or three separate actions, a fumbling, and a leap, and a fumbling; thus he was inexorably enclosed. The silence beat in his ears a cascade of infinitesmal sounds, the susurrus of dry waves in a shell, a monotonous crescendo that resounded now like a shouting in his trapped brain. He hung in his chair, waiting.

The finger made no move. The seconds passed. The room ignored them, deepening its impassive neglect of time. Time existed on other planes, not in these walls of soft texture and quiet-lighted night. Had Senate thought of the dawn, and of this as his lightening hope of deliverance, the stillness would have echoed back his hope, affirming in its weatherless shadow the perpetual nature of the night, the hours that would never end, for the room would expand itself to an infinity within the man-made hours, the limit of a dawn could neither be imagined nor hoped for. But Senate had no hopes beyond the immediate present; and his throat jumped drily—for if hope lay only in the present, then the present was the only opportunity for action, and it was only he who could act. The dreadful 'now' confronted him, certain as a sentence of death. A decision, with all its terrors of initiative and energy and watertight choice, had to be made—at once and by only Senate himself kneeling off his armchair alone in his room at night.

He saw that the finger was watching him. It had no eyes— but it crouched quietly surveying his every action. Since with no eyes it still appeared to see, he felt that it saw too into his brain, it knew instantly the very decisions of his soul; so that he tried vainly to disguise his actual thoughts, like an atheist boy daring to criticise God with only half his mind, and now having decided to move pretended with a voice of thought inside his brain that he had no intention of moving. But the finger saw through this duplicity. It crouched motionless and aggressive, taut with unpredictable movement, thinking hard, as a beetle thinks when it halts in its scuttling. The eyeless always sees more than vulnerable mortal eyes; curtainless windows, the dark sockets of a skull, the faceless heads of sculpture stare with what seems a perpetuity of fathomless knowledge.

A sudden shudder ran its cold through the nerves of Senate's back. He commenced to slide off his chair. His book fell. The finger drew itself in at the sound, fluttered for a moment, froze still again. Then Senate was down on his knees in front of it, his hands clasped in prayer, his lonely baldhead shining in the lamplight, a solitary bowed figure in the centre of the carpet. His lips muttered a wordless saliva, his aged mind sought for words, he babbled: "Gentle Jesus meek and mild look upon a little child. . . ."

The finger began to creep. It crept round in a semi-circle, moving quickly sideways, so that it passed outside his vision, away from the corner of his eye to some place behind him. His words trailed off at the empty carpet lying in front.

He shuffled round awkwardly on his knees. He dared not leave his knees. The finger crouched behind him, still pointing towards him, its single pellucid nail gleaming like the varnished head of an insect. Its direction accused, its crablike intensity of thought projected an ominiscient criticism.

Senate saw behind it his cheerful fire, its ash-caked edifice of coals. The finger was crouched on his own hearth-rug, crouched like some little pet animal, like some puppy! A soft and fleshy pet-thing . . . for a moment within his terror he warmed with an illusion of love for it, but instantly then this sensation passed—as the monstrous little nail winked in the firelight, as again he sensed the sharp vigour latent within it. Seeing it against his familiar fire and the dented brass fender, he thought suddenly: 'This is impossible. This is untrue.' The nightmare thought in a nightmare that this is indeed a nightmare and cannot be real; but instantly as if some watchful power is at work it is proved real, relief fades utterly, the image of hope is punctured and dissolves in a vacuum of terror.

Senate blabbing: "Suffer me to come to thee"—stumbled suddenly to his feet and shot his boot out at the finger. It darted quickly to one side. Senate stamped again, and once more the little thing evaded him. But as quickly as it moved, Senate was equipped with height and a wide range, so that the finger became like a quick-moving beetle, swift but out-distanced, and when Senate's boot struck the third time the leather crunched it into the carpet. Senate grunted with disgust, ground his boot hard. But when he raised it, not one but two fingers, smaller and palely nimble, darted from under his heel, leaving behind them a slough of skin. These scuttled away, turned, and then crouched regarding him, poised and again deadly still.

He groaned and rushed stamping on the two new wriggling fingers, stepping his legs high and dancing the mad leather down with all his strength. But as often as he crushed one finger, so two took its place. Soon, whirling alone in his room, his floor became alive with little pointing fingers. He began to howl, his cries fell dead on the felted night. He stamped harder and harder, his feet pranced with a ferocious lust, yet throughout even this he still held to a sort of consciousness, an intuitive despairing reason telling him that a direct entreaty had failed, and now this harsh abrasive effort was failing. What else . . .? How otherwise could he seek to circumvent these little evils? . . . But he felt he had destroyed his powers by two such extreme and earnest assaults, he had thrown his resources too far open and exhausted them beyond re-cuperation. What else? . . .

As his temper mounted even this last question receded. He lost sight of his room, and felt no longer concerned with his actions: although in a final moment of consciousness he was overcome by a sudden new disgust, for with cool eyes he saw his left hand, his own left hand for an instant clear and still and focussed bright. The middle finger was missing.

"And that," concluded the old sailor, "was the end of Senate."

The young man nodded. The little bubbles mounted con-tinuously from the bottom of the saucepan, the young man's eyes never stopped watching them. At length he said: "Well, and what of it? I've heard many stories like that. A man alone with certain pain of his own making, and finally this defeats him. The whole thing seems exaggerated, I am over-whelmed by too much of this creepiness, I am so surfeited with Senate's sinful little fingers that—if you'll pardon my frank statement—it makes for me a dull story."

It seemed that the old man expected such criticism, for he replied instantly: "In the first place, the significance of Senate's behaviour cannot be fully understood until Miel's story is told against it. And in the second place, Senate's story is the story of an extreme attitude, and such extremities are in their very nature dulling. There are no convincing stories of pure violence nor of pure pain. Just as there are no stories of pure happiness, nor of unallayed content. Such experience exists only by contrast. How can absolutes exist by themselves? And yet . . . people have always aspired to them, always have hoped to separate one absolute from the other absolute, pleasure from pain, good from bad, virtue from vice, seeking to retain one and destroy for ever the other, to separate qualities that are inter-dependent, that are essentially the complementary motors of each other's existence."

The younger man shrugged his shoulders and jerked the saucepan. The little bubbles wavered. Some tried to attach themselves to the side of the pan; but soon, left undisturbed, they continued their old course steadily upwards. "Then what about this story of Miel's?"

On mornings Miel left the slender pillars of his white rotunda and loped up the meadow to his wood. The high grasses rolled in a curve upwards, so that for a time their corn-feathers and golden cups made a skyline; this high curved crest seemed to hide a land of adventure lying beyond it, white clouds rolled along it, the stalks swayed sometimes in a wind that blew from unseen spaces beyond. Miel always walked up with a stirring of hope for something unknown, yet always reached the crest to find with feelings of pleasant relief that after all only his beloved wood lay ahead. It was inevitably there—his wood with its first tangled growth of birches and hazel and elder, its oak and ash and spruce and larch and its giant dark conifers lining up massively in the wood's core.

Miel's country lay in the north. His wood was a jungle, yet distinctly a nordic jungle. There were thin trees laced with a sheen of little leaves, leaves of clear green and silver green, birches and hazels. Though fragile these grew close and tangled as a jungle; and further inside this lace grew even thicker as there appeared the patterned leaves of oak and the dense green fingers of ash trees: and at the core of the wood rose dark firs bedded in dry and peaty forest earth. It was a fresh jungle, its moistures dispelled by the northern winds; the blackbird and thrush piped a clean and bell-like song throughout the warm wind-fanned northerly day—there was none of the croaking and laughing of horned tropical birds. Flowers abounded, odourless and virgin, for a warm atlantic stream washed the coast near Miel's wood; what might otherwise have been a grey land of fog and precipitous stone had become fecund and vegetating. There had arisen a nordic jungle of thin-stalked trees with small leaves, a silver-green tangle with a dark fir-grown core.

The yellow meadowgrass thinned to its edge and Miel trod the first green blades of the wood. He passed into the speckled shade of the birch leaves. The earth paled to a colour of dead leaves, thin grass-blades needled singly from this pale brown dust. Miel felt the cool pleasure of the shade—for above the leaves the sun was hot—and he walked on with his easy loping stride thinking how good life was in these woodland paths. And certainly life seemed good to Miel. Everything conspired for his content. His body inhabited this pleasurable and temperate land, his mind had resolved its most intimate problems—certain mysteries of purpose and desire and peace. Miel had no social worries, for he himself had been able to fulfil all the necessities of his fellow men. As now he walked along his woodland path he saw tributary paths and, at the end of these, glades filled with the white bodies of good people at leisure; he himself had provided this leisure, so that now there was no want to worry about. He was free also from political worry. Free too from domestic trouble—he and his wife and his children lived happily attuned in their white rotunda. Miel's body was sound and so was his active mind. His submerged senses had resolved their difficult equations and as for planetary influences—these stood in good relation for the astral Miel. No, Miel was untroubled, absolutely untroubled. From without and from within no forces disturbed his equable taste of the good world. Miel, one would have said, was poor material for a story—what could happen to Miel? To Miel loping through his lovely wood?

He traversed several glades through the oak and the ash wood into the resinous core of firs. Now he was approaching the clearing at the very centre of this wood—that was his favourite. He began to walk more slowly, humming and watching with pleasure the brown leaf-mould crumbling and sifting between his toes. Pale rhododendron flowers shone mauvely in the brilliant forest twilight. A chorus of children singing echoed through the leaves. Then the shade grew less, the sun filtered in long shafts from the roof of branches, and presently the clearing itself appeared. Standing under the last leaves, Miel looked out into a sudden yellow circle of sunlight and surveyed once more the nodding ranks of giant sunflowers that in their thousands he had caused to be planted.

High on their stems like flat-faced honey-cakes these golden-brown sunflowers filled the whole of the wide glade, their outposts nodded now only a few feet from where Miel stood. The dark firs lay behind. From above his head there descended a warm green sunlight strained through the last delicate screen of liquid leaves. And in front stood only the innumerable ranks of golden earthern ghosts silently swaying. Miel sank to the soft earth.

He stretched himself, lying with his chest open, his legs extended, his arms thrown back, his head pillowed on the leaf-mould. Miel lay sprawled like a cross at ease.

He lay at the centre of the wood, at the centre of his personal content. His achievement of the children's choir sang in his ears the music of good works done. Before his eyes stretched the deep blue summer sky and the round-faced sunflowers swaying in a wind of the present and of future recurrences of the present. Now with his head on the earth his eyes looked upwards so that all he saw of these was a forest of golden-brown circles set against the infinite blue. He smelt the earth near his nose, the earth of old leaves. He felt the cool green shade. His eyes were filled with only a vision of sunflower faces and their background of deep blue. The sun shone on them demarking clearly the yellow big petals and the flat brown centres.

They nodded drowsily. They were a hundred brown clocks swaying their faces at him, swaying away the time. They were clocks without time, unenumerated, peering at him without curiosity, drawing slowly back, swaying forward at him again. No sharp ticking from these clocks—only a slight tremendous movement as all together they swayed on the warmth of that noon-day sun.

The sun blazed, so that sometimes the sky condensed its blue colour to a vertiginous blackness. So much light was lanced into the great noon glare that colour disappeared largely from the sunflowers themselves, so that they too were merged into a violet black of pure heat against the blackening sky. But Miel lay in the shade, out of the heat, only feeling through his eyes the black brilliances beyond. Sometimes a breeze fanned the air, then dropped instantly overwhelmed: each of these soft murmurs rippled the heads of the sunflowers so that they bent forward and spilled their premature seeds. No other sunflowers in the world had ever been like these— Miel had fashioned them to flower and to seed at the same time. Now the nearest flower bowed forward and dripped its seeds into Miel's outstretched hand. He lay back to fill his mouth with their nutty sweetness. . . .

But, as he began to chew, a sudden desire mounted in his body, a desire which his extended limbs refused to satisfy— a desire suddenly to stretch! But to stretch violently. To shake his body. To scratch his skin on the earth and to grimace wildly, to screw his eyes and loosen his forehead and stretch his mouth wide so that his lips would smart. He knew suddenly a great impatience with the present. His limbs would no longer accede to the prompting of his brain, he lay quietly wishing to stretch, yet paralysed, perhaps by the nodding sunflowers, the dripping seeds, the hot curtain of blackening blue. The seeds flattened between his teeth, the flowers danced slowly against the sky . . . his eyes focussed on two great flowers, so that the others disappeared and only these two immense honeyed discs were left isolated and approaching his concentration.

Certainly now these big flowers lowered at him. They filled the heavens. He could no longer see the sky, nor even the radiation of petals—only now a mass of flat brown seed face, the brown belly of the flower. He felt the weight of an illimitable torpor. He saw reflected in the faceless face of the brown seed-growth the satiety of all his good walks, his long life, his goodness and his safe beauty. The brown mass lay over him, enveloping but never suffocating, covering him only with its sweet breath and its humming quiet growth. So much goodness, such a weight of peace—Miel felt himself yielded to these flowers, as involuntarily the perceptions are yielded to the anaesthetist, slipping away, the spirit and the senses by which he had judged and prized the world, the senses that had prized themselves, the keen fabric of critical feeling that was the only measure of his identity—slipping away, receding from itself to be lost in the sun of overlapping faces. . . . All over his losing body the latent muscles itched to move. Needs rose in him and burst vacantly for want of restraint. Bitterly he longed for the thousand little seeds to act. Bitterly he prayed that they would sharpen themselves into teeth, that such teeth would bite into him, assuaging his peace with pain, blessed pain, letting him taste at last the bite of sorrow.

The young sailor lay considering this tale, his eyes close to the small bubbles continually rising. Once, thoughtfully, he poked his finger at their enticing motion, wishing perhaps to touch one of the bubbles; but the water was boiling, he jerked his finger out and cursed. Then he turned to the older man and said: "You tell me to set Miel's story against the experiences of Senate. Perhaps, to arrive at a perfect understanding of both, I would have done better to listen first to a line of one and then to a line of the other . . . ?"

"That might be a way," the old man answered. "But I think I ought to confess that one line at least was not of Miel's telling."

"Not of Miel's?"

"No. I myself invented one of those lines." The old man rubbed a hand up his weathered cheek, feeling for bristles, feeling whether that line of his was as immaculate as his cheek was smooth shaven. "It was the last line of all," he added.

The younger man grunted. "I thought so," he said. "It's not true that a man should ask for pain. It's absurd—at least for a sound man."

"Yes, you're quite right—no normally sound man would ever consciously welcome pain. His brain, whose first function is survival, must necessarily be directed against bodily pain and its spiritual equivalents. Although pain is without doubt part of a complete state of living, although this is incontrovertibly the truth underlying the balance of all real experience, although all life would ring hollow without it— nevertheless man himself can never agree that this is so, simply because the minor engine directing him runs of its own purpose against such a pretension. Man needs pain, but no man will ever see the need."

At this the young sailor rolled over, scattering and crunching the pebbles, and pointed his whole sand-grimed arm at the old man. "That's it!" he cried. "That's just it. No man will ever see the need! *No* man! Why, from your own man's mouth you confound yourself!"

"I?" asked the old man's wrinkles.

The young sailor winked slyly. "Aren't there some," he whispered, "who have undergone more than their portion of sorrow, who first resent this, yet for whom sorrow must eventually become so much an individual perquisite that, like his other possessions, he must fight to protect it and so, against the whole world, make of it a virtue?"

In the Morning

"AND that," said the officer, pointing to a squat brick tower, shaped like a martello tower, that threw its shadow over them from only a few yards away, "is full of petrol."

The high curve of brick rose clear and pink against a wide sky of blue, fresh pink brick and its solid curve against the sure celestial blue; to one of the firemen standing with his hose just below, this quiet tower of pink instantly recalled southern walls seen against other blue skies—the terra-cotta citadel from some tale of Italian knights? As if to implement this impression just then a black rag of a bird swooped up over the tower, fluttered, went wheeling off at a slant skywards. A falcon? A young vulture flapping off this tower to the plain of fallen armour?

No, none of these, no more than a black rag of ash blown up on the hot air rising. And to the right of the tower now a stretch of black smoke funnelled and fanned upwards, as if beneath the roofs of the sheds opposite there lay imprisoned and snorting an angry battleship. "So be careful," continued the officer, pulling his mouth into the dry smile that pretends danger to be a delight for all. "Be careful she doesn't go up."

Eliot, one of three firemen holding a hose in the shadows of the brick petrol tank, smiled back and then looked from the blue sky to the room into which they were pouring water. This was a large room, part of a series of concrete sheds adjoining the petrol tank, and inside it was like night. It was as black as night everywhere but in the foreground, two yards from the window, where a stack of small black oil-containers burnt with busy yellow flames. The smoke from these velveted the room with black, the flames were like the glare of strong yellow candles. Thus night and fire were precisely enclosed within this concrete compartment: the reflection of the morning blue sky poured its fresh white light on the back of one's helmet, but the eyes in front were concerned with a dangerous compartment of night, where oil burnt, where stacks of little black cans might from some unpredictable erosion of heat suddenly blow up, perhaps one after the other, or perhaps all together, so that one moment would be still but for the little hissing of flames and water—and the next moment would tear aloud with powerful noise and a high gush of heat and fire, the firemen leaning into the window would be blistered or thrown back singed and ducking, the explosive flame might engulf the whole room, go flapping its sheet-tongue through the side-window against the brick petrol tank, piercing the brick with its million hot needles, baking the petrol to flashpoint—and one of two things might then happen. The flame itself might burn through the brick side of the tank; or the expanding vapours inside the tank might blow the top off, fountaining out live petrol on all sides. In either case the petrol would ignite, the tower and the firemen within its precincts would be smothered in a sudden avalanche of fire streaming far beyond them.

From the street outside the yard came the rumble of an omnibus on its daily round. It stopped, there was a pause, it started, geared up, and rumbled away. The firemen pressed up against the window ledge and watched their water-jet beat out the flame patches that honeycombed the stack of cans. Water dripped and slushed everywhere inside the room. Yet, as soon as one patch of flame disappeared and the sudden smoke of its extinction bellied up, then somewhere else another flame winked out from beneath, or from above, or from this or that crevice in the stack, a wicked winking yellow flame betokening an unknown source of fire within—who could know how much more flame resided there?—and then, as this new light disappeared beneath the prodding water, the first flame, miraculously re-ignited, would shoot forth again, flicker uncertainly, then flare brighter and brighter.

It was a ceaseless process. None of the firemen knew whether they had put out the flames they had put out, nor where the next flames would occur. They could only lean forward upon the backward drag of the hose, move the shaft of water like a broom from one flame to another, and watch, and wait, and shift the broom, and wait.

One of them suggested climbing through the window and raking the stack apart. "Get at it easier," he explained. But the officer shook his head. "It needn't blow," he said, "and you might make it." He paused, looking hard at the roof. "And another thing—we don't want any more stiffs, that roof's unsafe." He pointed to several large shapes of concrete, jagged and coldly heavy, that during the night had fallen from the ceiling. The heat from the fire had buckled the supporting girders, the invulnerable concrete had cracked and fallen. At any moment, this officer hinted, more might come down. "You want to use your loaf," he added, "not split it."

A slow smell of stale burning bloomed in gusts from the slush inside, the firemen grunted as they pushed or changed their grip, the water sputtered and splashed, the immobile petrol tank cast its shadow and made its silence felt—and Eliot suddenly noticed his wrist-watch. He still wore it, pressed now against the watery brass nozzle. Its hands pointed to half-past nine o'clock. He frowned, and blinked his eyes, as though he had remembered something unreal. "Extraordinary," he muttered. "Half-past nine!"

He thought this extraordinary because at half-past eight that morning, exactly an hour before, he had been lying on his own bed, in his own home, with the shape of his own wife shivering above him with a cup of tea. Through eyes slow with sleep he had registered her well-known form, bent forward a little with cold, clutching her kimono to her throat. Then behind her he distinguished the mirror and mahogany carving of the wardrobe that had been theirs for years, and nearer to his eye the white and blue tea-cup, and then flooding all round beneath his chin the flowered crimson of their old eiderdown. The curtains had been only half-pulled, they shed only a half-light on these familiar shapes and colours. The figure of his wife had been really no more than a greyish, solid shadow; the colours of the tea cup and the eiderdown shone only faintly, but were recognized by him clearly, for he expected them. He expected to see these familiar things when he awoke. They were the most usual accompaniment to this process of waking. For years in peace-time he had awoken to this same room and to these two people, his wife and himself; now, after years of war, nothing had really changed in the first moments of waking. External changes of mind and the cloud shadowing the world had not in the first slow seconds yet asserted themselves; even after four years, life in terms of war was still artificial, an unwanted fabric of duties and new experience superimposed upon an older, more real way of living; a relentless casing over, but no admixture.

So that, for all real purposes, it was to the old days of peace that he awoke. Some seconds later he recollected the war, that he was due on parade within the half-hour; this adjustment no longer sank inside him with its old nightmare lead, he scarcely noticed it—he was accustomed by now to the casing of war as he was to his old life, although the two had never intermingled —and with no more than a shrug of distaste at the late hour and at the discomfort of leaving his warm bed he settled himself to five minutes more of it and to his cup of tea. He lay then for five peaceful minutes savouring his familiar things.

An hour, less than an hour before! And now, by some extraordinary sequence of shaving, uniform, parade, boots, carburettors, tyres and a long recession of similar grey streets— here he found himself attached to a strange brick tower, an extraordinary tower packed with thousands of gallons of petrol that might blow at any minute! One moment the soft bed; the next this hard lethal petrol tank. And as if to emphasize the recollection of his bed, above the absolutely immobile tank there stretched this most peaceful blue March sky and occasionally there echoed from the unconcerned city beyond a rumble of daytime traffic.

'Of course,' thought Eliot, 'I must not fantasize my situation too much. It is, after all, easily explained. There was a short raid last night, the gentlemen in grey dropped a lucky one near this minor petrol dump, there was a fire, it was controlled, this is a small outbreak, and I am a fireman who happened to come on duty this morning at nine a.m. after a night's leave spent in my own bed'.

'And yet. . . .' He shrugged. For a moment the affair was nevertheless beyond his comprehension, and seeking an alternative to it in action, he heaved the nozzle over to another patch of flame. There was then nothing else to do but wait. He looked up once at the petrol tank, a dark quick look, pursed his lips, and returned his eyes quickly to the fire. 'What can I think about?' he thought.

He peered into the stack of black cans, forced himself to concentrate on them yet simultaneously searched his mind for some external idea. This effort to direct his thoughts was made too consciously, he remained preoccupied with the extraordinary nature of his present situation.

There was plenty of time to think. There was nothing else to do but think. These homebound services, he thought, made the most abrupt demands upon one's capacity for adjustment. If you are a soldier, you are extracted in one piece from your old life and set down in new clothes in a distant and new part of the country. All your old responsibilities are lifted from your shoulders, you are delivered body and soul into the hands of others who demand henceforth the devotion of all the hours of your life, and finally, perhaps, your life itself. The process, at the donning of a khaki cap, is complete. You are a soldier, disrupted from the old things, set among quite new things. From then on every facet of your environment has a connection with the forthcoming action in which one day you will be involved. You will have to make only minor adjustments between this new environment and the impact of real action. You are kept mentally attuned to the textures and concepts that comprise the action. But it is different with a fireman stationed on active service in his own town. He spends two days in his station, then one day on leave in his home; in this ratio the succession of duty and leave continues. Even from his station window itself he can still see the familiar roofs of his previous life. He has, in fact, never really left home, his nights in the station bunkhouse still represent to him emergency sleeping, a make-shift before the return to his real bed at home; he inhabits this bed less than the bunkhouse, but it still represents the life of his longest and deepest experience.

Living becomes in this way a series of sharp wrestings and abrupt adjustments. From the deepest home comfort in a few hours out under fire, from the flowered eiderdown with all its associations of peace to that part of the air-raided town, the fire, upon which the raiding planes concentrate their greatest bombload. Does this make the action more difficult to bear? The soldier goes to his action inured to its feel, with no old associations seducing his vigour. 'But,' thought Eliot, 'I'm not grumbling—how about the other end of the scale, how about the withering of a man's spirit after months in the marshy camp, in the desert without end? That's the other end of the scale—a lowering of your faculties through lack of the need to make adjustments. No, I won't grumble. Anyhow, why on earth imagine that either course should be easy? Too many people seem oddly to expect that a life at war, which in peace they foresaw as the end of life, should now by some miracle be made reasonable and pleasant. Absurd'.

Just then a sector of the stack of cans—that nearest the open window siding on to the petrol tank—collapsed. Instantly a high flame burst up as the cans scattered and oxygen blew in to feed the fire smothered inside. But there was no explosion. The tall new flame flapped dangerously at the window sill; the firemen swivelled round the water-jet to cut it down; the flame flared brighter, higher; a chattering school of portly brown birds bounced suddenly up from the top of the brick tank outside, sprouted wings, flew chattering away; the flame rose higher; they swept the cans with their hard broom of water, trying to cut the flame at its source; the force of water only dislodged more cans and the flame leapt suddenly to that size when it begins to hum, and then soon to roar like a fierce wind; it roared, and shot through the window and out of sight, searing up the brick tank; then, as suddenly as it had appeared, it diminished, its new bright glare sank away, a dark blueness hissed at the source of the flame and a drenching black smoke puffed up to mark its extinction. The hose-jet, sweeping away the barrier of cans, had happened to batter straight home on the flame's root.

The firemen relaxed and pulled their faces into those long

dry smiles. Eliot looked up at the tower and saw a new black smear licking the whole length of the brick up to the topmost curve. Then he glanced back at the little black oilcans. A new flame had started up at the back in a less accessible place than ever, shielded by a wall of those black-painted cans, burning its reflected light wickedly behind.

They turned the jet on it and again waited. From somewhere over the shed-top could be heard the echo of hammering; the sound rang freely in the clear air, and at times the voices of workmen—probably builders trundling bricks along some scaffolding—penetrated in leisurely gusts from their place of work in the outside streets. What will they feel, thought Eliot, when the tank explodes? That is—he corrected quickly his perversely wishful thought—if the tank explodes? Probably they would hear no sharp explosion but sense only an uneasy shifting of the scaffold—as though a huge power had turned in its bed, and the workmen's little ears were close to the pillow—and then long afterwards, for they had not expected it, a deep echo would travel to them, a remote sound but sudden, and they would look up knowing that something unusual had occurred, and see over the house-tops the huge plume of black smoke expanding slowly, very slowly, its convolute billow against the motionless sky.

Then since no distracting incident occurred, and Eliot was waiting and watching the same scene as before, his thoughts returned to their preoccupation with adjustments. He widened his vision to include others beyond his service, to embrace everyone within the city—surely their experience to-day demanded equal measures of adjustment? In the first days of air-raids, when raids lasted the whole night through, they dominated life in the city, so that people were more prepared for them and met them with a composure, if indeed unhappily engendered, that rose to combat the expected. Raids consumed a great proportion of the hours of the day by which people measured time. But now into a day of twenty-four hours the raid bursts suddenly, twists and prods its hot barb for only one vicious hour—and then there is silence. There has been a terrible interruption, but it was no more than that, an interruption, an alien force disturbing and accelerating the normal pace of things. . . .

Eliot's thoughts drifting were suddenly interrupted by what he now saw. The officer had climbed through the window and was hacking with his axe at the burning stack! The oil-cans fell away revealing clearly the fire behind them. The officer was cutting a way through for the water-jet. That was reasonable, for he was cutting carefully, but—what had the officer ordered only some twenty minutes before? He had forbidden any of his men to risk their heads beneath the splitting concrete roof—in fact exactly what he was now doing himself. Had the situation altered? No—and Eliot smiled. He remembered noticing how the officer had stood and watched, with no hosejet to occupy his hands, how these hands had fumbled now and again at his belt, how his eyes had continually ranged the fire and the tower, searching for some incident to occupy his attention, but in vain. Now, plainly, the officer was bored. He was so plainly bored that he had jumped inside, either risking the ceiling or forgetting the risk, so that at last he could do something. The possibility of death had receded beneath the huge weight of inaction. Eliot remembered his own perversely wishful thought that the tank would blow up, hardly a conscious wish, but nevertheless a shadow for a moment perceptible in the obscurity of his deeper desires.

Veering the hose away from the officer stumbling about by the stack, he thought: 'This impulse towards action—is there an alternative?' And he remembered suddenly that there was. He remembered a time during the period of night-long raids when he had stood over an unexploded bomb for several hours. The bomb had fallen in the street, breaking a watermain, and lying then without bursting in the crater erupted by the force of its impact. The crater had filled with water from the broken main. This was then the only water immediately available. There was a fire in the building opposite. Eliot's crew were ordered to fight this fire, and Eliot—who was that night operator of the pump—had to draw water from the flooded crater. There was no other source. So they had backed the pump towards the crater, and Eliot had lowered his heavy suction pipe into the water that puddled the dormant bomb. Then for several hours he had stood by the crater, listening to his suction grate on something beneath the surface of the water. On the wrought iron belly of the bomb, on some sensitive nipple that would actuate the charge? Occasionally he had greased his engine, modified his pressure lever, glanced by the light of his flashlamp at the quivering faces of the gauges and dials. And all the time, through the minutes and the hours, the bomb had waited beneath him.

But he remembered that at that time he had felt, after the first minutes, no impulse at all towards action. At first he had felt shocked, he had wished himself anywhere away from the lethal sleeper; he had tilted his helmet forwards, a pathetic move to shield his eyes with even this thin film of steel from the eruption a yard off of vast explosives; he had felt the need to watch the black water, to prepare himself for some preliminary message from the water, when common sense simultaneously informed another part of his mind that none would come; then as the anxious minutes extended he grew resigned, he was fixed there, without alternative, with only the knowledge that if the bomb exploded he would neither know nor hear anything. He was most apprehensive of a second's blinding noise before his extinction, when every nerve within him would scream for mercy, for escape, for relief from the sudden scalding unendurable tension, a moment of extreme anguish unknown to the living; but soon he had put this from his mind, it was too fanciful, it had never been proved. And then, after these first thoughts and their rejection, he found himself feeling—curiously, unbelievably and perhaps for the first time in his life— quite free! A strange sense of restfulness, of peace, of freedom from all desire and all need for action . . . at last he was experiencing a sense of pure rest.

Slowly he realized what had happened. It was simply that the bomb had assumed his personal initiative. The bomb had taken charge of his life and with it his conscience and every responsibility. Everything henceforth rested with the bomb. The bomb was God, Will, Fate. It was the arbitrary power that shaped his life—he himself could do nothing.

That, Eliot thought, was what occurred at the limit of this scale measuring the impulse to action. In degree one must act until some force as absolute as the bomb absolves one.

The officer had climbed back through the window. His leggings glistened with the black sludge from inside and also with streaks of thick creamy foam left spattered over the broken floor from the night's fire fighting. Eliot's crew had been using water for the purpose of cooling the remains of an old fire. The main fire had been extinguished by foam, they were cooling down these hot boxes which had now, with the astonishing tenacity of their heat, burst out into fire again.

Some minutes before, the officer had sent back a message for foam apparatus to be brought up. Now he told Eliot to double back to the Control Point and find out what had happened. The foam nozzles might have been at that moment entering the rear end of the sheds, somewhere behind the thick black smoke—but the officer could not be sure. The blaze was fanning up again, the burning oilcans had proved insistent beyond water. Now the officer wanted foam, quickly.

Eliot let go his grip on the hose. The Control Point was set out in the road, past the sheds. The shortest way there would be over the wall into the adjoining petrol yard. Eliot levered himself over this and dropped down on to an asphalt floor. Across this yard, intertwining and raised waist high from the ground, lay a network of oil-conducting pipes. They ran in every direction, over a space of many square yards between the petrol tanks. Each thick black pipe was an obstacle in Eliot's path, in what had now become Eliot's race. For suddenly, away from the static hose and the immobile tank and the waiting, his mind raced with new urgencies; he wanted to run; in his mind's eye he saw the flames hidden behind him rise higher and he saw again the black smear licking up the cold pink brick.

His fire-boots weighed his running feet, he had to swing himself over each thick iron pipe. For a few seconds there occurred a straight concrete causeway, then this dipped down by some steps into a basin, and rose up more steps, where yet more pipes faced Eliot, sweating now and breathless. Before him rose the buff brick façade of some offices, blackened and old. Beneath an archway and through a tunnel lay the road and the Control Point. He clambered over the last outcrop of pipes—they were too high to vault—and at last he was off the asphalt and lumbering faster over the cobbles of the cartway leading to the tunnel. On either side he noticed scattered everywhere rolls of steel hawser, iron sheeting, the rusted platform of a crane, hundredweights of girders heaped in orderly desolate piles. These rusted iron devices seemed inseparable from the working-man's hard world of cobbles and drays, goods yards and desolate scrap. He could scarcely see their use in a petrol yard, but would have been surprised by their absence. These hard-cast, barren textures were alien to his own world; they were removed far from the crimson eiderdown, from his clerk's life that saw no heavy iron at work, for whom the only great machines with which he came into contact, such gross necessities as buses and escalators on the underground, were painted a cheerful red or disguised with polished wood. At every introduction to these, the real textures of a mechanical age, he was compelled to make yet a further adjustment.

He ran on into the tunnel. His footsteps echoed in the hollow dark. His mind raced full of possibilities that had never occurred to him standing beneath the tank, beneath its very shadow. There he had been a small creature paralysed by the immediate and immense presence of his captor, only half his mind had worked, his blood had pulsed slowly, intimately, as though savouring itself during the last limited and precious minutes. Thoughts had passed through his mind; but slowly, not in the wild abundance with which they poured through him now as he ran. Where would the foam come from? How would he direct the foam men to the shed? Was there an opening at the back? Were they half-way there, lost perhaps among the maze of sheds, proceeding in a wrong direction? Where exactly was the Control Point? Perhaps they were already at work? What would happen to the men in there, by the tank? How soon? . . .

He felt a new fear for his crew. Parted from them, he saw them in perspective, a small group huddled back there, lost among the sheds and the tanks—and as he emerged into the sunlit street beyond the tunnel, he felt how hidden they were from the rest of the world. A car passed, and across its mud-guard he saw a group of fire officers at a street corner, the Control Point.

Above them, on a scaffolding, he saw those very builders whose distant voices he had heard from inside the yard. How unconcernedly they worked! How little—less than little, noth-ing!—they knew of the group of men hidden away behind the sheds! For these builders the raid had finished hours ago. They had slept, they had readjusted themselves to the pace of the working day. So it was with the rest of the city, except for isolated patches occurring suddenly round some street corners, where astonishing heaps of glass lay about the gutters and torn curtains flapped forlornly over their world of broken brick and plaster. Yet in these patches, dead and desolate, occurring suddenly and bounded then again by more acres of the uncon-cerned city, rescuers were tunnelling throughout the day be-neath creaking debris, little cries no louder than a baby's sob might be heard muffled through the terrible lathes and plaster —and at the next corner a man arrives suddenly with a barrowful of oranges, a crowd queues from nowhere, the oranges are gone!

Through the gates to that yard behind him a few men stood pouring water against their death. What would happen? What could happen? The fire might lick up and the tank suddenly blow. The fire might lick up and go on licking the round brick for minutes packing in more heat, but never quite enough. Perhaps the foam would arrive and blanket the cans with thick bubbling cream. Or perhaps suddenly beneath the weight of water lying on the floor above, or from a sudden access of heat from the fire below, the whole concrete ceiling might fall straight down on the fire, suffocating it at one blow, so com-pletely that for some minutes there would not be seen even the last smoke of extinction. Or perhaps the water from that single hose would capriciously take charge of the fire, the fire would quietly peter out! Or the little black cans would explode, two of the firemen would be killed, they would lie small under their sheets, just as Eliot had seen, some mornings back, three other bodies lying beneath sheets, laid temporarily on the floor of a grocer's shop derelict by blast, and looking in the waste patch utterly forgotten and small, the significance of their last contortion dwarfed by the greater wreckage of masonry in the street outside.

Eliot ran up to the officer in charge of the Control Point and gave his message. Foam was needed immediately at the rear of the sheds—had it been despatched?

Just as he spoke an immense shadow darkened the street, as though a cloud had crossed the sun. Eliot watched the glitter die on the officer's badges, and then turned fearfully to look over his shoulder at the sheds. From above their grey roofs an immense plume of smoke rolled upwards, stretching out into the sky, redoubling itself at every second, slowly coiling.

Eliot pointed and tried to speak. He pointed, but as the ominous cloud rolled up, threatening him heavily with the dreadful certainty of his fear, his throat only whispered.

" 'Sall right, mate," said the officer. "See the smoke? That's yer foam done that lot—she's out."

A Saving Grace

THE hour before dusk, when birds begin to rustle about their perches in the bushes, when the hot afternoon is grown old and cool. The house stood empty across the garden. Some windows were shut, others open; but since the sun was falling somewhere to the left and behind, this garden side stood veiled now in light shadow. Each of the windows, whether open or shut, presented a black rectangle without reflection. Their white sills and frames emphasized such a black rigidity, and within no curtains could now be seen—for the curtains were dark as the new shadows prowling now inside each hidden room. In that warm late-afternoon light the grass of the lawn—high and uncut—glowed liquid. Light shone through the transparent tegument of each green blade, though the tallest tips like feathered spears were tarnished with the sun's ageing gold. The grass led straight to the veranda, with its thin white pillars, its white trellised iron-work hung over with green creeper. From this veranda four black windows peered, and in the centre two glass doors stood open revealing a great mouth of darkness among the other blind dark eyes. In such a still air, the house isolated and empty seemed in some way to be moving within itself. One remembered that here was no deserted place—that it was furnished with well-known things, that only for the evening was it empty of people. The vibrations of living had never deserted it. It seemed merely to wait, busying itself quietly about many unseen duties—accumulating perhaps a little dust, sinking by a millionth of a fraction into the earth, expanding here with the heat and there contracting again into itself. It seemed concerned with holding itself together, holding itself in readiness for the return of its children, holding and waiting.

Meanwhile the sun stretched itself over a sky that widened with the cooling of the day. Such evenings, tranquil and clear, cloudless and of a still pristine loveliness—may seem not so much true in themselves as of the memory of other such times, immobilized in the past, irretrievable. They are thus themselves imperfect—for the other lost evening assumes the real raiment of perfection. The entity of such times is made up of a sadness, of the word 'nevermore'. They breed a lost melancholy that is not unpleasurable: rather, it is to be tasted, drunk like some opiate potion of non-desire, for reminiscence of this kind is no more than the ghost of hope, the remainder of hoped-for evenings evoked by the first summer weather now recollected, hopes that were perhaps never realized but which in themselves became the blood of life and now even as memories still invigorate with a shade at least of their ancient ambition.

Thinking thus . . . pondering that after all such melancholic mysteries are never so curious but have their explanations— so often in the simple terms of this or that biological decline— thinking and looking idly across the lawn at the house, the creeper-hung veranda, I was surprised suddenly to see not as before the empty dark square of the open french windows but instead the figure of a woman standing framed by the same inner darkness. She seemed to be wearing white, a broad white hat and a flowered white dress reaching to the ground. It looked from my distance like a dress cut in the fashion of some years past, and I thought—some visitor for a charity, some elderly parishioner wearing the dress of summers ago who had now wandered in through the open front door? So I was rising to show myself—when the figure moved, advanced and I saw who it was. Moreover, a large dog, a Great Dane, came pounding out behind her. I knew both. I sat down. They were my Aunt Hester and the dog Daniel. They had both been dead for what—thirty years?

Both Danny and Auntie Hester I knew well. Danny was my father's dog, a close companion; Auntie Hester was not a real aunt but a neighbour, intimate with the family, who had looked after me during my mother's absences (how well I remember her veil, her wide feather-brimmed hats, the air of perfume about her and the strangely exciting atmosphere

of the furniture of her house so different to ours. I suppose
Aunt Hester might have represented the first breath of a
woman other than mother, a stranger, intoxicating even to a
child and fabulous). So, knowing them indeed so closely,
feeling at the sight of them never criticism but always a close
and safe affection—for the first second I felt nothing odd about
their appearance, they were in my mind too familiar. Death
cannot age, no change can waste the shape of memory—so
this picture, momentarily realized after a pause of several
decades, hardly at all seemed strange. Until reason came to
say they were dead.

I heard all the old stories croak: 'Pinch yourself.' I did. It
made no difference. Aunt Hester walked onto the lawn, and
with Danny panting his tongue out beside her she stopped and
remained standing somewhere between the white tubs of
wallflowers. She stared towards me, though not quite directly
—more at the trees beyond my shoulders. The feeling was
that she was looking through me—rather than I, as tradition
would suggest, might have been looking through her. She was
certainly not transparent, certainly as solid as she had ever
been: the sun managed to catch and glow palely in the top
of her white hat, she threw a dark shadow along the ground
to her right.

Then—through the same window—stepped Mr. Chisholm!
Sun-yellowed flannels piped his long bowed legs, stretched
tightly at his paunch, and above the striped shirt and rowing
tie sat a straightly perched straw boater. His down-stretching
brown moustaches draped with gravity the roundness of his
redly genial face, his eyes glared a ceaseless weak exasperation.
He too was dead.

But I had scarcely realized his whole presence before my
real aunt, Aunt Connie, came out. She advanced, stopped,
and stood with the other two. (None of them seemed aware
of the other's presence, no word was spoken, no greeting made)
Connie was the Aunt with the bone. In her cupboard, deep
behind the cheeses, she had said she kept a long and thin white
bone. With this from time to time she had terrified me. Her
dark hair piled into an overhanging loaf on her frowning

forehead, her pale eyes with their dark circles, her long teeth
—these had lowered over me when sometimes I was alone in
her charge and she had discovered a misbehaviour. "Well," she
would say, pressing her lips against her teeth, "well, do you
want a taste of my bone? Do you want a feel of Aunt Connie's
nice white bone?"—then a pause, and slower—"Shall—I—get
—my—BONE?" Yet, Aunt Connie was as dead as the others,
long ago asleep under the granite angel.

Then the shapes of Ella and Bridie came out, edging and
quicker than the others, as though their black uniforms and
white cap-strings might soil the air, the pathway of masters
and mistresses. They stood close together, away from the
others and a little behind. And, instantly, as though chasing
these their maids came my father and my mother, leading by
the hand young sister May. May had died in a fire one night
in a boarding-house by the seaside—she had been only six-
teen: my father and mother had come back from a concert to
find the fire already dying down. Father now took up the
centre of the group, with mother at his side, smaller than him,
sallow and wistfully shrunken against his huge black-coated
frame. He stood erect, his hair and beard as black as ever, his
six-foot of height and great corpulence giving somehow the
impression of an immense black-coated butcher, a man of
thick white muscle and strong blood, certain of the stance of
his boots and the blunt thud of his chopper.

In a line they stood—Aunt Hester, Danny, Mr. Chisholm,
Sister May, Mother, Father, Aunt Connie and Ella and
Bridie. They stood without moving, though they were real
enough; you could sense a bloom of living about each figure,
as though beyond the immediate eye a small rising and falling
of breath could be sensed, an emanation of breath that can be
felt from the most immobile sleeper but never from the dead.
And from each one, darker than the more luminous shade of
the veranda, extended fur-black lengths of shadow propping
them up against the pinked gilt of that falling sun behind. A
solar exercise: of the nature of a photograph.

It is difficult to express the acceptance of these my dead
that I felt at that moment—can one recollect, for instance,

some almost parallel episode of unusuality and the way in which one's sense of personal ignorance placed this firmly, in the first startling second, within the reasonable plan of expected existence? Say—you are sitting in a boat moored to the side of a creek. It is your boat. The oars drift at the rowlocks; the painter rope at the bows is knotted loosely round an old pole protruding from the mud. You are idling, enjoying the sun, waiting for the time when the lobsters will be on sale in the cottage up the track behind you. So far, so good . . . then abruptly a figure looms between you and the sun. Breathing heavily, this figure is—you find—stepping into your boat, rocking your boat, picking up your oars. With eyes now fully opened you see that this is an old man in a fisherman's blue jersey, that already he has cast off the painter, and that the boat and the two of you are drifting out quietly over the leaf-green waters of the creak. The man picks up the oars. He rows! He says nothing. Once he looks at you, and without smiling, but gravely affable, nods. What, *what* do you do? . . . It's simple. Nod back. There is no other answer. You might think you would be saying: "And who in heaven's name do you think you are?" or: "Don't you know—you're in the wrong boat?" Or something similar. But these would be absurd, you could say nothing of the kind—for this man's absolute sureness of purpose, his passive calm, his lack of all effusive gesture, his nodding acceptance of yourself makes question impossible. He must, you admit, in that first upsetting second be right. It is you who probably have made some mistake. And so, though no reason as yet asserts itself, you decide to wait. Then—exactly then—is the moment of acceptance. No conscious reason has asserted itself. But since you admit his action to be right, you admit that somewhere, beyond your instant understanding, there is a reason quite logical for his visitation to your boat. You must assume your own ignorance, you give him a lien on a place, certain but as yet uncertified, in the scheme of things. In fact, although perhaps questioning the exact reason—you have nevertheless accepted it. So you are rowed across the creek.

It turns out of course that some minutes previously, when

you waved away a fly, this man who was the casual ferryman of the creek thought you were beckoning to him. He expected no further word, the district was taciturn, visitors known to be superior and silent to the natives. Moreover, he had a tumour of the palate. And think of it as you will, that tumour was the only coincidental extraneity. It could all have happened, and doubtless every day does, without such tumours.

In such a way, then, it was necessary to accept for those first perplexing moments the phenomenon of this group of dead people. It may seem in retrospect to have been a far more difficult case of 'acceptance.' But that is not so. The shock of sudden appearance was the same; the absence of all relation to usuality; the passive surety of their stance; the first moment of questioning one's own senses—in fact, of admitting them to be right. So that in extension, alone in the garden and in such a queer evening sunlight, the immediate muddled assumption was that I was perhaps a fiction of my own imagining, my adolescence was a dream, these my known adult superiors were alive as they always had been. And even then, quickly confirming my own adulthood from the material shirt and trousers beneath my eyes—nevertheless I could only be sure that even if these people were in fact dead, that then it was my own conception that death entailed disappearance which was at fault. What, at that lonely moment in real fact, had I to prove that death meant that they should not be there? An idea in my mind—that only. Instinct? There was nothing to confirm instinct. No written letters, no orders, nobody at my side to agree me right or wrong. I was alone—that is important—alone in a deserted garden, and with a mind shocked and therefore in the first place, self-admittedly, not to be trusted.

So—they were there, nine old friends, in a row. But not for long did they remain passive. For a time—how long I cannot think, such periods expand and contract outside the ordinary measurements of reason—they stood motionless, caught in the solar moment, immobilized in the photograph. And as in a photograph, their insistence on *being* grew as one searched further into the picture. Now as the sun sank lower, the shadow of the house welled forward and overcast their few colours in a mono-chrome suspense. They became more of a photograph, more faded, pitched in the lesser light of a lilac evening shade. There seemed, to loom above as in many dulled paintings and photographs, an appalling cloud like the emanation of God—a weight not so much of darkness as of an exclusion of light. It was as though some giant jelly-fish of doom hung over us the little fishes: or as though a fine black wind were passing. But now it failed to pass, it remained, hung on the air, grew steadily more ominous. With it, my awareness of the character of my old friends asserted itself. I felt the awe of the dark days clouding again my adult temples.

If they remained so still—then there was a reason for this? Waiting? For what? It was beyond knowing—yet now the supposition of such a pause, the pause that cannot be without an active ending, insisted upon some future threat. They were waiting, in fact, for something to happen. Something growing within themselves? A quiet malevolence simmering, soon to leap into the thunderflash of attack? Aunt Connie's thin bone? Father's dreadful butchery of the brows? The melancholy never-ness of my dear, unattainable Hester? The twilight was thickening, intensifying like the quiet mauve shadows in the dead hearts of these silent nine. . . .

Midges danced like white powder-flecks in the low-angled glint of the sun. The dew seemed already to be falling. The leaves, the deepening shadows grew moist. An emptiness, premonitory of the long dead night, seemed to be echoing across the world. Still I waited—then abruptly the sun disappeared. The photograph turned to deeply-dusked violet. The white clothes began to glow, the dark gathered into garments of fustier gloom. My senses ached for movement, the long tension seemed to be redoubling itself, gathering, running like a dark wave mounting up into itself, rearing ever higher to its all-flooding, mountainous descent. . . .

Now, at this last toppling, edge-heavy moment . . . out of the window came dancing, tumbling another figure. Absurdly short, round, bright-coloured ginger and purple and brown and pink! Simultaneously the sun blazed out again—it had been hiding behind a chimney! With a high whinny of laughter the little figure tumbled out, hands on hips—and proceeded then without pause to dance an in-and-out jig along and around the line of motionless figures! I could scarcely fix him, he moved so fast—but gradually he came together, a man, short, stout, chestnut-haired; with cheeks mauvely red with laughter; with hair thick-growing and waved on his head and round his devil-arched eyebrows; with gold teeth flashed in a white melon-laugh; with deep red side-whiskers cut square like long hatchets; with a blue shaved strength on his chin; with violet shirt, a pink tie, a gold-brown jacket and a summer promenader's white trousers striped brown; with a huge red dahlia roaring from his buttonhole, diamonds glittering his fingers, a pearl studding his tie! Never stopping he grimaced and giggled, postured and roared, bent himself double, kicked his legs in the air—never for a second did he stop moving. He jigged, he danced, he tumbled. He flashed his smile up at Father, down at May. He threw kisses, slapped backs. The sweat you could see gleaming all over his round carmine cheeks, his stout belly held firm with effort. And all the time he kept singing: "Kunckle, Kunckle—Kunckle's come!"—Then belabouring his balloon-pot with both short arms: "Play some music on the big, bass drum!" One moment he was a ball, the next a cupid spread-eagled in the air. He did tricks, trick after trick—he primp-walked suddenly away with his head turned backwards, you didn't know whether he was coming or going! He balanced himself on his hands, scissoring his tubby legs in the air! He put his hands on his knees and waggled them to and fro so you didn't know which hand was on what knee! He wiggled his feet only and travelled like a fat pillar of coloured salt side-ways! He conjured a stream of flags from Aunt Connie's open mouth, he took bright paper flowers from the seat of Mr. Chisholm's pants! Rabbits jumped from Father's pockets, Aunt Hester's bloomers fell elasticless to her feet! The two maids' apron-bows were tied together behind, they went circling round like a blind sack-race! On thoughtful May's head sat Kunckle's gay trilby, while Kunckle himself now

trailed the streaming bows of a bonnet! Kunkle! He blazed
like a full brass band! He sang like a singing saw! Clown!
Hofnacque! Hocricane!

And gradually, like wax melting, the stiffness left that line
of figures, one after another they moved their heads, shifted
their feet, turned their eyes from their queer lost horizons to
Kunckle dancing around them; the stiffness left their shoulders, their erect necks—it was as if a thousand fibres and small
muscles had eased each a thousandth of an inch. As rigidity
declined, so did the premonitory dangers. Like the raising of a
shadow, like that candle-red sun laughing out from behind
the black chimney, disaster lifted and a warmth was kindled
between them. No more could that stiff relationship—with
its set afflictions and its hard rule, its aggressive tensions for
fear the rule may be broken—no more could the dread casting
of private position gather its cruel eminence: Kunckle had
thrown it with his somersaults. So that now Father burst
suddenly into a gigantic laugh, so that Mother's strained face
softened to a smile and she took three steps forward and
round and back, then curtsied down to May. And Chisholm
and Hester were linking arms in a skirl of lancers. Ella and
Bridie were bent double back-to-back with red laughter, May
was dancing like some long-legged fairy, and at the centre of
this strange and tolerant momentum, this circling and postur-
ing of amused figures on the lawn in the last summer sun-
glow, this graceful motion of people leaning together with the
sway of their drapery surfing about the faster dance within—
at the centre stood Aunt Connie conducting musically the
movement with a white and slender wand, her bone!

Last, I caught sight of Kunckle—irrational, loveable,
tasteless Kunckle, like a tubby puffy steam-engine he was
prancing off into the veranda, I saw his coat-tail flying and
the white striped paunch of his bottom pistoning off into the
dark doorway. He paused once—to look round, flourish his
hat, blow a fine perspiring kiss back to the garden—and then
he was gone! But his company remained long after. Long
after, until, somehow, the figures of my old acquaintanceship
melted—and I was again alone with this empty, human house.

How Claeys Died

IN Germany, two months after the capitulation, tall green grass and corn had grown up round every remnant of battle, so that the war seemed to have happened many years ago. A tank, nosing up from the corn like a pale grey toad, would already be rusted, ancient: the underside of an overturned carrier exposed intricacies red-brown and clogged like an agricultural machine abandoned for years. Such objects were no longer the contemporary traffic, they were exceptional carcasses; one expected their armour to melt like the armour of crushed beetles, to enter the earth and help fertilise further the green growth in which they were already drowned.

Claeys and his party—two officers and a driver—drove past many of these histories, through miles of such fertile green growth stretching flatly to either side of the straight and endless grey avenues. Presently they entered the outskirts of a town. This was a cathedral town, not large, not known much —until by virtue of a battle its name now resounded in black letters the size of the capital letters on the maps of whole countries. This name would now ring huge for generations, it would take its part in the hymn of a national glory; such a name had already become sacred, stony, a symbol of valour. Claeys looked about him with interest—he had never seen the town before, only heard of the battle and suffered with the soldiers who had taken it and held it for four hopeful days with the hope dying each hour until nearly all were dead, hope and soldiers. Now as they entered the main street, where already the white tram-trains were hooting, where the pale walls were chipped and bullet-chopped, where nevertheless there had never been the broad damage of heavy bombs and where therefore the pavements and shop-fronts were already washed and civil—as they entered these streets decked with summer dresses and flecked with leaf patterns, Claeys looked in vain for the town of big letters, and smelled only perfume; a wall of perfume; they seemed to have entered a scent-burg, a sissy-burg, a town of female essences, Grasse—but it was only that this town happened to be planted with lime-trees, lime-trees everywhere, and these limes were all in flower, their shaded greenery alive with the golden powdery flower whose essence drifted down to the streets and filled them. The blood was gone, the effort of blood had evaporated. Only scent, flowers, sunlight, trams, white dresses.

'A nice memorial,' Claeys thought. 'Keep it in the geography book.' Then the car stopped outside a barracks. The officers got out. Claeys said he would wait in the car. He was not in uniform, he was on a civil mission, attached temporarily to the army. It does not matter what mission. It was never fulfilled. All that need be said is that Claeys was a teacher, engaged then on relief measures, a volunteer for this work of rehabilitation of the enemy, perhaps a sort of half-brother-of-mercy as during the occupation he had been a sort of half-killer. Now he wanted to construct quickly the world of which he had dreamed during the shadow years; now he was often as impatient of inaction as he had learned to be patient before. Patience bends before promise: perhaps this curiosity for spheres of action quickened his interest as now a lorry-load of soldiers drew up and jumped down at the barrack-gate. One of the soldiers said: "They're using mortars." Another was saying: "And do you blame 'em?"

There had been trouble, they told Claeys, up at the camp for expatriates—the camp where forced labourers imported from all over Europe waited for shipment home. A group of these had heard that a released German prisoner-of-war was returning to work his farm in the vicinity of the camp. They had decided to raid the farm at nightfall, grab as much food as possible, teach the German a trick or two. But the German had somehow got hold of a grenade—from the fields, or perhaps hidden in the farmhouse. At any rate, he had thrown it and killed two of the expatriates. The others had retreated, the story had spat round, before long the expatriates were coming back on the farm in full strength. They had rifles and even mortars. The news got back to the occupational military and a piquet had been sent over. The mortars were opening fire as it arrived: but they were stopped, the expatriates respected the British. Yet to maintain this respect they had to keep a piquet out there for the night. Not all the polskis or czechskis or whoever they were had gone home. A few had hung about, grumbling. The air was by no means clear.

When the officers returned, Claeys told them that he had altered his plans, he wanted to go up and take a look at this expatriates' camp. He gave no reason, and it is doubtful whether he had then a special reason; he felt only that he ought to see these expatriates and talk to them. He had no idea of what to say, but something of the circumstances might suggest a line later.

So they drove out into the country again, into the green. Rich lucent corn stretched endlessly to either side of the straight and endless road. Regularly, in perfect order, precisely intervalled beeches flashed by: a rich, easy, discreet roof of leaves shaded their passage as the foliage met high above. Occasionally a notice at the roadside reminded them of mines uncleared beyond the verges, occasionally a tree bore an orderly white notice addressed to civil traffic. And occasionally a unit of civil traffic passed—a family wheeling a handcart, a cyclist and his passenger, and once a slow-trudging German soldier making his grey way back along the long road to his farm. But there was nothing about this figure in grey-green to suggest more than a farmer dressed as a soldier; he walked slowly, he seemed to be thinking slowly, secure in his destination and free of time as any countryman walking slowly home on an empty road.

All was order. Birds, of course, sang. A green land, unbelievably quiet and rich, sunned its moisture. Each square yard lay unconcerned with the next, just as each measure of the road lay back as they passed, unconcerned with their passing, contented, remaining where it had always been under its own beech, a piece of land. And when at last the beech-rows stopped, the whole of that flat country seemed to spread itself suddenly open. The sky appeared, blue and sailing small white clouds to give it air. Those who deny the flatlands forget the

sky—over flat country the sky approaches closer than anywhere else, it takes shape, it becomes the blue-domed lid on a
flat plate of earth. Here is a greater intimacy between the
elements; and for once, for a little, the world appears finite.

The carload of four travelled like a speck over this flat space.
And Claeys was thinking: 'Such a summer, such still air—
something like a mother presiding heavily and quietly, while
down in her young the little vigours boil and breed . . . air
almost solid, a sort of unseen fruit fibre . . . a husk guarding the
orderly chaos of the breeding ground. . . .'

Such a strict order seemed indeed to preside within the
intricate anarchy—success and failure, vigorous saplings from
the seeds of good fortune, a pennyworth of gas from the seeds
that fall on stony ground: yet a sum total of what might appear
to be complete achievement, and what on the human level
appears to be peace. And on that level, the only real level,
there appeared—over by the poplar plumes? Or by the windmill? Or at some flat point among the converged hedges?—
there appeared one scar, a scar of purely human disorder:
over somewhere lay this camp of ten thousand displaced souls,
newly freed but imprisoned still by their strange environment
and by their great expectations born and then as instantly
barred. On the face of it, these seemed to represent disorder, or
at most a residue of disorder. But was this really so? Would
such disorder not have appeared elsewhere, in similar quantity
and under conditions of apparent order? Were they, perhaps,
not anything more than stony-grounders—the disfavoured
residue of an anarchic nature never governed directly, only
impalpably guided by more general and less concerned
governments? Was it right to rationalise, to impose order upon
such seed, was it right—or at least, was it sensible? It was
right, obviously—for a brain to reason is itself a part of nature
and it would be wrong to divert it from its necessitous reasoning. But right though reason may be, there was no more reason
to put one's faith in the impeccable work of the reasoning brain
than to imagine that any other impressive yet deluded machine
—like, for instance, the parachute seed—should by its apparent
ingenuity succeed. Look at the parachute seed—this amazing

seed actually flies off the insensate plant-mother! It sails on to the wind! The seed itself hangs beneath such an intricate parasol, it is carried from the roots of its mother to land on fertile ground far away and set up there an emissary generation! And more—when it lands, this engine is so constructed that draughts inch-close to the soil drag, drag, drag at the little parachute, so that the seed beneath actually erodes the earth, digs for itself a little trench of shelter, buries itself! Amazing! And what if the clever little seed is borne on the wrong wind to a basin of basalt?

Claeys was thinking: 'The rule of natural anarchy—a few succeed, many waste and die. No material waste: only a huge waste of effort. The only sure survival is the survival of the greater framework that includes the seed and all other things on the earth—the furious landcrab, the bright young Eskimo, the Antiguan cornbroker—every thing and body . . . and these thrive and decay and compensate . . . just as we, on the threshold of some golden age of reason, just as we are the ones to harness some little nuclear genius, pack it into neat canisters, store it ready to blow up all those sunny new clinics when the time comes, the time for compensation. . . .'

Just then the car drove into a small town on the bank of a broad river. Instantly, in a matter of yards, the green withered and the party found themselves abruptly in what seemed to be some sort of a quarry, dry, dug-about, dust-pale, slagged up on either side with excavated stones.

It was indeed an excavation; it was of course the street of a town. This town was dead. It had been bombed by a thousand aircraft, shelled by an entire corps of artillery and then fought through by land soldiers. No houses were left, no streets. The whole had been churned up, smashed and jig-sawed down again, with some of the jig-saw pieces left up-ended—those gaunt walls remaining—and the rest of the pieces desiccated into mounds and hollows and flats. No grass grew. The air hung sharp with vaporised dust. A few new alleys had been bulldozed through; these seemed pointless, for now there was no traffic, the armies had passed through, the town was deserted. Somewhere in the centre Claeys stopped the car. He held up his hand for silence. The four men listened. Throughout that wasted city there was no sound. No distant muttering, no murmur. No lost hammering, no drowned cry. No word, no footstep. No wheels. No wind shifting a branch—for there were no trees. No flapping of torn cloth, this avalanche had covered all the cloth. No birds—but one, a small bird that flew straight over, without singing; above such a desert it moved like a small vulture, a shadow, a bird without destination. Brick, concrete, gravel-dust—with only two shaped objects as far all round as they could see: one, an intestinal engine of fat iron pipes, black and big as an up-ended lorry, something thrown out of a factory; and leaning on its side a pale copper-green byzantine cupola like a gigantic sweet-kiosk blown over by the wind, the tower fallen from what had been the town church. This—in a town that had been the size of Reading.

Almost reverently, as on sacred ground, they started the car and drove off again. Through the pinkish-white mounds the sound of the motor seemed now to intrude garishly. Claeys wanted only to be out of the place. Again, this destruction seemed to have occurred years before; but now because of the very absence of green, of any life at all, of any reason to believe that people had ever lived there. Not even a torn curtain. They wormed through and soon, as abruptly as before, the country began and as from a seasonless pause the summer embraced them once more.

Claeys stood up off his seat to look over the passing hedges. The camp was somewhere near now. The driver said, two kilometres. Surely, Claeys thought, surely with that dead town so near the men in this camp could realize the extent of the upheaval, the need for a pause before their journey could be organized? Surely they must see the disruption, this town, the one-way bridges over every stream far around, the roads pitted and impassable? Yet . . . what real meaning had these evidences? Really, they were too negative to be understood, too much again of something long finished. It was not as if something positive, like an army passing, held up one's own purpose; not even a stream of aircraft, showing that at least somewhere there was an effort and direction. No, over these fields there was nothing, not even the sense of a pause, when something might be restarted; instead a vacuity stretched abroad, a vacuum of human endeavour, with the appalling contrast of this vegetable growth continuing evenly and unconcerned. That was really the comprehensible evidence, this sense of the land and of the essence of life continuing, so that one must wish to be up and walking away, to be off to take part not in a regrowth but in a simple continuation of what had always been. For every immediate moment there was food to be sought, the pleasures of taste to be enjoyed: what was more simple than to walk out and put one's hands on a cap-full of eggs, a pig, a few fat hens? And if a grey uniform intervened, then it was above all a grey uniform, something instinctively obstructive, in no real sense connected with the dead town. The only real sympathy that ever came sometimes to soften the greyness of this grey was a discovery, felt occasionally with senses of wonder and unease, that this uniform went walking and working through its own mined cornfields and sometimes blew itself up—that therefore there must be a man inside it, a farmer more than a soldier. But the grey was mostly an obstruction to the ordinary daily desire for food, for fun, for something to be tasted. The day for these men was definitely a day. It was no twenty-four hours building up to a day in the future when something would happen. No future day had been promised. There was, therefore, no succession of days, no days for ticking off, for passing through and storing in preparation. There were in fact the days themselves, each one a matter for living, each a separate dawning and tasting and setting.

Suddenly Claeys heard singing, a chorus of men's voices. A second later the driver down behind the windshield heard it. He nodded, as though they had arrived. The singing grew louder, intimate—as though it came from round a corner that twisted the road immediately ahead. But it came from a lane just before, it flourished suddenly into a full-throated slavic anthem—and there was the lane crowded with men, some sitting, others marching four abreast out into the road. The car whirred down to a dead halt. The singing wavered and stopped. Claeys saw that the driver had only his left hand on the wheel—his other hand was down gripping the black butt of a revolver at his knee. (He had never done this driving through German crowds earlier.)

"It's not the camp," the driver said. "These are some of them, though. The camp's a kilometre up the road." He kept his eyes scanning slowly up and down the line of men crowding in the lane's entry, he never looked up at Claeys. Then the men came a few paces forward, though they looked scarcely interested. Probably they were pushed forward by the crowd behind, many of whom could not have seen the car, many of whom were still singing.

Claeys stood upright and said: "I'd like to talk to these . . . you drive on, get round the corner and wait. I don't want that military feeling."

The men looked on with mild interest, as though they might have had many better things to do. They looked scarcely 'displaced'; they had a self-contained air, an independence. There was no censure in their stare; equally no greeting; nor any love. Their clothes were simple, shirts and greyish trousers and boots: though these were weather-stained, they were not ragged.

Claeys jumped down. An interest seemed to quicken in some of the watching men as they saw how Claeys was dressed— béret, plus-fours, leather jacket. It was because of these clothes that the military in the car gave Claeys no salute as they drove off; also because they disapproved of this kind of nonsense, and this may have been why they neither smiled nor waved, but rather nodded impersonally and whirred off round the corner. They might, for instance, have been dropping Claeys after giving him some sort of a lift.

So that Claeys was left quite alone on the road, standing and smiling at the crowd of expatriates grouped at the entrance to the lane. The car had disappeared. It had driven off the road and round the corner. There, as often happens when a vehicle disappears from view, its noise had seemed to vanish too. Presumably it had stopped. But equally it might have been presumed far away on its journey to the next town.

The men took a pace or two forward, now beginning to form a crescent-shape round Claeys, while Claeys began to speak in English: "Good afternoon, mates. Excuse me, I'm Pieter Claeys—native of Belge." None of the men smiled. They only stared hard at him. They were too absorbed now even to mutter a word between themselves. They were searching for an explanation, a sign that would clarify this stranger. They were unsure, and certainly it seemed unimpressed. "Good afternoon, comrades," Claeys shouted. "Gentlemen, hello!"

Without waiting, for the silence was beginning to weigh, he turned into French. "Suis Claeys de Belge. Je veux vous aider. Vous permettez—on peut causer un peu?"

He repeated: "Peut-être?" And in the pause while no one answered he looked up and above the heads of these men, feeling that his smile might be losing its first flavour, that somehow an embarrassment might be dissolved if he looked away.

The country again stretched wide and green. Claeys was startled then to see sudden huge shapes of paint-box colour erecting themselves in the distance. But then immediately he saw what they were—the wings and fuselages of broken gliders. They rose like the fins of huge fish, tilted at queer angles, grounded and breathlessly still. Difficult at first to understand, for their shapes were strange and sudden, and of an artifice dangerously like something natural: brightly coloured, they might have been shapes torn from an abstract canvas and stuck wilfully on this green background: or the bright broken toys left by some giant child.

Claeys tried again: "Gijmijneheeren zijt blijkbaar in moeilijkheden. Ik zou die gaarne vernemen. . . ."

The Dutch words came ruggedly out with a revival of his first vigour, for Claeys was more used to Dutch and its familiarity brought some ease again to his smile. It brought also a first muttering from the men.

They began to mutter to each other in a Slav-sounding dialect—Polish, Ukrainian, Czech, Russian?—and as this muttering grew it seemed to become an argument. Claeys wanted instantly to make himself clearer, he seemed to have made some headway at last and so now again he repeated the

Dutch. This time he nodded, raised his arm in a gesture, even took a pace forward in his enthusiasm. But now one of the men behind began to shout angrily, and would have pushed himself forward shaking his fist—had the others not held him.

It was not clear to Claeys—he felt that the Dutch had been understood, and yet what he had said was friendly . . . he began to repeat the words again. Then, half-way through, he thought of a clearer way. He broke into German. There was every chance that someone might understand German; they might have been working here for three years or more; or anyway it was the obvious second language. ". . . So bin ich hier um Ihnen zu hilfen gekommen. Bitte Kameraden, hören Sie mal. . "

The muttering rose, they were plainly talking—and now not to each other but to him. The crescent had converged into a half-circle, these many men with livening faces were half round him. Claeys stood still. Overhead the summer sky made its huge dome, under which this small group seemed to make the pin-point centre. The green quiet stretched endlessly away to either side, the painted gliders stuck up brightly. No traffic.

". . . Bitte ein moment . . . ich bin Freund, Freund, FREUND. . . ." And as he repeated this word 'friend' he realized what his tongue had been quicker to understand—that none of his listeners knew the meaning of these German words. They knew only that he was speaking German, they knew the intonation well.

He stopped. For a moment, as the men nudged each other nearer, as the Slav words grew into accusation and imprecation, Claeys' mind fogged up appalled by this muddle, helplessly overwhelmed by such absurdity, such disorder and misunderstanding.

Then, making an effort to clear himself, he shook his head and looked closely from one man to the other. But the composure had gone: they were all mouth, eyes, anger and desire —they were no longer independent. And this was accumulating, breeding itself beyond the men as men. They had become a crowd.

Knowing that words were of no further use, Claeys did the

natural thing—wearily, slowly he raised his arm in a last despairing bid for silence.

An unfortunate gesture. The shouting compounded into one confused roar. One of the men on the edge of the crowd jumped out and swung something in the air—a scythe. It cut Claeys down, and then all the pack of them were on him, kicking, striking, grunting and shouting less.

Claeys must have screamed as the scythe hit him—two shots thundered like two full stops into that muddle, there was an abrupt silence and two men fell forward; and then another shot and the men scattered crying into the lane.

Those three soldiers came running up to Claeys' body. They shot again into the men crowding the lane; but then the men, bottled up in the narrow lane, suddenly turned and raised their arms above their heads. The soldiers held their fire, their particular discipline actuated more strongly than their emotions. Two of them kept their guns alert, gestured the men forward. They came, hands raised, shambling awkwardly. The other officer bent down to Claeys.

He was almost finished, messed with blood and blue-white where the flesh showed. He was breathing, trying to speak; and the officer knelt down on both his knees and raised Claeys' head up. But Claeys never opened his eyes—they were bruised shut, anyway. And no words came from his lips, though the officer lowered his head and listened very carefully.

Through the pain, through his battered head, one thought muddled out enormously. "Mistake . . . mistake. . . ." And this split into two other confused, unanswered questions, weakening dulling questions. Broadly, if they could have been straightened out, these questions would have been: 'Order or Disorder? Those fellows were the victims of an attempt to rule men into an impeccable order, my killing was the result of the worst, that is, the most stupid disorder. . . .'

But he couldn't get the words out, or any like them. Only— weakly, slowly he raised his right hand. He groped for the officer's hand, and the officer knew what he wanted and met the hand with his own in a handshake. Claeys just managed to point at the place where the men had been, where they still were. Then his head sank deep on to his neck. Again the officer knew what he wanted. He rose, his hand still out-stretched from Claeys' grasp, like a hand held out by a splint. Then he started over towards the men.

Instinctively, for this hand of his was wet with blood, he wiped it on his tunic as he walked forward. Without knowing this, he raised his hand again into its gesture of greeting. There was a distasteful expression on his face, for he hardly liked such a duty.

So that when he shook hands with the first of the men, proffering to them, in fact, Claeys' handshake, none of these expatriates knew whether the officer was giving them Claeys' hand or whether he had wiped Claeys' gesture away in dis-taste and was now offering them his congratulation for killing such a common enemy as Claeys.

The Little Room

THE Nun Margherita was escorted with ceremony to the
threshold of her new little room without windows; but
there the Mother Superior and her sisters excused themselves
and left Margherita alone with the five appointed artisans,
who then immediately proceeded with their duties.

While three of these women artisans busied themselves with
lengths of plastic boarding—these looked almost like boards
of asbestos into which hairs and husk had been mixed—the
other two artisans erected a firm brass guard over the
manometer already cemented into one of the inner walls.
Thus the three women occupied with the boarding acted as
an impromptu guard over the threshold, while those within
were able at any moment to glance up from their work and
observe at close range any dilatory move on Margherita's
part.

But Margherita had removed herself quietly to the side of
the bed and seemed simply content to sit there and view at
her leisure the equipment of her new room, which, of course,
she had never seen before.

However, it differed little from all the other rooms in the
convent. The walls were distempered a pale green, the polished
linoleum reflected the same colour. There was little furniture;
only her bed, a simple affair of polished walnut with a green
silk coverlet, a small prie-dieu upholstered in similar materials,
and a table; a miniature electric fire stood in one corner; but
otherwise the room was bare, appearing thus with its shining
surfaces immaculately clean, orderly, but unvisited. There
hung about it an air of melancholy, the same that breeds in
the deadly clean gleam of all those small suburban parlours,
touched but unvisited, that day after day wait, dying of the
afternoon light, for the good rustle of dust, or for a book to be
thrown across their immaculate monotony. But of course no
such afternoon light ever penetrated into Margherita's room,

for there were no windows through which it might enter. Only in this way did the room differ from all other rooms; but that is enough, for the character of a room is conditioned as much by the angles of light diffused upon it as by any other decoration. Margherita's new room had no windows, then—but it was illuminated by concealed bars of bluish white electric light that cast upon the room what approximated an afternoon light, colourless, and originating from no definite source, perhaps thus even the more monotonous, for its very essence was artificial. This light illuminated with unwavering severity a bowl of large white daisies that the Mother Superior had placed by the prie-dieu as a gesture of her personal impartiality.

Up to this time Margherita had comported herself with commendably calm reserve. Such very placid behaviour might have been mistaken for complacency—but Margherita was in no way indifferent, she knew her position, and now she regarded the busy movements of the artisans with interest. Perhaps it was the very presence of these other women that enabled her to maintain a tranquil attitude towards such fatal proceedings.

Margherita was in process of being walled up. In a very few minutes the final boards would be nailed into place, and she would then be abandoned for ever to herself and her little airless cell. Then there would be many hours in which she could repent her sin. She had been sentenced for "the usual" —of which in fact she had been guilty on more than one occasion—and now it only remained for her to undergo the "prescribed treatment". For the moment, though, these artisans supplied her with feelings of company, it was difficult indeed to imagine life without people when these artisans were working around. Otherwise Margherita accepted as inevitable the process of her sentence—it was traditional and usual, she would never have dreamed of criticizing so venerable and deeply rooted a custom. If unpleasant things are expected, they are easier to accept—the more so if they are not to be accepted in the very next instant.

The three women on the threshold had almost completed

the fourth wall. They handled the light partitioning material with fluent ease, wielding their hammers and needles without effort, with the careless surety of workers skilled with their tools. They hammered the partitions together, sealing each socket with a nail, while along the floor they stitched deep into the carpet and on the ceiling deep into the tapestried frieze to ensure absolutely the exclusion from the room of all air. And at last, when only a narrow slit remained, they paused leaning against the new partition and chatting, for it was impossible to affix the final board until the other artisans inside had finished work on the manometer.

This instrument, of which only the dial showed, was already inset firmly into the wall. But since its function was to register the decline of oxygen in the atmosphere and since thus its slow needle would demonstrate to Margherita the speed of the approach of her suffocation, tempting her at some critical moment to injure the instrument in the belief, perhaps, that it was the agent of death rather than its mentor—for such reasons it was the custom to affix over the dial an outer trellice of brass wire as a shield against interfering hands. At all costs the manometer must be preserved—it was a refinement that was traditionally indispensable. How otherwise could the confined person be assured of a proper appreciation of the truth of her death? How could she grasp the full significances of her declining hours? For instance, without the exact message of the manometer, she might swoon prematurely, thus dying unnaturally early; or an optimism inherent in her character might decry the possibility of death, postponing in the strength of that belief even physical atrophies and thus protracting death artificially. In either case the dying would have been robbed of its natural proportion, and this was opposed to the convent philosophy. At all costs matters must take their allotted course. There must be no artificial stimulation, no short cuts, no illusions whatsoever—real experience according to the laws of nature afforded the prime base upon which all matters, including the suffocation-confinement, must be ordered.

Of course, it had been argued that illusions were illusions

according to natural laws—after all as themselves the illusions they occurred within the machinery of natural minds, they did not occur anywhere else—but nevertheless the highest intendants clung to the conception of an arbitrary norm which they styled as the real experience of a majority. Yet—came the constant complaint—how could any majority be proved more real than its minority? People on the sliding scale between the flesh and the spirit were difficult units with which to deal—there might be more of one sort but was it the right sort? What was the evaluation of a "real" person. There might, for instance, be a majority of units far too fleshy—but this majority though convincingly numerous might also be convincingly sub-real? In a ceaselessly changing world among ceaselessly changing inhabitants, who was real, at what stage, now? Glib answerers maintained easily that there was no change, that the old world was the same and that human nature never, never changed. And that was the kind of answer given by the intendants, who, at this stage of their doctrine, smiled with pitying distaste at their interlocuters, raised their white eyebrows and sucked at their hollowed cheeks, invoking then such ready panaceas as "common sense" or even—could this veil a conspiratorial return to the flesh?— "horse" sense.

However, such problems did not concern Margherita as she watched the artisans finally stand away from their task and then survey the fitment with satisfaction. They turned to Margherita with smiles, as though wishing to be congratulated on their skill, and for her part Margherita thanked them, nodding her approval and smiling into their faces. For some minutes the three of them chatted about the manometer; then the artisans began to wander about the room, fingering the bed and the walls awkwardly, now quite plainly worried as to how they might take their leave. Margherita, too, found their company increasingly irksome—there was an emptiness now in their relations with her, almost as though they had left her already. No longer had the three of them a mutual interest. The only subject of meaning to all of them, the manometer, had been exhausted. The atmosphere became really embarrassing, so that Margherita felt almost glad when the three artisans in the corridor began to yawn very loudly, and finally to summon the two inside, complaining that there were many other duties to perform, that valuable working hours were being lost.

The two inside leapt at this chance, they jostled each other in their haste to bid Margherita farewell. In a few seconds they had disappeared through the remaining slit in the wall. Margherita was relieved to see them go. Only when the final board was being nailed into place did she raise one hand towards them in a slight gesture of restraint. Then she wanted the two artisans back. But then it was too late. She was alone.

For some minutes she stood in the centre of the room, slowly tasting the new silence, the breathless silence, and the first sensations of being quite alone. The four walls, the floor, the ceiling—in fact six walls and their eight immaculate corners. Her eyes slowly roved these surfaces, one by one, and then suddenly she realized their similarity—there was no opening whatsoever, no familiar shut door, no window frame, only the plain unrelieved walls. It seemed impossible, no place could be like this. Perhaps there was a door behind her. Her senses told her there must be a door. She spun round— to face a wall. The door was eluding her, it contrived to exist behind her all the time! But spin as she might the door was too clever—it disappeared every time, just in time! Once she thought she had caught it in the corner of her eye, a misted rectangle just fading, like a shadow left on the eyes by a strong light. Several times she pretended to turn one way, then suddenly spun round in exactly the opposite direction. She tried even to disguise her thoughts, as if the omniscient door could read her mind. But every tactic proved useless—the door was too clever by half!

Then she looked up at the concealed channels from which the light came—it seemed to her that the fanning of this light might be heard. She strained her ears. Yes—a buzzing, a slight continuous whirring! For a moment her striving senses brought this companionable sound, but as her hearing relaxed so the noise faded, there had been no noise after all, nothing there but silence, a silent light, motionless, painted.

She shrugged her shoulders. The room was impassive. Nothing moved, it projected no character whatsoever. It was bare, yet compact. It gave no sign of warmth, but was not cold. It echoed no sounds, nor did it consume sound. Whatever happened in that room happened by itself without the aid of the room, against a neutral background that neither projected nor absorbed. Margherita walked over to the bed and sat down. Her footsteps clattered on the linoleum an exact sound, unechoed, unmuffled. She rested her head on her hands and stared at the floor. What was there to do?

Yet the room without character seemed nevertheless to be alive, to contain invisible and inaudible motions, as if its function were to hide things going on just outside its walls. It radiated the impassive energy of a surgeon's waiting-room with its connecting door shut and watchful; it was like the interior of a large refrigerator, where there was no actual movement but the sensation, almost perceptible, of ice forming somewhere behind the walls, perhaps within the walls themselves. Of course, there lay also about this room a strong foretaste of doom—that was only natural, and Margherita felt it herself, though as yet she had not been moved by any deep apprehensions, remaining so far resigned beneath the weight of inevitable traditions. For all their massive ponderance, traditions such as these impose themselves gracefully, their approach is foreseen, they come slowly, with no sudden shock, with the footless tread of encroaching lava.

She rose from the bed and went over to the manometer. Through its brass screen the dial could be seen distinctly, its needle steadily pointing to a number, never quavering, encircled steadily by imperturbable spikes of enumeration that, of course, never moved. This girdle of numbers, some red, some black, lay engraved and meaningless. The units rose in hundreds, their many "O's" and the enormous aggregate signified nothing to an imagination accustomed to count in simple threes and fours. These figures were vacuous, inestimable. If they expressed anything to Margherita, they expressed only an infinite plenty—thousands of "O's" to go before anything could happen, thousands of pounds of oxygen to eat, hundreds of cubic hours to pass. Margherita turned away from this impossible instrument, walked over to the electric fire, switched it on, careless that the ravenous little filament would squander her oxygen, careless with her wealth of hours.

Many years had passed since Margherita's novitiate, she was quite accustomed to solitary confinement. The idea of loneliness held no terrors for her. She went to the prie-dieu and on her knees addressed a prayer to the organization in which she believed. Presently she rose and went again to the bed. There she sat in contemplation. The glowing filament burnt at her air, a quiet and hungry bar of vermilion silently murdering her. But Margherita hardly thought of this acceleration; really she had not yet appreciated that she was about to die. She had often considered death, but never her own. She could never imagine her own death, in fact she had never tried—the idea was inconceivable. Even now there was no startling evidence to direct her thoughts. She was whole, healthy, fed, warm, breathing. Her hands were still hands, they told her beads, each finger was as sensitive as ever; her body filled the inside of her, she felt the usual pains in her left shoulder and a cramping discomfort down on the left of her back; her mouth felt pleasantly fresh, her eyes a little tired; this was her body as she had known and felt it inside her every day. The idea of its disintegration simply could not occur to her. Despite the disciplines of humility, an animal self-confidence assured her of life; her entity lived; and since its function was to live it could not consider itself dead, nor would it be capable of beginning to think in so negative a direction. Certainly these present surroundings implied death to her thinking brain. But here also she was deluded, for the tradition and its ceremonial had outpaced its truth, so that now only the idea was true.

Nevertheless after some hours Margherita became restless. She had meditated but had not been able to lose herself in meditation. This was ordinarily a difficult exercise, but to-day the power eluded her altogether. Something distracted her. Perhaps something in the room? But why, she thought, should this pleasant little room prove so distracting—it was like all the other little rooms in the building? Yet unlike the others this room disturbed her. Then she realized—it was of course the absence of windows. She thought: "Alone in my ordinary cell, however absorbed I become in my meditations, I am always accompanied in some measure by the presence of the window. A little square of sky, a little square of the infinite." (But there was more to it than that. There were the small shadows, for instance, that surround all windows—the shadow just above the top frame, where in all the room the shade seems deepest, and again beneath the sill where it is really deeper, for the floor reflects no light. Windows and doors are deeply impressed in the child's first consciousness; they are the exits to mysterious regions, the entrances through which the first shapes of terror may approach, the first images of love. They are more than doors and windows, they are rectangles of infinite drama, mystery, and hope. They remain forever a mental comfort; one should never move far away from these facts perceived in the first moments.)

Margherita stared with greater curiosity at the green distemper surrounding her. She saw this closed expanse for the first time windowless. The first feelings of uneasiness disturbed her, so that still seated in an attitude of meditation her eyes glanced quickly from one side to the other, urgently revealing their whites, her eyes moved but her head remained still. Deprived of meditation, the full vacuum of these enclosed hours revealed itself to her. This artifice for solace had crumbled, she did not know how else to occupy herself, she had no further means. Loneliness descended and, thrown open against herself, she looked down at her monotonous empty hands and at her feet without direction. She could see, as if they were plainly laid out in layers, the hours that remained for her in the little room—an endless staircase of hours, not descending, as in reality they must, but instead ascending. She could see the stretch of these hours but never the limit. Because they had really to be experienced now, minute by minute, they appeared endless; outside the room, thinking of another in her position, she would plainly have seen the limit, she could have contracted the period into a reasonable perspective for criticism. But now she was the subject, the hours had no clear ending, indeed life itself seemed monotonously long.

Then, strangely, this very idea that life was endless provided it with an ending. By "endless" she had really meant "of immeasurable length". But by virtue of not being able to measure the tedium, and thus endowing it with a proportion, though of a length unendurable, she had really now envisaged an absolute length—and a length must have an end. So for the first time she saw the possibility of an end to life. Perhaps, appalled by the great staircase of hours, she began to hope for an end, and her wish enabled her to feel it quite clearly—so clearly that, if those misted hours had really formed a staircase, she might have seen the fringe of the topmost carpet, the brass rods, the level space of the landing. But the hours were not of carpet; they were a misted succession of grey apprehensions formed sometimes into the letters of the word "hours", sometimes with no form but only weight, and so the final hour could never be seen but only perhaps felt; she was still defeated by the appearance of the final hour, death was still inconceivable.

Yet . . . she had felt the idea of death, if not of her own death. She could think of death on the one hand and of herself on the other, and know that these two ideas were related, although perhaps she could see no form to the link. And so, sitting on the green bed, her hands still clasped, in the lonely room where nothing moved, not even the heat, not even the light, where everything was quite still, where she alone could be heard to move and the rustle of her gown sounded deadly exact and solitary—there Margherita began to pity herself. She could say to herself: "I am to die." And now, in a remote way, to feel this, to regret it as the first unshed tears began to swell below her throat. She felt suddenly small, neglected, abandoned by those she had known and the environment that had nourished her. She had been left alone! Not one of her sisters cared, perhaps they had even ceased to think of her. She crossed the linoleum to the prie-dieu and tried again to pray. But 'I am to die', she thought.

All through her prayers she felt the weight of death. "This person, this 'me' that I am, this familiarity of hands and memories and close wishes and dry disgusts, this well-shaped shadow lying about my inner thoughts—all this is going to die. It will cease to be. There will be nothing more of it." Then she thought through the words and the half removal of herself in prayer: 'It cannot be?' And then: 'But what of God?' 'Where will God be if this 'me' ceased to pray here beneath him? I feel Him in my prayer, it is in my thoughts that He takes a shape. If, then, there is no me to feel Him . . .?'

Many hours later she crossed herself and rose. Her mind had grown drowsy, the air before her eyes had become confused and thick. Perhaps a glass of water? She went to the bed and looked for the jug. There was bread laid out—but where . . .? They had forgotten to leave her a jug. That was too bad! To think that they had forgotten such a vital detail of ceremony! Such casual behaviour belittled the ceremony. Could the ceremony have been as important as she had imagined? Perhaps they had not thought it worth while to devote their energies to the ceremony, perhaps they were impatient for other things. It might be that even now one of them—perhaps the Mother Superior herself—had remembered the jug and had personally questioned one of the artisans; yet even if the artisan had answered truthfully, which was to be doubted under the circumstances, then it was probable that the Mother Superior had nevertheless dismissed the question of the jug from her mind at the first opportunity. It was plain that her old companions had no further interest in her, their thoughts had skipped easily away to other matters. She, Margherita, was finished with. They had even hurried the ceremony of finishing her, so that an important detail had been neglected, and this showed that Margherita had been forgotten even before they had gone. How thoughtless these people were, how treacherous their affections!

Margherita felt this neglect deeply. Now that the ceremony

had been exposed as unimportant, it seemed equally unimportant that she should die. It seemed now to be a mistake,
and without point. All her efforts were to be of no purpose, she
would die unseen, unheard, unfelt for, even unremembered.
Hopelessly she took up the bowlful of daisies and drank the
bitter yellow water from among the stalks, several of which
fell untidily across her face as she drank.

She replaced the bowl and her eyes remembered the
manometer. She hurried quickly clicking over the linoleum
and peered through the brass shield.

She gasped—with surprise, with shock, with fear, and then
for the first time for breath itself. The manometer needle had
advanced to within only ten units of the blue-starred danger
mark! Soundlessly, with no show, no hesitant jerk, slowly it
had revolved on its inexorable sweep, sweeping down the
units with its remorseless steel stick. 'If it would quiver!'
Margherita thought. "But it's steady, steady as the hand on
one of those electric clocks. You can't see it move," she whispered, the words chasing themselves fearfully, "yet it moves;
you can feel the time shortening; but from minute to minute
you can't see how short it is; for as soon as you fix on a minute
it has gone; the hand has already approached some seconds
further on." She put her fingers to her face, scrambling at
her features, as if she needed in some way the reassurance of
their shape. "And what happens? Does the speed increase?
Still imperceptibly, but nevertheless increase? Does the
pressure rise at a compound speed?"

Her hand on her face came away wet, as streaming wet as
if she had stroked a rain-spotted windowpane. She gasped for
breath. Then, trying to concentrate, she took carefully
exercised long breaths and paused in between these with her
lungs empty. She seemed to be breathing not air but weight.
It was so heavy to breathe, it took a pull—she perspired with
lack of breath. Then, suddenly agile, like a cat wide-awakedly
springing from half-sleep, she whisked her arms at the cord
of the electric fire—the plug snapped out and rolled on the
linoleum with an empty clatter. To have left on that bar
biting through the precious minutes of her oxygen! She stared

down at the plug, panting, her hands with their white scrubbed knuckles clenching and unclenching.

Why had she attacked the cord so savagely? Because the air in the little room had grown hot, uncomfortably hot? Because the needle's advance had thrust her suddenly far up her staircase of hours, so that this sudden proximity with the end had flooded her with an equally abrupt desire to live? She had not felt this desire before. In the endless hours death had seemed remote, inevitable, but remote. Now it was dangerously close. She looked in all directions, moving her head slowly in the heat, but with thoughts that raced, to find at all costs a way of spinning longer the hours she had wished to compress. But these hours were now remorselessly compressed about her ears, they weighed above her eyes in the blanketing air, air that was thinning yet thus grew thicker, and her eyes finally returned to the needle, which even in that short time had encroached upon two further units.

Desiring life, her regrets took form. She no longer pitied herself as one neglected. She strove now strongly to recapture what might have been. Her regret now consumed the past: 'What I could have done—in that long time!' The sensation of growing physically smaller which had distinguished her mood of self-pity now reversed itself in these positive regrets; she felt herself grow larger with the striving of thought, her mind attacked, she summoned at each possible resource, she seemed to grow large with the strength to attack. The time that had been wasted, the opportunities missed, the effort unpractised! Now in the shortening moments she thought back upon her past as a compartment of time whose every minute should have been utilized with faultless efficiency. She imagined only an inexhaustible energy that had been voluntarily let to waste; she forgot the necessities of rest, of disorder, of lethargy, of melancholy, of digression—all the negative inclinations through which incomplementary struggle the positive energies exist. No, in Margherita's sweating, panting, leadening brain there thrummed only the one-faced regret that the minutes should have been more used. She could have done this, she could have done that; she could have planted this avenue of limes, she could have blessed that maritime charity; she could have proceeded with her journal, she could have seen to the re-equipping of the dairy; she could, standing on a hill once at dawn, have appreciated more fully the message of the iridescent skies, she should then have exerted her senses so that forever after she could have re-created that dawn; she should have multiplied her lover by many lovers; or she should have disdained him, incarcerating herself within a shell of virtue shaped by tireless impeccable effort. Whatever it was, she had left it undone. However much she might have done, she could have done more. However much she had seen, she had not felt deeply enough. However much she had felt, she had not stored those feelings deeply enough.

As again she rose the bed groaned—the sockets of its wooden frame seemed to complain beneath an invisible pressure. She dragged over the short linoleum journey to the manometer. Her feet lifted heavily, every such effort was made beneath a great weight. Her head nodded. She had made the journey from bed to manometer many times. Each time, even as her steps grew slower, as the needle swept closer, even within an ever-increasing desire to lie down and sleep—her desire for life mounted. As she looked through the engineer's brass at the dial she saw the needle encroaching, as steadily as the sun's shadow, upon the second unit beneath the blue stars.

Gasping, with slack shoulders, she dragged the prie-dieu from its place and set it by the manometer. She knelt beneath this dial and stared, not for a moment longer daring to leave it. Who knew whether the needle might not suddenly spring forward? If she stared, she could superintend its motion and know intimately the speed of her decline.

As the oxygen thinned and the pressure weighed more heavily, as the time shortened and the blue stars approached, as the units increased their pace and her grasp for life fought at their speed to slow it—sorrow for the past changed to a more virile regret for the future. The vague images of matters in which she was not ordinarily interested suddenly enthused her—the building of the new wing at the southerly aspect of the old convent fortress; how appalling that she would never, never see this! The installation of an electric laundry—this would occur, many other changes would occur, but she, dead Margherita, would never, never see them. . . . Gripping the sides of the prie-dieu and staring through the brass shield she thought then of the problems of doctrine, of behaviour, of prayer that would now never be solved. She thought with growing envy of the great goodness of life, the browning bloom of autumn fruit, the ice-slush on the February roads, the draughts of winter, the huge dusty leaves shading their green midsummer trees—and above all the skies that went with the seasons, the skies to which she had looked for consolation . . . a thousand good things she would never feel nor see again. She would never see them. There was no hope left. Yet—it was still inconceivable that there should be no hope! Hope was bred in her living veins. But a new weight of reason was cruelly forcing at her senses, crushing out hope. With her pale scrubbed nails she began picking at the little brass wires of the shield. One finger-nail weaved like a worm through the square and thrust itself straight at the needle, smelling at it, but yet inches away. Her mouth began to mumble, sagging, letting water.

How many hours had she endured in that room? A hundred? Days perhaps? There had been no measurement. The last hour of all dropped its lead on her nodding neck, she slipped from the prie-dieu on to the floor. Her finger pointed still at the manometer, but weakly. Her veil fell aside, revealing the nunnish pate bald as an ant's egg. An intolerable weight of sleep pulled her down, pulled at her eyelids, her puffed breathless lips, the muscles in her blueing cheeks. She forgot about the future.

Her eyes craved only for some taste of the present, the sight of birdflight, the colour of a flower, the pressure of her man's arms, the lick of fruit. How strong these could have tasted! Her lips opened and her tongue came swelling out, ever fattening, gently to lick the air.

The vision of the taste of fruit faded, as in their order the wish for the future had faded, the regret for the past, her first incapacity to believe in death; and now lastly as a swimmer out of her depth she began to struggle, her fore-brain gone, only now like an animal, thoughtless but to move, the instincts alone in charge. The naked head lurched from side to side, her arms weaved slow frog movements, weakening at each thrust. Before long they stopped moving altogether.

The Windows

I

ALTHOUGH Broome had lived in this house for nearly fifteen years, it is to be doubted whether he ever saw it. Similarly, did Broome ever see his wife? That, too, is open to question, although not perhaps in quite the same way.

Broome had good sharp eyes. A pattern of wrinkles surrounded them, and in these lay old evidence of scrutiny and sceptical experience, as though Broome were accustomed to screw his eyes up the better to adjudge clearly his perspectives. These eyes of Broome's could stare clearly through the rifle sights, survey keenly the plans of the bridges he built. They could soften, too, when they regarded his wife. And on occasions they would sit back in themselves, glittering wisely, during his grave talks with Son. Broome's eyes, in fact, performed the ordinary offices of eyes in an ordinarily efficient manner. They were good eyes, in fine condition for a man forty-five years old.

One May morning, when the trees smelt heavy with blossom and the young leaves glistened wetly, Broome stood on the gravel drive in front of his house and looked up at the dark, white-framed windows above him. Each window implied a room in his household. The barred lattice by the ivy looked out from Son's bedroom—the nursery of ten years before. A thin window high up under the eaves belonged to one of the maids. Lower down three broad squares, with sunblinds already shading them, reminded him of his wife's bedroom, a room of cool atmospheres, of perpetual afternoon shade. Two smaller windows, he saw, were open. Through one of these the pink bathroom tiles glinted. And through the other, one could just make out the curve of the staircase ceiling.

Broome puffed at his cigar and fidgeted with his watch-chain. Although the sun was warming his back, although his breakfast had settled well, although a day of open leisure lay before him—he felt restless.

He stood looking at the house and wondering what he wanted to do. The morning was under way, it was eleven o'clock. The clattering of breakfast dishes had died down. He could hear his wife upstairs telephoning for more food, while—he could imagine—the maids hurried about the bedroom laying out fresh-smelling sheets. Someone splashed water in the the bathroom. From the back of the house a tin bowl rang on the stone kitchen yard. A dog barked, once. A sparrow fluttered from the ivy, hovered and flew away. And over the whole façade of this household of his shone the morning sun outlining already with black shadows each red stone pediment, each false arch. It flashed into golden glitter the high weather-cock, it bleached the white-painted eaves and the white banisters of the front balcony. The sun shone through beech-leaves and the leaves of a sycamore, freckling the cool edge of the lawn, burning the gravel yellow, making of the sheltered woodsheds and garage a moist village of shadow. The air paused expectant of heat. Somewhere high above a silver fleck aeroplane hummed.

Broome blew out thick-tasting smoke and watched it float serenely into nothing. Then turning suddenly on his heel, so that he made a sharp scrunching sound on the gravel, he walked a few paces up the drive—but immediately turned back, to resume finally his exact position of a few seconds before. His mind felt unusually blank, as though it screened a secret wish of which as yet he knew nothing; and in fact could only vaguely recognize as a wish at all. Rather than investigate such fancies Broome liked to reason according to sharp facts and deadrock circumstances within immediate grasp. Yet—that morning this was not easy. Quite without thinking, he began to gaze closely at a corner of one of the eaves above, The white-painted woodwork jutted out against the blue sky. and with its crown of dark-red tile and the soft shadow beneath, it formed a picture for him that had become strangely significant. But of what? Irritated by the wasted minutes slipping by, he shook his head, shaking it to clear his mind, trying to assimilate the morning as certainly as he clutched the comfortable weight of coins in his trousers pocket.

He thought: 'This is absurd. A sunny morning, the whole day in front of me, and here I am wasting my time like a bored child. Everything is in order. My house, my garden, my health, the company of my wife. Everywhere there are jobs to do, games to play—matters that ordinarily stimulate me. There's time enough to waste later on! Or if you wish to idle, idle properly. Make up your mind to taste your leisure. Lay yourself on the wicker chair underneath the cedar, and make up your mind to do nothing. But at least, decide!'

He took a step towards the garage. The car waited—he would visit the club, perhaps enjoy a turn of bowls. But in the very instant of this decision he paused, during the one step forward he entertained and dismissed three or four alternative plans—to transplant the cactus, to mow the lawn, perhaps after all to spend the morning in the wicker chair beneath the cedar. Again he stared at the white-painted eave, losing himself easily. And then suddenly ne became particularly conscious, in his vague irritation, of the shape of his body, particularly the nape of his neck, as if someone were watching him from behind. But no one was there—he scarcely troubled to look. He knew that in his mind's eye it was he who was looking at the back of his neck, critically perhaps, or if not critically, certainly very closely, so that his body began to feel smaller than it was and oddly defenceless.

His wife called down to him from the window above. "Broome. What are you doing?"

How her voice echoed in the morning air! A moment ago it had chattered, talking into the telephone, like a voice talking into a pillow. But now it coiled out to him, sounding nearer than he would have imagined—the window was just above his head—and curiously clear against his own muddled thoughts. He looked up. "I'm not doing anything. Only smoking."

"In that case can you run me down to the station? It's high time I spoke personally to the goods people about these hens. The telephone seems to paralyse them."

He listened carefully to the open window, noticing with

surprise that the sky reflected in the darkened glass. He pictured his wife and smiled gratefully as in a second he reviewed certain qualities about her that he had always admired, and which perhaps still formed the focal point of his love for her. Small matters, like the quick flicker of her eyelids, business-like as a bird's wing: her calm white hands drawing a thread: her straight neck with its frail determined chin. "I'm sorry," he said. "But I promised myself to transplant the cactus this morning."

Her head poked itself from the window. She smiled pleasantly, with no hint of displeasure, and said no more than: "I'll manage."

Broome then walked quickly across the drive and through a gateway of shrubbery to the greenhouse. There he waited, doing nothing. He picked up a cactus pot and only some minutes later discovered that it was in his hand. A few weary flies buzzed through the stillness. He stood helpless, he was waiting surrounded by objects which had no use for him. Pots, watering cans, twine, sticks, trowels—such things lay within reach but aloof, as though they had turned their backs on him, or perhaps had not even gone so far as that, but were instead looking straight through him, a man who had no existence for them.

Why had he come here? Broome frowned at the weathered whitish panes. "Why didn't I take her down to the station? I would have quite enjoyed the run—and her company. Why, in the middle of my indecision, when a decision is suddenly offered should I reject it by making an alternative decision? I like my wife, I love her. It's not as though I want to avoid her. What's wrong—to-day . . .?"

As he stood there, as, holding his breath with guilt, he heard the car drive away, as he then slackened his shoulders with relief—he repeated the words "To-day!"

It must be admitted—that was an exaggeration. This state of indecisive mind had been growing on him during the last few weeks. It had begun with the first days of warm weather. It had coincided with the appearance of the leaves. It was then that he had begun pausing, right in the middle of some decided errand, inexplicably, obsessed involuntarily by the appearance of some quite ordinary object. Yet to him at such a time the object became suddenly extraordinary. A garden roller for instance would assume an unbelievably profound significance. An open window—from the kitchen, perhaps, with its chequered curtain blown out and hanging limp on the ledge— would seem isolated from all its immediate environment, projected and independent of the rest of life. The white eave and the painted balcony at the front of the house were in particular interesting, almost reminiscent. But of what? That he could never decide. Nor be sure indeed if these things were actually reminiscent or not. Perhaps instead he was merely more aware of life, more interested in the process of living. Certainly his desires were satisfied, and desiring nothing, he should appreciate more the pure fact of existence: he had his house, his son, his wife, his security. Yet finally—he dismissed these thoughts and attributed his strange behaviour to spring fancies!

But now, since weeks later this condition of mind had remained constant, had even grown stronger, he dismissed the possibility that the spring alone could be the cause of his trouble. Why, for instance, had not the spring weather similarly affected him on previous occasions? Perhaps, then, this was a symptom of his age, some critical change of life, the inception of a new cycle? One could not be sure. He stood, in the closed silence of the greenhouse, bewildered, guilty, an unwanted cactus in his hand, still undecided as to what he wished to do.

The pot dropped to the floor and with a crash broke into a mess of red fragments and crumbling earth. "There!" he said, "I did that on purpose!" (His eyes had become obsessed with a pattern of flies in a corner of the remote glass roof, he had forgotten absolutely about the pot in his hand, it had dropped.) He stooped to pick up the pieces, murmuring to himself the specious psychological explanation as though it excused him.

A knife-pain ripped into his finger. He snatched his hand away from the pottery, saw the plum-coloured blood swelling from a long cut. A heavy drop splashed onto the tiling. With a sense of relief, he pulled out his handkerchief and wrapped it round the cut finger. His indecision vanished. He walked briskly back to the house.

Upstairs he knocked on the door of a back-room. A sound like a skirt rustled as though to hide itself, and then, muffled— his sister-in-law's quiet voice. As he went in, speaking about his cut finger, he was struck by the smell that made this room different from all others in the house. A smell of linen, of sewing baskets, of all clean folded cloths : and with this a brisk scent of lavender mixed with the smell of a stronger medicated soap. A saucer of water lay before the gas fire. The bedspread and the cupboard paintwork were white, pale red roses patterned the wallpaper, a sewing machine stood on a dark wood table. The room faced north, and to Broome's sun-dazzled eyes it seemed that his sister-in-law sat in shadow, although her chair, an old rocking chair, stood by the daylit window. He distinguished her black head and her white starched dress, but her face was blurred in the greyish dark of the room.

Yet, presently, as he sat on the stool at her feet, while she bandaged his cut finger, he looked up and saw her sallow face and pale eyes more clearly, perhaps, than ever before. Once again he found himself drifting away from the immediate moment. He began to study intently this face bending over his finger. How clean the skin had been washed, how soaped and shined it looked! Then, as her eyes were lowered to his finger he noticed the lines forming about her mouth, lines of resignation, of long distressed patience. This sister-in-law must have been distressed by the years, by her lonely spinsterhood ; yet how clean and compact she kept her plain face, how vigorously she scrubbed it! He looked closely at her ear beneath its lank black hair, no longer a fresh ear, no longer exhaling warmth and tenderness : yet immaculate.

The face bent over his hand, and Broome heard the rustle of starched linen from her collar as she moved her arms slightly, firmly, to the deft knitting of her fingers. 'I'm looking up into a face,' he thought. 'It's a long while since I sat and looked up at a face, a face bending over me, with my head close to a lap.' He glanced down at her hands which were scrubbed like pale clean vellum, at her colourless finger nails, and then he saw beneath the skin several clear mauve veins. The fingers twisted and knotted his bandages with an astoundingly simple efficiency.

He spent the rest of the morning talking to his sister-in-law. He made no decision to stay in the room, not even at the critical moment when the finger was finally bandaged. He merely remained where he was, talking casually, standing at the window in silence while his sister-in-law sewed. Perhaps in a sense, he was still drifting through the morning: no direct decision had been made. Yet on the other hand no alternative now presented itself. Without questioning himself, as though it were the most usual thing—although his visits to this room were in reality most infrequent—he remained idly chatting, his eyes resting now on the white bedspread, now on the gas-fire, now on his sister-in-law's placid, colourless face. He made no move even when the car returned crunching across the gravel drive away somewhere in the front of the house.

At one o'clock his sister-in-law dropped her sewing with a sigh, and they went down to lunch.

II

Now in his forty-fifth year, with a cut finger, Broome sat in his garden. His wife sat by him. They sat beneath the cedar in the centre of the lawn, and over the tea-table they discussed amiably and contentedly topics of the household, a letter from Son, a dinner party for the following week. From a window above came the ticking of a sewing-machine, a routinous noise that in its suggestion of labour emphasized the leisure of a summer's afternoon on the lawn.

"She never seems to stop," said his wife. "I wish that sometimes we could get her to go out. She never sees any new people. She'll end up an old maid."

Broome frowned. "She seems contented enough."

"But it's the wrong sort of content. Everything else has

passed her by. She falls back on this artificial apparatus—as if it excused any further effort."

"I thought she'd always liked sewing—surely it's not so sudden a preference as you make out?"

His wife nodded. "In a way you're right. I'm exaggerating. Really, it's that she has always been quiet, always detached from us. Well—if she likes it . . . but that machine gets on my nerves, she plays on it as if it were a child, it seems to absorb her so, yet it's only a machine, an artificial thing . . ."

"Artificial . . ." Broome repeated the word drowsily and then suddenly found his mouth forming another word—"Nonsense." But he never spoke it, for the reasoning that prompted it, a succession of surprisingly clear thoughts, set out in order like the ordered roads on a map, disappeared as abruptly as it had arrived. He could not recapture it. His mind drifted. His eyes wandered up to the high windows beneath the eaves. There they remained.

A pink May tree, a drooping yellow laburnum, one high lilac bush with its blossom already withering—these rose in shapely progression towards the red stone wall of the house. Then up the wall itself ranged the white-framed windows, each a secretive mirror absorbing a dark reflection of the trees and the sky, until high under the white eaves themselves lay the smallest topmost windows, windows of never-visited box-rooms and maids'-rooms, back-windows with a hint of a hidden curtain, windows that lie at the top of steep carpetless stairs which are mounted, tentatively, only on rainy afternoons when the house is still and quiet.

Broome watched the windows and felt himself grow small. Into his mind there drifted impressions of a black enamel pram, a white parasol, a tarred road glistening and smelling in the hot summer sun. The shadow of a cloud passed for a second over the house, then disappeared. The windows came to life again, their sleeping summer's life, a dead life in the potent sunlight. Why, thought Broome, why, why?

His wife talked on. He did not hear any more.

III

During the next two weeks Broome relapsed further and further into the possession of his intermittent wonderings. These grew deeper, more frequent. Soon every sound, smell, taste, sight took on the same deep, new, inconsequential significance. He ceased to visit his office. He made every excuse to be alone, to wander in the garden, to be free only to stand and peer at things. Everything he saw pulled at his heart with a yearning for . . . he could not tell what.

He began to visit his sister-in-law more often. His visits were never an occasion. His sister-in-law never ceased to sew— with her head leaning to one side, squinting a little with her pale eyes at the needle, at the stitches passing out of the machine.

Then one afternoon, as Broome stood looking down at her colourless hands, her lustreless hair, he became conscious, quite suddenly, of something intolerable in the air, an intolerable oppression, as it were the root of the monotony of all afternoons, of all the continuous tickings of clocks, the monotonous tappings of sewing-machines, the hours, the long incidentless hours that lay between tasteless meals, the uninterrupted vista of the day's dying light that seemed imperceptibly to start dying immediately upon the last stroke of noon.

He stood appalled at so suddenly receiving the full weight of this monotony, in the dull white-painted room, above the lank hair of this woman bowed over her sewing machine.

In the heavy silence a sparrow fluttered out of the ivy with a sharp thunderclap of leaves.

Abruptly he bent down upon his sister-in-law, grasped her white-starched shoulders, and then raised her slowly from the chair. At the first touch of his fingers, she shivered—and sat terribly still, like an animal curled at the smell of danger. Unmoving, her shoulders bowed, her head to one side, he lifted her to her feet. Then, as he turned her to him, her eyes, small eyes with short lashes, squinted quickly up at him. A sly, frightened queer glance. But powerful—it brought to him a sense of his own face. He saw suddenly his own eyes, dull and swollen, he felt the pressure of a frown between them, he realized suddenly that his lips were munching. Quickly—he softened his face. But his sister-in-law had seen it. The fear faded from her eyes. In its place—a slyness of recognition passed over her tilted face, passed not like a light but like a shadow.

Controlling himself, Broome said, "Come for a walk." His voice was pitched too high.

"A walk? I never go for a walk."

He had to speak over the lump in his throat.

"You must come for a walk. Now!" His voice steadied itself. He added more casually: "Just a stroll along to the bridle-path. It'll do you good—please. . . ."

Without speaking, with no assenting movement of her head, she turned to the door in silence. They walked down the stairs and out into the garden. He never touched her. But she walked as though led, her arms down to her sides, her head tilted, as if she were listening, yet robbed of the power to hear.

They walked across the lawn without exchanging a word, and then entered a grass-green avenue between beech-trees and slim silver-birches. At the end of this avenue stood a stile, and beyond it the bridle-path. The avenue lay in a premature leafy dusk, lit only by a green phosphorescence shining from the fresh shoots of grass. Broome saw the stile many yards ahead along the straight avenue. He measured the distance to himself. His sister-in-law's white dress hovered beneath his shoulders, his brain thundered with the milling thoughts. What had he nearly done? What was he going to do? What intense purpose seemed to be forming from his erupted emotions?

As he walks forward, as the stile comes nearer, one matter is decided. He will take some action about his sister-in-law. In some way, he must affect her, he must enforce his impression—possibly before the stile is reached. The stile becomes a boundary, a limit of time by which certain things must be done. Broome's heart begins to pump loudly, so that he hears the acceleration of his own blood in his ears. Yet they are walking quite slowly.

And then gradually, from the torment of his dimmed mind, a purpose precipitates. The white shoulder in the corner of his left eye gives him a sudden, unexpected clue.

He has recognized in the white shoulder a similarity to the white shoulder of his nurse! Now his mind leaps back to the windows—and thence to the days when as a small boy, he used to look up at the high windows of his old home, and wonder what strange rooms lay behind them. He sees how the white eaves of his present house are like the eaves of his old home. He remembers watching them on summer afternoons lost in the past—a misted time that seems now to exist some-where about his knees, waiting to be re-experienced, waiting round his knees, just at the place where his own boy's head would once have been. One by one he sees, with mounting excitement, the objects that have recently so fascinated him—the garden-roller, the painted balcony, a laburnum tree, the white back-room with the sewing machine. He sees clearly that these all had their counterparts in his childhood. He tries to picture, as a whole, his present house. But that he cannot. . . . He sees only the eaves and the windows and the other dis-connected objects. He realizes—he has never seen his house! All he has ever seen has been an accumulation of separate images—each a recollection. Perhaps, he thinks, one can never see anything but this. Perhaps all matter once experienced is never experienced again, but occurs again only as a recollec-tion of the first experience: perhaps one is continually re-experiencing one's virgin awareness . . .

That must have been so with Broome—Broome, certainly, who had submerged so forcibly his first sensibilities, who had manufactured from his ambition an artificial world, a world constructed above and clear of the river of his first associations. Now they, the inalienable associations, were finally reclaiming him.

The stile draws near. As his feet tread further along the grass avenue, he wonders suddenly: 'Forty-five? The "danger-ous age?" Surely—it can't be that I am just veering off into my last adventure? Is this the frantic discontent of a middle-aged man wishing above all things to grasp at his receding chances of romance?'

Then he looks down at the dull black hair beside him, he sees again the scrubbed, polished hands at his sister-in-law's cuffs. "No," he says. "This is not the last lust. This is . . . a sort of relapse." And then—as one does at some moments of crisis—he penetrates for a brutal second the screen of his vanity, he reviews himself for once quite clearly. He sees how his wife was a creation of his own, how her beauty and her elegance were objects of his imagination but never of his love. He sees his life, and he does not want it.

He looks down at the white shoulder and his hands yearn to the whiteness and they clutch it. The stile is only a yard away.

Broome seems to fold down over the figure at his side. His lips press into her face: and then he finds her mouth.

Who knows why the white body surrenders? Who knows why the dammed up desire of years should so suddenly be spilled? Who knows why it flows out with such instant acquiescence? Who knows why there is no struggle, no cry even—but instead a limpness of absolute surrender in the white body in his arms? Is this soft reciprocation not, after all, the liberation of desire—but perhaps of a personal love, a long hidden love for Broome himself personally? Perhaps Broome's teeth—for he bit straight into her cheek—decided her surrender. It was a shock greater than the shock of his embrace, so that her natural rejection of his embrace was overstepped and excused.

A week later they eloped—possibly for ever—and Broome's wife was sadly telephoning the police.

The Boiler Room

ON the day this happened Piesse arrived at the boiler-house feeling bad in his marrow. All through him, in the inside of his bones, under his muscles, in his brain under its heavy skull he felt bluish and soured, not because he was cold, not even ill, but because for some reason a disgust filled him, so that he shivered against the sight of everything, men and things, with considered hatred and some sort of a remote contempt.

He could not have said exactly why his lips pursed—as if he had licked a sharp lemon—when he saw the blackened brick wall of the school to which the boiler was attached; nor why he turned away his head quickly as a boy, pale and smiling, nodded from across the street; nor why he raised his boot to kick at a pile of refuse upon which some cats were crawling, lowering the boot then and not kicking only from weariness and a foreboding that his action would only disturb things and make things move, and that then they would be even harder to endure.

He stared hard at the daily paraphernalia of the school-yard—the swings, the stone steps and the tiled washhouse—but his head was bent a little forward, as though even in this deliberate self-assertion of his contempt he was afraid of some power behind or above him. Yet the air above was anything but oppressive, it was fresh and light—the white wintry sun shining low had made one pale golden sheet of high clouds—and a dry, brisk morning echoed with invigorating sounds, tram-bells, the barking of frisky dogs, a sudden peal of treble laughter from one of the classrooms above. Once, looking up at the black branches of a tree veined delicately against the pale sky, Piesse began to wonder why he felt so bad on a morning like this: but while he was still looking at these branches, he wondered instantly why he had ever felt good about things at all, on any morning, anywhere, ever.

Some boys were leaning out of an upstairs window, fluttering an overcoat and a piece of ragged cloth. Piesse stared at them, not understanding, vaguely knowing only that they were playing some game of absurd importance to them. He frowned, resenting, feeling that their action was a personal affront. Then a little girl in a red cap ran out of the school door singing. She ran past him, a small ball of clothes on white legs, and disappeared suddenly hopping round the corner of the gate. He stopped and stared after her, grunting out a noise of contempt, and then turned again towards the boiler-house.

Sailor was already there, squatting in his blue overalls on one of the iron rails, and intent on a part of his forearm bared of the sleeve. Some long hairs had furred over a tattoo pattern. He was cutting these with an old razor-blade, and at the same time hummed a tune right back in his teeth, so that the sound hissed out like a whistle. Without really raising his head he nodded good morning to Piesse, who felt immediately a new accession of disgust, resenting instantly this new proximity. Though the two of them had worked closely together and amicably in the lonely boiler-room throughout the year, to-day Piesse just stared hard at the black eyebrows jutting out over Sailor's two little deep-set eyes—as though he now saw them for the first time. Fat, piggish Piesse walked over to the shovels, crushing the coke-grit under his iron-shod boots. "Eight-thirty," he said.

Not hurrying, they began their work. They took the various jobs slowly, often pausing, wandering over to the doorway, smoking cigarettes. Occasionally the sailor made a remark, or grumbled out a joke, or even asked Piesse a question. Piesse never answered, only grunted acknowledgment, keeping his eyes down at his job, or anywhere away from the old sailor's boiler-suit and from his face, and sometimes he pressed his lips together tighter and made no answer at all. But this hardly mattered, for Sailor's questions were not framed to be answered—they were facts believed by Sailor, merely stated as questions; for he was a close man, needing neither the acclamation nor the opinions of others. He was proof against

Piesse's mood. He shovelled coke to himself, he talked for himself. When he was resting he seemed always to be adjusting something about his person, setting himself independently ship-shape. In the afternoons he would spend long periods sewing, or washing out a shirt, or gathering together old scraps and junk—wood, dustbin iron, even rags—to take home and make into something. Piesse was irritated that the sailor remained unaffected by his silence. He thought darkly of this as an insult. Yet if the sailor had criticised his mood, or, worse, had tried to cheer him up, his insides would have seized with rage. He resented Sailor's presence, either way. He avoided meeting his eye, straining to do this. But whenever the sailor's face had turned away, when the coast was clear, he glanced quickly over at him, letting his eyes rest for a moment on those overalls, savouring a swelling resentment. Then, as Sailor moved again, he flicked his eyes down instantly. At all costs he wanted to avoid the sailor's eye. And when he was looking down, hard, so that his throbbing neck arteries darkened the room around and above him, he became terrified that perhaps the sailor would quietly be watching him. He was afraid then that the sailor would question him, cajole him into speaking. Furiously, sweating with both fear and attack, he polished the brass of the big thermometer. He felt he would burst.

The two big boilers stood side by side, separated by a few feet and a protective railing. Their massive round iron sides were rusted brown and then greyed over with dust, but the railings encircling them had been painted bright green, so that in their rough cast heavy skins the two boilers looked like huge dormant pachyderms enclosed by a bright fence, truncated featureless monsters, but alive. They never moved, never quivered, made no sound. Yet they seemed to live. Of huge weight, they enclosed within their bellies a tremendous sleeping power, hundreds of compressed degrees of heat, piled up energy bursting to split free.

Sometimes Piesse or Sailor would open the mouth-doors and then the red middles could be seen. Inside—one could not see too far, not all the secret by any means—a mass of red coke nuggets burnt beneath slight, slow-licking flames like the little devil flames in an old picture of hell. As the door opened a fiercely-singeing breath would blow out, fanning into the air already dry and hot. It would perhaps be Piesse's job to shovel coke into this inferno, or to rake out with his long iron the golden clinkers.

Their jobs were various. Coke lay piled in two hills, one reaching to the ceiling in an alcove by the door and the other smaller hill ranged opposite the boilers. They had to shovel coke from the big pile to the lesser pile, wheeling a light iron wheelbarrow in between. From the smaller hill they fed the boilers. They had to rake the boilers, to clean the thermometers and pressure gauges, to polish a little brasswork, to adjust the valves round the school buildings, to inspect the safety steam escape, and many similar tasks. But their main work was below in the boiler-house, shovelling.

They had worked together for a long time. It was a slow, lonely job, in a colourless place, a cell segregated from the rest of life and from all the soft textures—but they had always managed well with each other. The alienation of the place had brought them together, so that their confidence was close. They knew and respected each others' fancies and small habits, they shared the two pictures of each others' homes and wives and children. Sometimes they took a drink together at dinner-time, and once Piesse had spent a Sunday at the sailor's house. But on the whole, although their companionship in the boiler-house had become very close indeed, they kept their home lives apart. They quarrelled seldom and then on trivial matters that were adjusted without malice and soon forgotten.

But to-day, like a pile of coke suddenly falling, Piesse's equanimity had collapsed and in the void a venomous worm pullulated at every moment more viciously.

Towards eleven o'clock he was shovelling from the small coke-hill easily into his shovel. The light, dried slag scooped easily into his shovel. It was no effort to lift this stuff, light as pumice and holed like dry lava, and so Piesse went on thinking. His resentment festered and seemed to go on swelling inside him—yet he was not an unselfconscious man, so that even in the course of his rising hatred there came to him sudden flashes of tranquillity and extraordinary calm query. At these moments he forgot the sailor and wondered what could be the cause of his mood, abruptly surprised at himself. Why should he behave so oddly on this ordinary morning? What was this dry hate corroding him? How could the people and the things about seem suddenly so difficult to endure, so worthless? He noticed that he found them worthless; that was because the people themselves seemed to attach to their actions such vital importance.

He looked back on the morning and remembered that until he had left the house his mood had been normally cheerful. Then, as he thought, he recalled certain distressing emotions. A cab-driver had shouted at him when he had crossed the road, and standing on the opposite curb a man in a black hat had laughed. Something about the hat, which was broad-brimmed and clamped down over the man's ears—something there had irritated him. At least he recollected a distaste when now he thought back on the episode. Perhaps it had been the man's face, with yellow carious teeth smirking at him from a hard grey stubble on the lip above? And then the post office had refused to meet an order for money, questioning his identity so that he had begun to believe that he was not perhaps himself after all, and would never again be able to prove this. That had made him furious, and perhaps had frightened him, too; although, of course, he had realised even at that time that the notion was ridiculous. Apart from these two mishaps, he could recollect nothing unpleasant about his walk to the school, except that the latter part of the journey had seemed to grow duller and duller, and that his breakfast had returned upon him. Something had upset his digestion. Now he felt blown out inside, too unwieldly for his frame. But, he argued to the grey nuggets of coke, it was absurd to think that two such insignificant troubles could have affected him so deeply. Things like that happened every day. Although it was not to be doubted that his depression had overtaken him only during his walk. Or had it? What about the previous

night, or had it been the night before . . . hadn't he been
dreaming of something that he could scarcely now remember,
but something certainly disturbing? His mind drifted back,
settling upon this or that experience of the previous days,
remembering, accepting, rejected, even inventing things that
possibly had never happened. He jabbed viciously at the coke
and it grated drily on his iron shovel. The moment of detachment passed. Again the atmosphere closed in darkly around
him, he felt himself redden, and suddenly he wanted to sob.
Everything became dull, unendurably dull again, so pointless
as to seem almost aggressive. He flung the last shovelful deep
into the boiler and slammed the door shut.

As he bent upwards, by chance he came face to face with
Sailor for the first time. Sailor had just turned from polishing
a strip of brass on the second boiler. They had been roughly
back to back, and now suddenly they had both turned, and
they were standing face to face.

Piesse was short, so that now he found himself staring a
few inches away from the V in Sailor's blue overalls, a V
crested by a dark shag of hair and a roll of woollen undervest.
In that second, with Sailor perhaps still moving, he raised
his eyes slowly, as though drawn by an exterior will to do so;
he felt even then a perilous seizure slowly looking up the sailor's
neck to his chin, nose, eyes.

The sailor was a lofty man, lank, thin and still gawkish in
his heavy bones. Piesse had to look up at him and felt instantly
aggressive, wishing to cut down this disadvantage. For a
moment neither of them moved. They were shocked at seeing
each other so closely so suddenly, surprised by the coincidence
of turning together. They were shocked then to a standstill
before the laugh that relief should have brought. In that
moment Piesse studied very carefully each feature of the face
above him.

He saw the sailor's skin, sallow and even purple beneath the
eyes. He saw thin, hard lips and a patch of black stubble
where the razor must have slipped. Further up, on the sailor's
high starved cheekbones, several long single hairs straggled
from black pocks in his oily, open-pored skin. Then—the eyes,

small and deep-set like a monkey's eyes. They were pale-grey eyes, ringed with tiny black lashes. All around them the flesh was coloured an ill lilac, shadowing the little eyes more deeply, and from the corner of each there stretched beneath the flesh a purple swelling, like a teardrop bruised in the blood itself. Close down above these eyes jutted a bony brow, overhanging them with two thick bursts of bristling hair. So that beneath these and among the black lashes the eyes appeared like little old things, childish and simian, weak and secretly crying. Piesse shuddered.

All at once the lips split open and the sailor smiled, showing suddenly two rows of large, perfectly white teeth, false, and shocking bright, like enamelled tin against his sallow lips. Piesse shuddered again. With horror he realised that the smile was meant for him—the first direct act of the sailor towards him that morning. His jaw set like sudden ice. Then, somehow, the shovel seemed to fall forward from his hand, perhaps clumsily pushed forward as his hands lost their feeling of things, perhaps pushed by an automatic intention far, it seemed, from Piesse's brain—yet whatever somehow pushed forward hard and quick, so that the handle struck Sailor in the crutch, bending him over abruptly in sudden pain.

The sailor grunted redly, with his hand to the soft part, and then still grimacing raised his face, stretched with pain, and swore. He swore at Piesse's clumsiness right into Piesse's face, spitting the words out through his clownish teeth: "You bitch! You f—g . . . bad-tempered . . . awkward . . . sod!"

Bad-tempered. The word bolted through Piesse's mind and stuck, shutting out everything else. So all the time Sailor had known it! The bugger had known it and nursed it up to himself! Superior? Smirking over the tattoo mark, all to himself?

Piesse clenched his knuckles into a ram of bone—and smacked this hard into the sailor's teeth. He heard the teeth crack before he felt the pain in his knuckle. He saw one white tinny tooth slide out on to Sailor's lip and fall. Then the sailor spat and coughed—the fractured denture and perhaps more teeth must have caught in his throat.

The face opposite Piesse underwent a sharp series of change, as though its muscles were directed by external strings. The changes were each absolute and different, jolted with kaleidoscopic clarity.

A face of disgust, screwed up by the pain and the things he was spitting out.

Then abruptly a new face—as his eyes flickered up to Piesse and the whole expression slackened to something idiot and quite surprised.

This passed as the black brows darkened and Sailor's face set stiff in fury. He clutched up the shovel in his long hands and swung it high above his head, rising again to his full height, poising on his toes, glaring madly before he brought it swinging down at Piesse's head.

Piesse crouched back suddenly terrified. But not at the sight of the shovel about to strike him. Rather he was appalled at the thought of what he himself had done. Like a child he covered his mouth with his hand, as though he had said something wrong. He was ordinarily a passive man. The extent of his sudden action shocked him. The violent broken moment brought him suddenly back to a normal sense of values; he saw now clearly the relationship of himself to others and how he had so violently acted in what seemed now a very distant dream of madness.

But in a rapid instant this terror of what he had done passed and he was assessing the danger of the oncoming shovel. Though a passive man, he came from a boyhood on the streets where boys fought. He recognised the moment before the hard knocks came, so that now he was able to rouse himself. He never could have felt the disadvantage of being in the wrong. Fighting was ingrained too naturally in his muscles. Now he was quick with anger and resource, and still crouching he stretched out his hand, grasped the long clinker iron, and not pausing to weigh it or first draw it back, he lunged it with all his stocky force hard into the sailor's stomach.

Just then, from above, a bell rang. Instantly the air was full of the sound of running feet and the chattering of children's voices swelling out all over the playground as they ran out for their morning break. It was a crystal sound, echoing shrilly, but in some way pure and excited, like the sighing and shattering of windglass.

Piesse fell forward on his lunge. The iron squashed into the sailor's stomach, but never penetrated, blunted off by the resilient overalls. Yet it threw him off his balance, so that he keeled over on one leg, bringing the shovel down clear of Piesse's head, but heavily on to one boot, cutting through the leather and smashing those toe bones beneath. Piesse gave one high, quick grunt as the pain shot right up and through all his body—yet agile and crazy for survival he leapt instantly upright again and faced the sailor afresh, now with the clinker iron back across his shoulder to swing it against the second shovel blow. The sailor held that shovel now like a bayonet and on a level with Piesse's face.

Then they were at it.

In that muffled dry air the irons cracked heavily, not ringing, but dull and hard. Coke-dust gritted beneath their boots and was flung up in a choking cloud round them. Against this fierce motion the walls and coke-piles and the boilers waited. The walls there were whitewashed, streaked with grey dust, bare but for picks and irons hung in the corner. So that the room was all grey and white, with only the green rail to colour it. The massive iron boilers slept their tremendous sleep; the grey slag-piles rustled sometimes and fell, but for the most seemed to wait. White bricks, grey coke and heavy iron made up the big bare cell. The air was dry and stifling, clean in the media of dust and grit, radiating arid heat. From the ceiling hung one yellow electric bulb, weakly charging the air with ceaseless night, slow-ticking nightmare night, bare and vigilant as the air of a fever ward by night-light. This was made more dismal by the doorway, through which could be seen the white day.

The moving shadows of the two men flickered with a greater urgency against other still-cut shadows. Both men moved awkwardly, yet with swift surprising strength. The bony sailor looked too thin to support his shovel, his knees knocked together; he was all bone, long, and his elbows jutted heavily and at precarious angles from a narrow tubular chest. And Piesse—with his fat round belly and splayed feet— was too comfortable a man to have a clinker iron in his hands. Piesse was piggishly comfortable, with a sandy-haired piggish pink face, prominent teeth, naked near-set eyes—and his big feet splayed out, giving him a loutish but innocent waddle, like a fat boy anxious for a game. He lifted these feet quickly, yet by nature still planted them flatly and at absurd angles. He moved them now with ferocious agility, and from his flabby body there emerged a secret and horrible strength, as unforeseen as the surprising force knitted from the sailor's complexity of bones. Both men were badly developed—in no sense the picture of two fine males fighting. But despite their deformity they had lived hard lives of manual work, and curiously from their warped bodies there emerged the un- gainly strength.

For a few seconds, no more, they sliced and parried with the two brutish tools, circling each other, but never hitting through. The shovel and the iron were both too clumsy to be driven with dexterity through the opposite guard. It was easier to parry than to strike through, though Piesse with his iron could hardly sustain the full smashing weight of the shovel.

Then, suddenly, the shovel swung the sailor off his balance. Piesse saw his chance, drove the iron straight for Sailor's eyes. But the eyes moved and the end of the iron caught instead the flesh beneath Sailor's ear, tearing it and blackening the the blood that now suddenly started out. The handle of the shovel caught Piesse's knuckles, numbing all the fingers. He dropped the iron, caught it again with his well hand, swung it up again—this time above his head, one-handed, like a man with a lasso.

His mind was swimming with the pressure of his effort— and also with the chattering of the children playing above, which seemed to grow louder and more confused. It was like the murmur that rings in the ears before fainting, as confused and as suffocating, yet now much louder. Piesse could not shake off this sound. He was, then, still self-conscious, he had not excluded completely the outer world beyond his effort.

Rage should have reddened out all these other things—but perhaps Piesse had remained after all conscious of his first act, of himself in the wrong. He had been able to fight, but nevertheless deeply inside him he felt the blame. The external world of criticism had remained.

With the iron above his head and the sailor stumbling still off his balance, he thought in that fractional second of the children, who suddenly reminded him of little frog-like vermin, untold numbers of small, busy white frogs, each with two legs and two clutching hands, squeaking and preying and eating. Their faces were old, yet small and bright with predatory vigour. He did not quite see their faces, yet that was his blurred feeling about them. And still the chattering screamed louder in his ears, fearful music, the windglass in a gale.

One voice above the others suddenly emerged as a child ran shouting by the door of the boiler-house like a gull swooping and disappearing then instantly on the trail of its own lonely shriek.

Piesse brought the iron down. But once again the sailor parried, catching some of the blow on his tattooed arm. The flat of the shovel slammed across Piesse's chest. Piesse struck again—and then abruptly grew afraid. He backed away, then raised his long, hooked iron again, trying to fight the fear. But it persisted. He was afraid not of his enemy, nor of pain, nor of death. He never thought of death. He was afraid instead of being afraid, of the act of retreat, and in a flood his self-criticism took charge of him, blaming him for that first blow at Sailor's teeth, and now merging into a fear of all criticism, of running away and the odour that would follow him. He gripped his iron and swung it—while above the lonely voice passed again.

But now the child was screaming louder, in greater excitement, and was suddenly joined by two others. They all screamed close by the door, whooping with glee, stamping and in joyful panic screaming, higher and higher. . . .

It seemed that another voice joined even these—as in the same sudden second—and that this last voice would even scream higher in the end than the others, for it seemed to have a greater force beneath it, and to be piping, louder and higher, hissing its cry venomously, as if the child were screaming as a snake might scream, erecting its cry swiftly, a screaming sound that blew out like a knife . . . the top of the boiler thermometer had blown off.

Both men recognised it at once and turned dazed to see the steam pouring from this deafening new whistle.

Number Two Boiler had been overstoked; the furious heat still rising inside had forced the thermometer up and over the danger line, had blown the cap and actuated the warning whistle; something had blocked the escape valves outside; it was only seconds before the big boiler would burst. And as these seconds ticked, the boiler still slept, with murder breaking inside it, crouched for the spring beneath its hood of sleep, while on its side a little panicked brass whistle hooted louder, screaming out the danger call like a furious elvin parasite.

Piesse felt a great lightness flood his mind. The boiler was going to blow, but the warning whistle sounded to him more like a siren for freedom. The sailor had turned his shovel on the boiler door, which now swung open, blowing out its hot wind and bringing a fierce muttering from the overstacked coke inside.

Even during his sensation of relief Piesse's mind managed to flash for an instant back to the child, to the earlier morning, to the group of boys hanging out of an upstairs window overlooking the school yard. Automatically, beneath his relief, he swore. He swore at himself for a fool. How could he have never taken in what they were doing? Had he been mad? For now he saw quite plainly that what they had been doing was this: they had been dressing up the boiler escape pipe, using it as a prop for a stuffed effigy, perhaps of one of the masters, binding the clothes firmly over the steam escape pipe, clogging and stuffing this firmly with cloth.

Piesse had not stopped moving and now shouldered up against the sailor, lunged into the furnace with his iron, scooped out the first red coke. It fell glowing over his boots. Before he kicked it aside he had brought out another rakeful.

The sailor was raking, too. They went at it hard, crouching back a little against the heat—with the idea that they could protect themselves by those pathetic inches from the coming jet of scalding water.

They raked and sweated. The ear-splitting whistle never ceased. It blinded the room with sound, urging them like a single long stroke of the goad. The steam came down off the ceiling and clouded them, so that now they were alone with the red mouth and this new grey blanket of steam obscuring everything else. The air was wet with it, the sweat poured off their faces close to the furnace heat, the monotonous shriek enclosed them. They worked shoulder to shoulder, in absolute concord. The sailor's bleeding ear bent near Piesse's face, the furnace glare showed on Piesse's ripped knuckles. But neither noticed these things. There was only one thought between them—to save themselves, to rake out the fire, if possible, before number two should burst.

Building Alive

AS on a fleet and smooth naval pinnace, intricate with grey cocks and rope and white-painted enumeration—we six on the Heavy Fire Unit drove swiftly through the quiet Sunday streets. Sometimes at odd corners or through a breach in the skyline of tall buildings the huge buff plume showed itself, calm and clean as sand against a pale bluish sky. We as well felt clean, in our blue flaired tunics and silver buttons, too clean for what was coming, conscious of this and awkward at a time when smudged khaki and camouflage net were the equipment of action. The streets were too clean; there were no people, the people were all hidden away cooking their Sunday dinners; one church bell pealed ceaselessly to an empty town caught in the Sunday pause.

Then, gradually, the immaculate polish showed a ruffling, stray scraps of paper suggested the passing of a crowd, a weed of splintered glass sprung up here and there on the pavements, another and invisible weed seemed to be thrusting the window frames from their sockets and ahead, as this tangle grew denser, the street hung fogged with yellow dust.

Our destination lay within the dust. Once inside it was easy to see, only the outer air had painted it opaque. But it was like driving from the streets of a town into sudden country; nothing metropolitan remained to these torn pavements, to the earthen mortar dust and the shattered brick returning to the clay. The fly-bomb had blasted a pause within the pause of Sunday morning.

Ambulances already. Two or three people stood about, handkerchiefs to their red-splashed faces. In the silence a loud-speaker called for silence. The rich living voice appealed to the dead rubble, coaxing it to make tapping noises. And men with long detecting poles weaved to and fro through the mist like slow shrimpers. We were ordered round the debris to search the broken buildings on either side.

At the top of the first flight of stairs, dark and rickety, a light shone through a crack in the unhinged door. The door came off easily. A single shadeless electric bulb hung over a tailor's table, shone weakly and yellow against the large daylit window beyond. On the table lay a pair of trousers, an iron, slivers of glass and splashes of red blood, comet-shaped, like flickings from a pen. Every lightly fixed furnishing of the room had shifted—bales of cloth, doors, chairs, plaster mouldings, a tall cupboard—all these had moved closer and now leant huddled at strange, intimate angles. Plaster dust covered everything. There was no space left in the room, there was nobody in the room. The blood led in wide round drops to the door, the tailor must have been 'walking wounded'. Had he been one of those outside, fingering blindly for the ambulance doors? The yellow bulb on its single string burned on, the only life in this lonely Sunday workroom, the only relic of the tailor's shattered patience.

Then, under the steady burning of this bulb, against its silent continuing effort, other sounds began to whisper. My number two, Barnes, looked at me quickly—the building was alive. Our boots had thudded on the stairs. Now for a moment, no more, they were quiet. They were silent, the light was silent, but falsely—for beneath these obvious silences other sounds, faint, intractable, began to be heard. Creakings, a groan of wood, a light spatter of moving plaster, from somewhere the trickle of water from a broken pipe. The whole house rustled. A legion of invisible plastermice seemed to be pattering up and down the walls. Little, light sounds, but massing a portentous strength. The house, suddenly stretched by blast, was settling itself. It might settle down on to new and firm purchases, it might be racking itself further, slowly, slowly grinding apart before a sudden collapse. I saw Barnes glance at the ceiling; he was thinking of the four floors still hanging above us; he was thinking perhaps, as I was, that the raid was still on and that any other explosion within miles might rock through the earth and shake the whole lot down. Walking in such houses, the walls and floors are forgotten; the mind pictures only the vivid inner framework of beams and supports, where they might run and how, under stress, they might behave; the house is perceived as a skeleton.

Then through the stripped window came further sounds—a distant explosion from the south, and above this the purposeful drone of a second bomb flying louder every moment. The gallows that would mark its course! To each dreadful roof gallows along the bomb's course a black sock would rise to swing like a sentence rather than a warning of death. The sound approached like a straight line. It approached thus for many people . . . everyone on the half-circle of its sound fanning forwards would attach the bomb to themselves. It could drop anywhere. It was absolutely reasonless. It was the first purely fatal agent that had come to man for centuries, bringing people to cross their fingers again, bringing a rebirth of superstition.

Down in the courtyard they were carrying a man out from the opposite block. We caught a glance of him through the twisted framework of an iron footbridge. They had laid him on a blanketed stretcher on the grey rubble. He lay still, bloodless, only his face showing, and that plastered with the same sick grey dust. It lay evenly on him, like a poisonous mask—he looked gassed with dust. Once he struggled, his head turned from side to side. He seemed to be trying to speak. It was as if his real face, clean and agonized, tried to be free and show its pain.

Now, in the long moment it takes these bombs to fly their swift distance—now the drone was already changing its note. The first remote aerial wavering, like a plane engine far up and away, had strengthened and bolted its direction upon our area. It was coming all right. We waited, though there was no time to wait, no real time but only the expansion of a moment so alert, and listened then for the drone to sharpen itself into the spluttering drum-beat of a jet-engine. But beneath this sound, separated from us by widths of sky, the little murmurs of secret life, fearful in their intimacy, could still be heard. And still fixed in a second's glance at the wounded man below, our eyes absorbed the whole courtyard, the waste of rubble between tall, torn office buildings. The iron bridge hung darkly between. Across it a new nest of broken pipes splayed up, a hydra head of snaky lead, but halted, paused like the rest of it. Only the oncoming sound moved deliberately, but this too was fixed, mounted on a straight, straight line that in its regular, unvarying crescendo provided only an emphasis to the stillness of the courtyard. A whole architecture, all that had ever been built, all the laborious metropolitan history had been returned to its waste beginning. The virgin scrap, the grey mortar earth, the courtyard wall torn and stripped into the texture of ancient moon-burnt rock—all these passed, taking breath. Only the little sounds sucking themselves in hinted at a new life, the life of leaden snakes, hesitating and choosing in whispers the way to blossom.

The drone was diving into a roar. We crouched down beneath the window. My eyes now near the floor found themselves facing a gap some three inches wide where the outer wall had loosened itself from the floorboards. The wall was leaning outwards. I saw my hand steady itself on a book of cloth patterns; the fingers were bleeding, the hand removed itself instinctively from the cleanish cloth, cut itself again on more glass on the floor. The bomb was above. We held our breaths, not in all that sound daring to breathe for fear we might miss the cut-out. It seemed much darker near the floor . . . the floor grew as dark as childhood. Only the amazing crack in the wall remained clear, gaping its draughty mouth. The noise grew deafening, a noise now as heavy as the shadow of a wing. Then, in a burst of anger, it seemed to double up on itself, its splutter roared double, it was diving, at four hundred miles an hour, without ever cutting out, heading like all mad anger unrestrained on to the fragile roofs . . .

The wall, like a rubber wall in a Disney cartoon, sprang out at my eyes, bulging round, then snapped back into its flat self. That happened, distinctly. Whether despite the crack it had actually expanded into so round and resilient a curve, or whether the noise and the windclap of the explosion jarred this round illusion within my own round eyes—I do not know. But that happened . . . just as the silence fell again, just as the glass rain spat again, just as an iron tank went tumbling down outside, and—it seemed a long time after the explosion, we were already up at the window—the wall of the building opposite across the courtyard wobbled and then heaved its concrete down on the wounded man and his rescuers below, burying them finally. It seemed, even at that time, extra hard for the man on the stretcher.

Swiftly the life of the house blossomed. The trickling from the pipes gushed free, cascading noisily into the courtyard. Tiles, plaster, gutter fragments and more glass lurched off the roof. A new growth was sprouting everywhere, sprouting like the naked plumbing, as if these leaden entrails were the worm at the core of a birth, struggling to emerge, thrusting everything else aside. But the house held. It must have blossomed, opened, subsided upon itself. We raced down the stairs to the concrete mass below.

As we picked, hopelessly, at the great fragments, it was impossible to forget how hard it was on the man on the stretcher. It seemed, stupidly, that he alone had had no chance.

One Sunny Afternoon

SUMMER, three o'clock, the afternoon: fair weather, no hint of a storm, no presage in the sometimes slight breeze. An ordinary day. Axmann was lying in his bedroom.

Outside the sun glared, dazzling the green-painted window-frames, drowsing the leaves—but this Axmann never saw, the shutters were no more than one inch open. Through slight fissures—two heart-shapes cut in the wood, the inch-wide vertical bar laced with transparent curtain—a weaker light was reflected up to the ceiling, cutting there its incandescent patterns and its filigree pools of lace, diffusing over the remaining room an aqueous dust of greyish, softer light. No colours, no sharp shadows obtruded—Axmann lay protected. And cool. No sound. The clattering in the kitchen had ceased, the sink now would be clean and drying, the plates and cups ranged moist and white on their shelves; the floor new-swept, the draining-board watered fresh as boat-wood. Half an hour previously the back-door had been slammed, footsteps had receded and died into silence. Axmann was thus alone in the house, and felt it. This was the afternoon.

Such an afternoon may be left to continue, may seem without end. Ordinarily there looms a line, imaginary but palpable as an equator, drawn to represent four-thirty o'clock and tea-time. But alone in the house this line that may otherwise be drawn so implacably now fades, dissolves, vanishes. At three o'clock one is safe, one may stretch out on the bed and softly, without dozing, taste all the quietude of this slow, shaded, cleansed, effort-past time of the day. Quiet—though in what at first seems such silence small new sounds soon begin to assert themselves. Linen sheets affirm their rustle; a light low breeze arises from nowhere to touch a scrap of paper by the skirting-board—and then as abruptly withdraws; a dripping tap can now be heard three rooms away, not unpleasantly, for it rings on the tin basin beneath, and irregularly, never crashing the forehead. Occasionally the outside world cries in the distance—a train whistles, a motor-gear grates into motion, a sudden bird stumbles squawking from some bush—but these though louder than the little noises in the room sound nevertheless remote, with neither the impact nor the meaning of the rustlings and scutterings so close. Only when a direct attack is made on the house—the shell of the protective house—does that sound scream into dreadful definition. A knock on the door! The intense electric postman's ring!

But that afternoon no knock came, no ring. Axmann remained alone, undisturbedly resting—and at such an ease that much of existence seemed actually to have been suspended. The small sounds, the light, the idea of time were all held in suspense. That pale light hung with the sense of being absolutely there, fixed out of time, with no dying, no change, no effort to promote further its existence. So the sounds, so the presence of the cool sheets, so the half-open door, so the sense of empty shade in the passage unseen outside. These facts were fixed—there was now no decay, none of the chemistry of all matter changing: the room and·its atmospheres were immobilized, pleasantly frozen in the grey amber of that summer's warm shade.

So for the moment Axmann continued to lie on his bed. At such times it is possible to discuss at length one's own life, to take stock of the whole situation, for here it seems is a pause from which the past and the future, each sufficiently now separated, may at last be surveyed coolly and in some fair perspective. Axmann lay thinking—unashamedly of himself, of what had been and what might be expected.

Expected. *Expected* . . . there grew curiously a division in the meaning of the word, a division that in the mind's eye took on some darkening shape—a division, it seemed, that had to do both with the expectancies of conscious ambition and the expectation of something unrealizable exactly but that one always had known, certainly, would happen. The difference there in the two expectations between the artifice of conscious hope—and the truth, always hinted, never made quite clear, of some deeply set iron-tracked destiny. There was plainly a 'something' that had always been going to happen—an idea, as elusive as it was nevertheless certain. And in this very certainty lay a sense of menace . . . it grew plainer, as the thought developed, as its presence took weight, even as with such a weight its elusive quality perplexed the more—so very nearly did it take shape.

Axmann made no attempt to shake away this growing unease. In some measure a premonitory sadness charmed him —into lying passively, still, surrendered in such a quiet tickless room. Through dozing eyelids he now watched the door; and in the triangle of dark thrown at its slightly open top slowly he became more conscious of the emptiness of the house, the absolute emptiness. But emptiness suggests presence: he began to feel how he was there in one small room at the end of the house, one box at the end of numberless other boxes inter-linked by the long straight passages, all of which were empty . . . all of which were furnished with chairs and carpets and light and shade, but empty of people and so the recipients of presence. Therefore—what might not be happening at the other end of the house, unheard, never seen? What shadow might not be darkening against the wall, what cupboard door slowly swinging open? The silence, the motionless cool light seemed to create an echo as now he began to listen for the emptiness—and as he smiled slightly at such ordinary childish imaginings. But however much he deprecated these with his reason—they were not easy to quell. Childish, ordinarily animal —their essence was strong. Reason told against them. Reason also whispered: 'It has been. It could be. One day . . . one day as to-day . . .'

So that soon, making no attempt in his relaxation to dispose of these fancies, but rather in passivity inviting them—the sense of unease was allowed to thicken. Expectation was chang-ing already, subtly, to apprehension. There came upon the air that physical gloom that precedes an unpleasant visit, the gloom that soon reaches to the pit of the stomach, the phrenic gloom of the dentist's parlour. Guilt—even with the dentist a sense of doing wrong. But guilt of what?

Slowly the sense developed, it gathered a forceful wrath,

it grew upon itself like a grey summer cloud thickening to thunderous purple. Such a sense gathers form . . . yet without shape. And now as Axmann began to watch more closely the top of the door, the skin of guilt imposed on the deeper cause itself intensified and became projected out of imagination into the full reality of predicament. A force of premonition, exactly as powerful as the dread that grips a bad dream, thrust with its full power into the room. (Yet it was afternoon, it was light summer outside, it was pleasantly coolly dusk in the sun-shaded bedroom.)

He never moved. He was concentrating on the top of the door. Since it was already ajar, it suggested an entrance. Immobilized in mid-swing, it seemed to be waiting before the full circuit of its motion should be completed. Above, the long grey triangle of shadow cut clear and still against a plaster frieze—white ivy—and against the cream picture-rail. That place on the wall, that higher reach of the wallpaper of lilacs and pink birds, had seemed to him always remote. Years ago, as a child, he had lain recuperating on the same bed, looking up at the same strange birds and lilac flowers—and even the sad golden sunset moving round the room had never really brought that high and unfrequented place nearer to life. No marks up there, no nails; it was an airless, plastered place, never humanly touched. And now across this desolate wall, this high wall whose lifelessness had so often at sensitive moments brought a melancholy shiver—now curiously there came creeping a strange sense of life.

For a moment it was difficult to know. Then reason jerked suddenly clear. Movement—there was a moving up there. He opened his eyelids to see clearer, closer—and for a further instant as the lashes receded from that muddled, half-dozed focus they flickered and he thought that such a flicker must of course have caused the first movement, out of perspective, so that it had seemed to galvanize the upper wall itself. But then his eyes were widely open and he saw at once he was wrong. There was certainly movement up there. The shadow cast by the door was lengthening, spreading along the wall. Moving then no more than his eyes, with the eye-muscles

themselves already stiffening with dread, he looked at the door.
It was opening.

No sound. It was slowly swinging open. But this time it was
no chance wind, no cat. There was a hand grasping round the
door, a hand wet and red.

One thought, stoney, terrible, crashed down and seized his
brain. . . . Simply: 'It's happened. At last, finally, *it has
happened*. . . .'

This without confusion, in a moment of appalling clarity—a
crystal-sharp stasis of realization, seen as words, felt with the
full weight of a whole lifetime. Now. At this very moment.
No retreat. Nothing but to realize, to go on realizing it, while
its reality grew greater and greater . . . it *had* happened, after
the years of waiting, the long years and the days and the
minutes—after all that spacious time this expected crisis had
finally, finally occurred.

How many times, nervous or upset or suddenly awake from
a dream, how many times had he watched in lonely rooms the
doors of cupboards, of wardrobes, of the rooms themselves?
How many times had they seemed to his childish apprehension
to have been about to open, to whisper forward a fraction—
only to remain shut? And, sometimes, on similar occasions, a
cat had strode forth, a parcel toppled down—to bring what
acute and blessed sense of relief? But this time . . . now
behind the hand behind the slowly opening door he imagined
the perspective of order and cleanliness throughout every foot
of the house, the furniture, the china, the pictures still dreaming in their places, still unaffected—but now forever removed
from him by this that stood between. A great remorse entered
and held him—for the times he had walked about among those
peaceful companionate furnitures and had taken in them no
delight, of them no notice. Given the chance again, the earthly
beautiful chance, how he would work to notice them, delight
in them, love and care for them! But now there would never
be that chance . . . nevermore. From now on, unalterably, the
difference had been driven. This that was slowly opening, this
he had always feared to happen *had* happened. No retreat. No
advance. Only the moment, the rooted tremendous moment.

But the door never opened fully. Instead, with one adroit step, the long step that a figure may make sideways from behind a screen, there appeared suddenly standing there a man—quick, jerked into being by the stride of a puppet. By Axmann's door, against his own wall, within his loneliness this visitor stood and with eyes stared down straight towards the bed. The afternoon light played softly on, the shimmering lace-pools of sunlight shone still luminous on the wall, a picture framed in black hung as usual without movement—yet inter-posed against these familiar hour-long things and the half-dark of the doorway stood this figure! There, sculptured in flesh and cloth and light, with no spectral question, there in the room.

But stood still only for a second—a long second of recog-nition—before it began to move forward across the small room, its two red wet hands raised in a gesture of appeal, or as though bearing tenderly some invisible burden. And from the lips, smiling coyly in a thin butterfly crescent, there came words, crooned and crooned over again with each step forward: "Baby," crooned the lips, "baby . . . dear baby."

Axmann lay concisely frozen. There was no jumping back through the window, no leaping to his feet, no statement of carefully selected words to question such a strange intruder, none of the bravados so rehearsed in his imagination. He lay just still—alert and hardly breathing. A dry oxygen of fear told his gripped lungs that this could be nothing human, that at last, in some palpable daylit form, a ghost in the sunlight had come; that some loss of his reason had made it so—or that there had occurred some cosmic eruption, some change of all things, a rising of the dead, an end to the world on a peaceful summer's afternoon . . . perhaps in the streets and everywhere these things had begun to walk. Doubt turned his senses over—could he have ever known anything, had the old trusted planes never been, had this been happening all the time, was the memory of his old safe room an illusion? But in that long moment of the figure's approach—a moment as long as the reflected pattern on the wall, as long as all such watery delicate sunlight in whose glassy gleam there resided the length of all long dying afternoons, of hours and hours of patient time, of

time of a melancholy length—in that moment he knew that
whatever this visitor was, man or ghost or madness, it had with
portentous certainty occurred, despite disbelief, despite reason,
despite——

"*Baby . . . dear Baby,*" came the soft voice, up and down in
its singing appeal, as though itself were hurt. And in that
expansive time all the features of the mouth and of the rest of
the face, the visitor's clothes and the impression of how he
moved were instantly and in every detail known to Axmann,
exposed instantaneously it seemed on his nerved consciousness
as a photograph on a sensitive plate, all in a second, so that
time still expanded endlessly after he knew all these things.
The small round mouth, its thin faint pink lips wet, curved
into a shape of coy blandishment—that remained nevertheless
in this way so curved and crescented that there was in it a
cruelty, a cat's curved smile, the curved incision of the winking
parrot. And like a parrot in other ways—quite round eyes,
brownish flecked with red, showing a thin line of white all
round the staring surprised discs; and a small nose, suddenly
bent, giving a hare-lipped look; in a white-skinned heart-
shaped face, big-headed and point-jawed; under short,
scarce, nut-brown hair. His suit was dark, hanging loose—as
though he were very thin, thin from the want expressed now
in those raised arms that appeared in some desperate way both to
entreat and to offer. No tie, dust on the shoulders and a sleeve.
Blood gloving both hands.

He simply came up to Axmann, looking down at him
with what seemed a strange unbearable compassion. He sat
down on the bed, sideways, but never letting his eyes leave
Axmann's. He leant over and somehow, for Axmann was not
undersized, took him in his arms and lifted him—like a baby—
on to his lap. More even than his cold fear, those parrot-staring
eyes held Axmann moveless. And the man's arms were like
iron, implacable as iron, implacable perhaps too as the fierce
compassion that stared from his face held slightly sideways.
". . . *dear Baby,*" sighed softly this face above Axmann's, a face
now bigger for being above. And gently, but in that iron grip
tender, the visitor swayed him from side to side.

Even then, awkwardly placed across the lap of another full-grown figure of his own size, arms pressed straightly into his sides, feeling gripped and strangely weak and gangling—even in that unusual position Axmann was not consciously sure that this form holding him was properly flesh and blood. So unpredicted, yet so always feared, this sudden advent and its aftermath still held the continuity of a single episode, a single shocking episode—nothing else had happened, no change, nothing but the smooth completion of the visitor's approach. Thus it was not absurd even to sit on that dusty lap. Once, for a dimly strengthening moment, Axmann opened his mouth, beginning a question, as though seeking consciousness during a dream, struggling against the powerful dream. But then the stranger's eyes had seemed to open a fraction wider, the circling whites had seemed almost to shine—and in this shining there could be felt the expression of love and compassion and yet still at the same time another and an opposing quality, a projection of inexorable possession and a terrible potential anger. Somewhere in Axmann's bemused feeling, somewhere mixed among his lungs straining for breath and his cold milked will, he saw the look of a loving saint, the impassioned cruel potential in the soft eyes of martyrdom; and then also the look of a nurse, yearning down with eyes whose love is near to hunger, whose eyes are never separated from her mouth, whose hands grip too tight.

Suddenly the parrot-face bent closer, one hand crept round Axmann's shoulder still thus enclosing him in the bend of his arm—and picked up Axmann's hand. The eyes now turned and peered down at the hand. A look of unendurable pity passed over the face, the lips still curved upwards seemed nevertheless to droop. Now the voice changed its words and pitifully declared: "*Baby . . . poor Baby. Baby's got his gloves on.*" Then, moving his other hand to Axmann's fingers: "*Take, take, take . . . poor baby's gloves off. . . .*"

He had been stroking and feeling the fingers. Now abruptly the left hand closed over the wrist and the other caught hold of Axmann's smallest finger and pulled. The voice rose: "*Take . . . take. . . .*" The one word came now reiterated with every sharpening tug, rising shriller, punctuated as the pulling grew stronger and more vicious. Then a shuddering effort seemed to convulse and expand the whole encircling body, the voice shouted its one word high, the hands pulled like hands prising and parting a chicken bone—there was a dull snap, Axmann's finger stuck out loose and long. Jabbering quickly the hands caught another finger and were already bending it in its socket when the thunderous impact of that first shocking pain cleared in Axmann's mind and at the same time cleared everything. He snatched his hand free, twisted round and now his face above this visitor jabbed out both hands and gripped the neck.

But the other was still strong, the vice tightened again— though now Axmann too had his grip and a sudden strength. Fear had milked him, now pain got him back that strength. A ferocious strength too, pain-maddened as madness strengthens. And so for a second they sat there, interlocked, the stranger's face comically surprised, with pursed lips still smiling, mocking surprise and sly, archly severe with baby for being so naughty. But then this baby—who was in agony and angry, who saw how much blood there was about, who saw the stranger straight now as a human enemy—this baby was straining with all his painful might at the neck, this baby despite the other's vicious power was succeeding. So that in another moment the parrot-face ceased altogether to smile, grew bright with rage, changed its mood with the fearful efficiency of a nurse who one moment may croon and the next raise the hidden hand in torture as she sees her authority denied—just so the face began again to jabber but now in an urgent whisper. And—fought. They both fought. Though neither loosened their first grip. They only swayed together more powerfully, strenuously tensing the hard muscular strain and heave: not searching for further advantage; but like bull animals locked in a mutual death-grip so that neither moved but merely waited for a weakening.

Outside the window, in that gardened summer peace, in the streets tarry and hot beyond there sounded a sudden commotion of automobiles—accelerations and the shuddering bounce of braked tyres on macadam, doors opening and voices emerging; from somewhere a whistle, running footsteps, the sudden electric doorbell, hammering.

Axmann heard these sounds and the growing hammering on the far front door—but from inside, from inside the muffled quiet bedroom. He kept straining. He saw too, above the whispering face opposite, slightly to one side and above the opening and shutting crescented mouth—that play of aqueous summer light on the wall, fragile and old and caught in its terrible stasis.

The bed creaked. It creaked its message to Axmann's brain, a message of tensions and supports and leverings. Risking everything then, but never loosening his grip, he jumped sideways still sitting but so that his legs took on a new and powerful bracing purchase, so that his feet seemed to grip the floor. For a moment his socks were about to slip on the polished floor; but they held; and Axmann was on top, throttling hard at the parrot-face. Breathing sounded like drumbeating then in the still bedroom, the linen smell gave way to the wet reek of sweat, and all the time for minutes it seemed the bed creaked and the eyes grew wider and wider and looked always with their circling whites more surprised, more as if about to wink like a wise, sly, humorous, cruel bird.

After the police had broken down the door, when they had followed the blood-trail to that room, the stranger had been finished. He was dead. Axmann fainted across him. When Axmann came round, they told him, after certain preliminary questions, that his visitor had been a man who had murdered, some streets off, his wife and baby.

My Tree

IMAGINE my predicament: To find myself in my poverty the owner of a great resource, so great a resource that I cannot begin to assess the final extent of its dimension, which can seem to me only infinite, of endless potentiality—and yet I am powerless even to touch it! I, Peter Wedekind, assistant polisher, twenty-eight years, seated in the garden adjoining my room in this derelict northern suburb!

Behind me lies the room itself, with its stained walls, its greasy couch, its curtains of ragged green tablecloth, its ink-stains, its soiled cups, its breath of damp. The mould breeds in each dark corner, desolate clouds of damp creep up the wallpaper, the little spawns of dry-rot leap unseen from board to board, the crumbling earth encroaches from beneath the boards. Once I measured a little roll of earth that had thrust itself from beneath the loose skirting board—it had advanced an inch in a night! Something was thrusting into my room; or perhaps the earth itself—terrible thought—was on the march!

But here I sit in the flowering summer garden and my room lies behind, almost forgotten. The garden accompanies the room—it is mine, absolutely mine, according to a legal arrangement with the landlord. The grass is mine, the flowers are mine, the anthills, the weeds, the stones, the twigs, the earth. I can do what I wish with all these things . . . I can dig a trench straight across the garden, or, if I wish, I can erect mounds. Then I can raze these mounds to a level, I can administer water and create a jungle of hungry living things. Walking past a bed of flowers, I can run my hand through the leaves and petals. I can touch, I can measure, I can know, I can possess.

Yet, sitting here among the sunlit flowers and the green weeds, the sun never warms me. I sit in the shade.

The shade is cast by the branches of my tree.

Its bole, which must measure three feet across, stands embedded in my earth just a few paces in front of my chair.
From there it climbs to an incredible height, shooting forth
all manner of branches, extending in numberless tiers its
ascending patterns of leaf.

I cannot judge how high this tree is.

I have walked round the houses to the next street and from
there I have seen the top of my tree, which rises as high, but
no higher than the surrounding chimneys. Yet I sit beneath
it, and looking up I try again to estimate its height—but now
it is different, I am lost in the branches and the leaves, layer
upon layer, pattern upon pattern, as they recede up to the
sky, as they achieve so great a height that my eye can never
discern the topmost leaves, as the sky seems to lower itself
towards my tree, so that perhaps—as I sometimes think—the
two meet. Seeing it thus, I cannot imagine that this is the same
tree that only topped the chimneys—and if it was, then which
version of my eyes must I accept as true? Perhaps one can only
judge these things from where one stands from minute to
minute—yet I cannot ever believe that the tree has not its
own true identity, its own exact size, its independence of my
miserable self.

It is such a huge tree, such a giant to grow in this tiny
garden. And it is all mine! It is mine utterly, to keep, to stroke,
to chop. I could go at it with a hatchet, hacking at the bole
so that the bark flies grizzling all around! Nobody in the world
could stop me! No policeman could grip me for touching my
tree, no neighbour could go crying to the authorities. It is all
mine, irrefutable, indefinitely mine. And yet—I am powerless!
I cannot posses my tree, although it is mine. Of course I could
cut at the bark, I could pick at the leaves, I could attach to
my head a dental mirror and scrutinise the inner recesses of
each dark wormhole. But such a survey would contain only
the few feet of trunk immediately accessible to me, and those
few feet represent no more than a fraction, a pitiable fraction
of the whole. I could extend my survey higher from the rungs
of a step-ladder, but even then the fraction would merely be
doubled and thus remain a fraction. I doubt whether any

ladder would be tall enough to reach the top, even a builder's ladder, and in any case I could never climb such a ladder— I have no head for heights. I know so well that if I penetrated to any distance from the ground my mind would wash blank with the grey vertiginous fears, my thoughts would scatter and lose themselves, I would be out of my depth, bemused, giddy, sick with the profundity into which I had entered, and I would be sent clambering to the ground, humiliated beyond belief by my own possession. I am therefore beset with an insurmountable obstacle from the very first—I know myself to be physically incapable of ever understanding my tree. Physically—even on the very lowest plane I am decisively defeated! But that does not prevent me from devoting endless hours to theoretical research, to speculation, to dreams. This I cannot stop. It is too much—to possess and not to know! One is doomed to a life of hopeless speculation.

My garden, you see, is no more than twenty or so feet long, no broader, a mere patch. I value it, but I see that it is finally not more than a patch. And then—monstrous, incredible, freakish—there grows out of this miserable patch a thick tapering trunk of wood and fibre and leaf, so that, perpendicular, it is perhaps four times as long as the flat patch, perhaps twenty times more, and beneath the earth its roots twine, oh—for ever. I cannot see my roots. I cannot touch my high branches. I can walk and stamp all over my patch, but these other things that are mine I simply can neither see nor touch! Never, never, never!

I can tell you—the thought of this has begun to sicken me, to bring the sweat to my neck, sometimes to make me cry with a child's fury. Who knows what my tree is capable of, who knows what I might not possess? Completely unknown to me there may be nests, great nests tucked away in the uppermost branches, even in the lower branches that are carefully screened from me by other branches, still lower, almost accessible! There may be holes in which live companies of squirrels—squirrels I have never seen, whose footsteps will never reach my ears, they are so high, so soft, so hidden.

And sometimes others attempt to penetrate my tree.

Though in their journeys they penetrate higher into my tree than I have ever done, I can at least console myself that their journeys take them only over a single path. They can only know that part of the tree upon which they have actually trodden. I refer, of course, to the cats; often these inquisitive cats can be seen clawing their way up the bark and losing themselves in my leaves. At this point I never fail to experience an unbearable agitation. The cats disappear into my property with their searching eyes, their ready claws; and I—I the owner!—cannot know from this point whither they go or what they see. Later I observe them slinking down, sometimes with a surfeit of calm in their yellow eyes, sometimes running down the vertical bark in terror, so that the noise of their scampering claws sounds like a single screech of tearing paper. Then it is that they disappear over the wall with little howls of terror. But what have these cats seen, what have they done? Have they found in some crevice a nest of fine fat white suckling spiders and filled with these their silent cats' bellies? Or have they met, face to face, round some strange contortion of branch, a great bird that has flown at them with its red eye, its sharp clucking beak—so that terrified they have fled earthwards?

Yes, perhaps a bird! You see, there are the birds, too. I haven't forgotten about the birds. These birds come from everywhere, flying into my tree, nesting there, hopping up and down my branches, chirping, cooing, invading me easily on their flowing wings; and never telling me, never. For how could they? I do not chirp. I'm no bundle of feathers and egg. I am the owner, the man. Yet these insignificant vagrants know each a little more than I. And what of the larvae, the locust, the rare scarlet butterfly, the ancient kite, the jackdaw's diamond, the murdered pelvis dropped once from an airship and since bleached white in its new crutch of high wood? All these treasures of mine may be up there—all hidden from me, immutably inaccessible.

But sometimes, I forget my irritation with these possible treasures. Then, for a while, I can lose myself in a peaceful oblivion. I sink into contemplation of the great beauty that

resides in my upward leaves. From where I sit, at the base of
the bole—at some point about the middle of the tree with the
unseen roots beneath and the ascending trunk above—there
I can see quite clearly a certain proportion of my tree. That
part is no mystery. The mystery begins above and below this
point. As for the roots—I can dismiss these with a certain peace
of mind; that is because they are beneath me, and for that
reason it seems that they at least are accessible. If I decided
to dig it is quite possible that finally I would unearth each
root, even unto each thin white fibrous end. In this way these
roots present the illusion of a task already accomplished—
though in my deepest heart I know that I would never have
the patience, nor indeed the strength, to dig so much or so
deep. No—really the roots do not worry me. But the ascending trunk—that is quite a different matter. In these airy upper
reaches lies my true agony.

How beautiful the leaves are! They are shaped like little
green hearts. As I gaze upwards, a thousand of these are
trellised against the white blue sky. It is as though in the sky
there resided the waters of a distant estuary wandering through
the islands and inlets of a green land. And how green this land
is! The lowest leaves, in shadow, seem to shine with a dead
green, like leaves touched with the phosphorous of twilight.
And higher there are more leaves, whole planes of leaves, upon
which the sun shines from above, so that they appear from
beneath to be liquid and yellow as underwater plants. It
seems as though wet green blood itself shines like a heart-
shaped light from within each leaf. And further, further,
higher, higher, until the leaves are small, flecked with shadows
and touched into fire by a high sun that seems to belong to
.another day altogether. Curiously, this appears like the remembered sunlight of some time of holiday from long ago.
This sunlight is so aerial, so high, fresh, pure—like the crystal
light that shines on the very top of a tall flagpole white against
the holiday blue sky.

And through these green leaves—green as a dry water
rippling in shadow and wind, in light and the interplay of
shining and fading greens, in calm and storm, in pattern and

in sudden gusts of chaos that as suddenly decline into a fresh integration—through these green leaves there burrows upwards the great bark trunk. Black and grizzled, ridged and furrowed with fat bark, this trunk winds upwards like a giant worm searching. It burrows into the green, it seems no longer to support the leaves. And from it spurt auxiliary snouts, its branches, elongated and on the smell. And all around the green leaves play, ceiling on ceiling, devouring the branches as often as they shoot forth. Sometimes these leaves look to me like little green lice clustered round the old serpent, eating at him with their millions of tiny teeth—and yet the serpent continually throws out new limbs as the old are chewed off, for in its stubborn body lie eternal resources, a sluggish yeast-vein of rising sap, an accreting breeding life.

You see. First I think of the leaves as hearts—and the next moment I am talking about lice! The longer I gaze up into the tree the more morbid I become. I begin my contemplation lost in its beauty, I end by hating each leaf with all the enslaved disgust in me. I hate the tree. I hate my own tree. I defend myself against humiliation by hate. I hate because I cannot have, I cannot reach, I cannot know, I can neither touch nor understand nor solve. Yet even so I must continue with my efforts. I must hate and search, and do both these at the same time. Also the beauty, the mystery tempt me . . . and more than this . . . perhaps more than anything else, the thing that tantalises me is the knowledge, an indisputable but utterly unproved knowledge, that hidden in the tree are great potentialities, great resources, and an ultimate meaning that is of essential value. Somewhere in the deep sea of pattern lies a spring to be touched, a leaf to be turned, a branch to be swept aside—and all will be revealed. But . . . though this is possible, it will never be done. At least, never by me. That is the most terrible part. I know from the start that I strive in vain. Yet I must continue to strive. I am a slave to what I have and I do not have it.

The days and the nights drift by. Each evening as I lie on my couch and watch through the windows the setting sun turn my tree from green to black, I sink deeper and deeper into the tireless stupor that controls me. My wakeful hours are spent in ever more feverish speculation. I lie down exhausted, yet constantly turn over in my exhausted mind the barren fruit of the day. Food is no longer a pleasure or a ritual: I do not see people: I take no interest. This maddening tree steals me—why does it stand there? What is it? Why do I own it? To what purpose? These are questions that can no longer be avoided . . . the smaller topics of living pale and disappear beside such fundamental questions. I feel suddenly that at twenty-eight years of age my life is halved, and I only have a few ever speedier years in which to solve the question. There is no time, I must concentrate on the one matter.

Last night I lay down as usual and watched the twilight deepen around the great shadow of my tree. The air seemed to darken and grow purple, yet at the same time the moon rose, and the distant sky grew lighter. I watched the silhouette of the three appear through this alternating weirdness of shadow and cold light. My eyelids drooped. As my vision became blurred, so the outline of the tree grew sharper in the gradually ascendant light. In this way the tree remained constant—yet I was lowering myself into a half-sleep. With a last whirring sigh, as though it were stretching its arms into a yawn, the clock gave a long tick and stopped. There was only silence. It was so utterly silent then that the air seemed to be dripping all around, like a rain of silence. In this still atmosphere I sank deeper into my lethargy, watching the tree, which never once looked at me, but stood out aloof in the night garden. Yet, though physically sinking, though my blood was running slower and my tendons relaxing—somewhere in the core of my neck a stimulation bristled. I grew more and more alert. Perhaps the silence had put me on my guard. Abruptly my thoughts became clear and momentous. They loomed hugely and with absolute definition, so hugely that they seemed in danger of toppling over, like those last vivid thoughts struggling beneath the anaesthetist's cup.

I thought: 'They are wrong. We do not grow old continuously. We grow old only in fits and starts. We grow old only in terms of our realisation of our age. For five years we decay, and then suddenly one morning we face the mirror and see a new face. It is only on that particular morning that we recognise the face, and then only does it become real. So with our minds—we are sporadically waking up to new stages. A cycle of behaviour completes itself, and suddenly one morning we are faced with a new mind. The residue of its memory may not be new, its manner of working may remain the same. But it is new in the only matter that really constitutes a mind—the food it seeks. A mind is a mind not by what is in it, but by what it seeks. On a few mornings in life we wake up with new minds, we are faced with changed vistas, we realise a different plane. Just as if we had aged.'

Either this obsession with my tree had begun a new age of thought, or in that very moment I was entering upon a new phase. The thought was not new, it might have occurred to anyone . . . but, new or old, every thought must at one time be personally realized. And in the moment of personal realisation it must bring with it all its intrinsic shock. A moment of great detachment, and at the same time of great selfconsciousness, it is like the second that curtains the first thoughts on waking from sleep, when the brain acts clearly, yet the self is distant: the self is distant, but it is preponderantly somewhere, and at the time one cannot but be aware of its tremendous power, all its forces can be felt to gather and hesitate before flinging themselves in grand assault upon the virgin brain.

So I realised with a shock what a change had occurred in me—the time for speculation was past! This was a time to act! I decided then, once and for all, upon a series of excursions.

Once and for all I decided to challenge my vertigo and climb the tree, climb to the very top, climb along each branch, scouring with my eyes each inch of bark, leaving no single leaf unscrutinised. But it would be wrong to approach this matter with a ladder, it would lie too far off the trunk, it would bypass too much. No, I decided in favour of staples. I went to the shops to purchase iron staples, prongs to hammer into the bark as I ascend. But alas, the shops could offer no more than two staples. I wished for four, they offered me two. They offered me only half what I desired!

So a ladder it had to be. A ladder—I knew as soon as this certainty was thrust upon me—a ladder that would provide no return. For ladders disappear. Ladders go. It is almost as if, as one ascends, the rungs beneath wither and fall off, the wood itself disintegrates, shreds into a paste of disbelief— how could one have reached so high, on what possible engine? And, in actual fact, as soon as one has left such a ladder for the branches, as soon as the ladder is left untenanted, leaning innocently against a tree—then someone will be there to take it away.

Of course, I need not do this—I could cut down my tree. But would that not in itself defeat my purpose? Would the tree not collapse within itself, would it not begin to change even in its swift downward rush, would it not be a different tree and destroyed by the time it could touch my hand?

I know too that I could come to terms with my curiosity, I could temporise for the rest of my life, I could compromise. But then how sluggish, how deceitful, how impotent life would become! My bones would grow soft.

I could move away, I could find another garden . . . but then there would be another tree.

No, the ladder it must be, the climb from which there is no return—and where perhaps there is no destination.

Journey into Smoke

A WIDE fan of sudden bright light unrolled itself against the night as the warehouse to the left of us collapsed. Down in the dark alley it was as though a floodlight had been switched on. Flashlamps and the odd small fires dimmed beneath this blaze of theatrical daylight and for a few seconds the new light held, illuminating our scene fiercely, wavering only as its power increased, as an arc-lamp wavers in its effort towards greater intensity. Not until then did I see that Hegel and Sid were standing ankle-deep in a dark red slime.

I had heard that one of the heavier aerial mines had fallen elsewhere in the district, but, of course, I had never expected to see anything like the stuff that clung around those two pairs of boots in front of me. Instinctively, I glanced down at my hands. I had been straightening up hose on the ground and naturally my hands had felt wet. But now, in that bright light, stretched out in front of me, fingers taut and spread in the nervous moment—those might not have been my hands at all. They were two new hands that had by chance nestled into the cuffs of my tunic. They seemed to be wearing skin-tight red rubber gloves that glistened wetly, like the gloves of a surgeon, like the oiled body of a camera nude. The thought came to me, slyly, almost humorously, that I ought to retch. On such occasions, I thought, people retch. But standing there in the company of my red hands, I had no desire whatsoever to retch. At a moment like this, the stomach really disappears and one is all head. These moments, reputedly so subjective, sometimes produce a most immaculate detachment. So I just stood there, independent of time, suspended in that sudden sphere of momentary light, absorbing the whole scene upon the clear and leisurely film of a detached mind.

There are painters who rely upon a fairly abstract combination of textures to define the composition of their pictures. Our floodlit alley-way appeared then to be very much like one of these pictures. For a moment it lost its reason and became a startling erection of thick pigments. Straight ahead, a high bare wall, scarred by blast and splinter, washed by huge streaks of pulverised brick and plaster, so that the regular mortar lines had disappeared and all that remained was a high mass of brown and pink. At the bottom a regular square of black was the doorway through which we had been ordered to enter. Then the dry pink abruptly stopped as that wetly varnished rich red plane upon which we were standing flushed across a straight horizon two-thirds down the canvas. And then there was nothing else in the foreground but the rich mass of dully glistening red. Otherwise, a hazed brushing of smoke here and there; one darker streak of blacker smoke that bubbled up from the dark square doorway. And somewhere the silhouetted figures of Hegel and Sid, although these were of no significance.

The light went out. Reality reasserted itself. The flashlights relit themselves, torch beams filtered between the darkly moving shapes of firemen, mutterings and shouts and the sludge of heavy boots were switched on by the dark like a sound track. It was cold again and it was wet. I wiped my hand up against my legging and felt it stick to the oilskin. At the same moment I smelt a thick smell that was gassing up from the ground. I knew then that this ankle-deep slime was nothing worse than molasses. A bomb had blown a dump of molasses across the alley.

Now Hegel, Sid and I were up against the doorway that led to our job. None of us knew what the job was. An officer had doubled up to us and he had just pointed down the alley to this door and said: "Get in there—quick. They want hands in there—and quick!" Then, as if he had never seen us, he had gone running up the alley. I don't think he had actually stopped moving at all. In the white mist of smoke we had only recognized him as an officer by the glint of fireglow on his brass epaulette. And so there we were, up against the black square opening, smelling closely the thick smoke that bubbled out of it.

A foot of draught blew below the smoke and we could just

see that there was no floor within the doorway. There were only some steep steps. The building looked like a kind of warehouse and this doorway probably led straight into a large vault. Hegel was the first to go down. He went down slowly. It was no use rushing matters when you didn't know where the next boot was going to. Hegel went down slowly into that black hole—just like a diver. Yes, in his heavy rubber boots, with his legs encased in black oilskin, with his thick belt and axe and rope, with his dark high-buttoned tunic and his steel helmet curtained round by a loose green oilskin gas shield, in all this heavy fireman's gear Hegel had very much the quality of a deep-sea diver. He lowered himself slowly, feeling for the steps with his heavy boots, so that it looked really as though he lowered his heavily weighted self against a strong resistance in the bubbling sea of smoke.

He disappeared. Sid—we called him Sidley the Kidley—followed. Sid was one of those spare, tall, big-boned men whose limbs move in all opposite directions at once. He·was as awkward as a marionette, and it seemed that his compact uniform and his boots and his leggings were the only means by which Sid was held together at all. So Sid swayed down on his tall knock-knees and then I followed.

The steps were wooden and rickety. They were steep, like a ladder, so that I had to go down with my back to the smoke and my stomach close up to the steps. As my face came level with the draught of air that always lies beneath smoke, I took a last good lungful of the fresher air outside. Then I was down in the black smoke—and at exactly that moment my boots touched water. I felt my boots slip on the wood and I heard a dull splashing. Three more steps and I touched floor level. The water was well above my knees. I dragged my hand in it and felt that it was warm. Somewhere ahead in the long blackness there was a pretty big fire to heat all that water. In any case it was a big fire to have occasioned the water at all, for this was a lake formed from the accumulated gallons poured in by the fire-hose ahead. I kicked around under the water to find the hose-line and reassure myself that there was a fire-hose ahead. For that could be my only objective. We three had been sent in to help other firemen already at the seat of the fire: somewhere underneath the water there would be a line or two of hose to show us the direction of the fire. That is about the only way of finding your way about in smoke. As it was, the fire was too far ahead to show through the thick fog that blackened everything out. And only rarely could I make out Sid's torchlight—although he was perhaps only five yards ahead of me. We had each to work our way individually along the hose-lines. That was the only way. And at last my boot touched a firm roundness which I knew to be the hidden snake of hose; then I could edge along it, kicking it with the flat side of my boot, holding my arms out in front of me to sense in time any obstruction to my passage, my eyes fixed only on the limited yard of light my flashlamp circled on the black surface of the water.

The smoke, thick and burning with smell rather than heat, kicked at my lungs. I bowed my head against it, much as one bows one's head against a rainstorm, for no effectual reason. The smoke enveloped us absolutely, but occasionally I bent right down to the water's surface where there was a light draught of pure air. But it was impossible to trudge against that weighted water doubled up for long. So that after each breath of pure air I half straightened up again and once more the smoke came swilling and blackening my lungs. It is no joke to walk through dense smoke—when you are breathing heavily under the weight of your equipment, when you are enclosed within a tight, fearful sphere of darkness, when you are in a building that is breaking up, with hell knows what ingenious pitfall quietly awaiting your next foothold. Perhaps the floor just finishes, abruptly, with a deep drop a foot ahead; possibly you'll step into a bucket of acid, or against a machine-saw; or perhaps a naked electric cable lies waiting like the poisonous fin of a hidden stingray.

But just then I remember that despite everything I was thankful for one concession—the smoke was not hot. It stifled but it did not burn. The heat would come only as we approached nearer to the fire itself.

That room seemed endless. I had already kicked and

stumbled through about forty feet of water and rubble, but still there was not the ghost of a glow of fire to be seen; nor were there any sounds of firemen at work—no mutterings and heavings of men straining against the back pressure of huge hoses, no regular roar of water crackling into the fire. Instead, only the immeasurable thick darkness that cloaked us with an oppressive illusion of infinity. Though faintly, from every side, I heard the steady dripping of water from what beams and ceilings lay above; and from farther off, from quite another world, the muffled echoings of gunfire and the bursting bombs. I began to feel lost. I felt that the dark water extended around me for ever. Then I felt that perhaps this was not a room at all —but instead a passage, a narrow passage which was closing in on me as I walked farther along it; soon it would grade itself down to a narrow tunnel and I should be crawling through the water on hands and knees. With this thought I felt the beginnings of panic. I was shut in, enclosed, muffled in a fearful blackness that was airless and palpable. So that I forced myself on faster, stumbling over strange shapes deep in the water, kicking with almost loving kicks the blind hose that was my lifeline and my only remembrance of the free air. I stretched my arms farther forward, instinctively gasping towards the fire for which I now longed. And I caught hold of Sid's jacket. At the same moment he began to curse—a long litany of most definite words that coughed out of him into the smoke and were quickly muffled.

He was struggling hard. By my flashlamp I could see the water churning white as he thrashed it with his twisting body. He had caught his boot in something beneath the water, something that held his boot secretly fast, like an underwater clam. I started to tug at his leg. Now we were both coughing. The smoke was choking us at every sharp breath of effort. Then I bent right down into the water and began to search around his boot with my hands. I felt all the way down his leg until my fingers touched his ankles. And there I found what held him.

In the fighting of fires the unforeseen predominates. There is nothing that might not happen. Apart from the vagaries of the fire itself, one is encompassed by disintegration. One is enclosed by material that is breaking up, perhaps slowly, perhaps suddenly in a quick pang of disruption and relief. The world is warping, blistering, weakening, sagging and falling. The knot of the builder's old artistry is being loosened by slow fingers of heat. And as well as this, in factories and warehouses the fireman must contend with machines and materials new to him, inanimate personalities that must ordinarily be skirted by those who are not their technical masters, and personalities that in the heat of the fire may easily go mad. A lurch against a switch will start the quiet machine rolling, a few hundred gallons of water may swell up a roomful of grain so that the walls burst and the building moves to collapse. But ordinarily these unforeseen enemies occur singly and the fireman's alert sense of the moment has a chance of overcoming their secret attack. In his thick uniform and heavy equipment a fireman feels himself a capable unit; and however ephemeral are the material cloth and rubber, their very weight and thickness together provide him with a buttressing against his elemental enemies, both physically as the uniform gives him a weightier, stronger momentum, and mentally as he feels himself a protected yet aggressively compact unit. But that night, and at the moment my hand touched Sid's ankle, the unforeseen enemies chose to occur together.

Whatever held Sid's foot cut my hand open deeply. This happened as soon as I touched what felt like metal. It happened beneath the warm water, so that I did not feel the pain to its full degree. But before the sharp slicing had tremored away from my nerves—the water suddenly flung itself up at us in one great wave. A white and dazzling light screamed through the darkness. The air and the smoke hummed with the slow crack of a suppressed power exploding. The stone floor quaked and every separate tissue and organ in my body seemed flung peacefully, serenely out of place. Then, after this thunderous, blinding impact—the roof above us began to fall. Its new voice of rending laths and plaster, of splitting beams, of tearing brick and mortar was real and understandable in comparison with the elemental moment before. The pain came back to my hand. Sid's foot had freed itself. Together we ducked. We ducked right underneath the water. And the debris began to fall. It fell away to the right of us and we were not touched.

Part of the roof had fallen and now the stifled smoke rushed freely away into the upper air. In a moment it had thinned out sufficiently for the moonlight to filter through the great hole in the roof. And so we saw each other again—Sid, Hegel and I—three black figures in the calm, ancient light, with the wisps of white smoke still trailing thinly around us. We stood there bent still in our frozen attitude of wonder, still arrested by that eternal second of movement and change.

We were in an immense vault. The roof was high and the far walls were constructed of heavy grey stone slabs. Perhaps they were grey only in the moonlight. For the moonlight seemed to soften even the charred black water that stretched all around us like a deep and mysterious lake. There was no colour in the vault but grey and black, no movement now except an imperceptible thinning of the last white mists of smoke. Iron girders supported what was left of the roof. Iron machinery stood against the walls. Iron, stone and water composed this hard new world. There was neither softness nor colour. And the moonlight deadened further these remote, cold textures. It was like standing in a cathedral divested of the warmth of sanctity, a sacred and cool place with no humanity. It was unreal. Again I began to feel lost; again I felt the stirrings of a rebellious vertigo. The wet, grimed figures of Hegel and Sid looked lonely and helpless. The moonlight had sterilized all sense of companionship. I felt that each one of them was as individually alone and lost as I was. But automatically we began kicking along the hose again towards the grey end of the vault where no fire-glow yet showed. And as I ploughed forward through the water I saw that now the surface was littered with small floating shapes of paper, hundreds of them, scattering the water like a countless flock of inch-long ducks. I shuddered when I understood the surreal truth—they were toffee papers, stilly floating, unutterably forlorn.

Suddenly, from behind a projection far ahead in the wall, a fireman appeared. He came out backwards, almost scudding in the water. He was being pushed back by an invisible force. He seemed to be struggling with something beneath the water. He was bent nearly double and he was struggling hard. And just then—the unbelievable happened! For into that cold vault of moon and iron, through the nauseous smell of smoke and disintegration, braving that fearful atmosphere of unreal things—there came the homely aroma of toffee cooking in a pan! Golden, nutbrown toffee! The thick rich toffee of a schoolday kitchen, broiling away over a cheerful gas with the winter's afternoon darkening outside! The aroma, strong and magnified, came mushrooming over us, warming the air, colouring the greyness, livening the blood in me with its excitement of beloved nostalgias. Hegel and Sid must have smelt it too. For all three of us started forward with fresh vigour. The vault had lost its horror. The air was warm and human. Real things were with us again. I have been told of a single butterfly that cheered an acre of muddied Flanders trench. I have heard a single church bell toll softly over the bombed and burning City of London. Now again a single remembrance of the real life of other days counterbalanced that strange edifice of terror which the night had woven around us. We plunged on through the water, free of the blind hose-line, exerting every effort of our warm whole bodies towards the fireman struggling ahead. I caught up with Sid and I saw that he was smiling. Hegel was nearly running. Hegel was a short man, and when he ran his legs raced in a regular circle, as though he were pedalling a bicycle.

The fireman ahead was still scudding backwards. We threw ourselves on to him. He managed to shout, "Radial branch adrift!" and then we knew that underneath the water the heaviest of all fire-hoses was snaking backwards with terrific force. How he had held on so long was a miracle. The radial branch was a kind of monitor braced on a steel tripod and never manhandled without it. But now, with the three of us throwing all our weight on to it, we just managed to nail it down. Its tremendous back pressure of water tugged like a steam engine. But we held on, sweating and cursing, until at last other men arrived. Then we were able to send back a message for the motorman to turn off the water.

A little later, having rearranged the radial branch, we put the fire out.

The Eye Man

EARLY winter, the sun reduced and distant in a high blue mist. Mild cold cleansing the air finally of the autumn, the last leaves and the dark odours—as though a new atmosphere had blown down from some mineral mountain, clean, fresh, and the sun to help, the sun coldly drying out all those damp gatherings of fallen leaf. The dead pulp of a felled tree, worm eaten ochre stuff that a week before you could have picked out in sodden pasty chunks with a finger-nail—now this was drying and appeared white in the fresh morning's light! Along the avenue the other trees had sprung free of their rags: now they sprayed firmly a new tracery of naked branches glistening, brown and already denticulated with early buds; here and there a few leaves remained, squatting the branches like isolated birds—or, when the sun touched their paleness, pure and solitary as the first leaves of spring.

Indeed, walking up the avenue to the hospital in such a mild, crisp air, this seemed to be some kind of a spring day. The old season was plainly dismissed, the first clean day of winter invigorated both the air and the light. The lungs smelt it, one could drink the clarity of the sky and the whiter look of the houses, the sudden keenness of the trees. Possibly the elation of that atmosphere had much to do with what was to happen: though such air could never really have penetrated into the tiled interior of the hospital, infused as it always was with its own air, quiet, grey, suspended. But perhaps a foundation was laid, a quickening that was afterwards, inside, to be reflected.

At the hospital they were going to look at my eyes. The time had come when my good eyes had gone red-veined and sore: now the specialist was to examine them. Eyes, my vital fish-soft eyes—what would the specialist do? Was there to be a prodding with thin steel picks? Surely . . . the Sister would clip back the lids, exposing the eyes to all light, to the cold

daylight of tall hospital windows, to the aching bright glare
of the lamp intruding across on its white enamelled arm? . . .
While behind the specialist would be moving somewhere and
my body would sit and wait, thinking of the shadow by the
basin behind my eyes, a shadow of hands and washing sounds
. . . who would prepare the syringe and the smarting
drops?

So through the hospital doors, into the grey hygiene where
white tiles and sterilized steel waited quietly stainless or
moved smoothly beneath the grey veil, a veil of a grey so
pale that it could be felt more than be seen—for nowhere in
the hospital corridors did there occur a bright enough light,
all that appeared at first so white lay as beneath a coating of
the finest grey dust. That intendants and nurses walked
quickly and quietly, that the trolleys and body-length chairs
moved on such silent wheels—these movements were also
veiled, hushed in the suspended air. One had to press slightly
on the toes to pass along the stone floors of the corridors, the
ringing of heels would have sounded too sharp a blasphemy.
It came, then, as a relief when the bright nurse whisked up, all
starch and soap and skirts and braced black calves, and
answered my whisper in quite an ordinary voice, neither loud
nor soft, neither hushed nor too cheerful: "Eyes? You'll find
the dentist's room up on the right."

"Excuse me, nurse—it's my eyes . . ."

"You'll see the sign—DENTIST—second door up."

Before I could explain she had gone. So I entered the
dentist's room and sat down on one of the five chairs grouped
round the dental chair.

Those other chairs were occupied. Nearest the frosted window, beneath a sharp northern light paling down on his
boyish head, there sat an old workman. His hair was brushed
like a boy's, cropped at the back, and with one short straight
lock brushed down across the forehead; his eyes shone round,
blue and inquisitive; he had a boyish grin and sat twisting his
cap between his knees. Next to him, a little lady with pained
eyebrows, a down-drawn line of a mouth, wispy eyes and her
neck bent forward as if to avoid some perpetual threat from

behind—all these features were tilted plainly by years of complaint and self-martyrdom; on her head she wore a knitted commando's cap, and when she spoke, in a wavering complaining treble, she never said a word that was not pleasant, polite and cheerful. Next to her another elderly lady—but this one huge, white-faced, silent; she had been brought in by the Salvation Army trooper who was at that moment busying about settling her; finally she was arranged upon the chair with the poise of a stone monument, weighted against the years, massively secure; a card was placed in her hand and she was left, grasping the unseen card, staring at the dentist's chair until some nurse should come and bring her to life. But the lady next to me was different again, she was a 'sporty' one, about forty, with orange cherries dangling above the black fringe that combed across her forehead, with a badly shaved back to her shingled neck; when she talked, she kept winking, she spoke knowingly about 'ones over the eight.'

The five of us sat in an uneasy semi-circle and stared at the vacant dentist's chair. A reassuring dust-sheet draped it; and this white sheet, a slop-pail, the bare atmosphere, and the common purpose that linked us all suggested somehow that we were five people in process of moving house. We had arrived, the furniture had come. This was the hiatus when we rested among the packing cases and looked around with hopeless eyes at the hours of toil ahead.

As I sat down there came a knock on the door and in sailed another, a woman draped in flowing flowered garments, a miscellany of coats and jackets and skirts and overskirts that all seemed to be rather pieces of curtain and embroidered table-cloth than the ordinary stuff of dresses. She wore beads and gold and jet and cameo minutiae—they hung everywhere, from her ears, her wrists, her neck, her bosom. Her pale hair strayed from a loose bun. Her face had the texture of crinkled freckled paper. But the years had left only a vague impression of age, as indistinct as her tiny receded eyes peering red-rimmed from behind a pince-nez. One ear was stuffed with cotton wool. To the other she held poised a curled tortoise-shell ear-trumpet. She pivoted herself on a stick of yellow indian wood, yet managed still to sail, for some reason—it instantly occurred—like a duck with rickets. Yes, this faded apparition of the pale brownish garments whose failing apparatus was patched with so many medical engines —so that one wondered whether she hid automatic steel legs beneath her skirts, whether her yellow hair was a toupet covering the silver plate on her skull—this lady jerked and sailed like a ricketty duck.

(But why . . . why? And then something about her motion reminded me of an earlier scene that morning. In the first place her proportions were anyway duck-like, and the horny trumpet suggested a beak. But above this her movements recalled a visit earlier that morning to the rabbit run. I had walked down the aisle between the hutches, each with its rabbit's shivering nose, until at end I saw a lonely hutch where, among so many fat rabbits' fat fur, something black and feathery whirled. A black rabbit with feathers? We looked closer. It was whirling round in a bath of sawdust, bouncing its plump body about as though it had no legs. It was a black hen. Its legs and its claws were tucked close to its body—all withered, I was told, by early rickets. In fact, a live legless hen bathing in a bath of sawdust. How it whirled and rolled and bounced! Every so often pausing to eye us with a coy red eye, then again tossing its head wildly and scuttering off among the clouds of sawdust. And again it would pause, this time covered completely with the pale dust—and then, with an impetuous flourish, shake the dust away, extend its neck in royal approbation of each glistening black feather, nod, and in the next instant throw itself into the sawdust again with a frenzied cluck of delight.)

She sailed straight for the dentist's chair and arranged herself upon the dust sheet. There she waited, head back on the head-rest, as though she had come to see about her eyes but would make no objection to a dental extraction while she waited.

Suddenly a door behind the chair opened; a nurse's white cap emerged, a puppety finger beckoned to the workman. . . .

Through the thin parting of the doorway, in a bar of glittering yellow light, I caught my first glimpse of the specialist.

It was a bright-lit picture framed by the doorway, the sudden and not unpleasurable shock of finding an unsuspected room recessed within one's own. The man himself sat bowed over his desk, a desk littered with bright things—for a moment he was the waxwork figure of a jeweller imprisoned in some arranged scene. Then the bright alchemy of glittering objects and the warmth of light took charge—a power began to radiate from the rich warm room. A moment before the dentist's chair had seemed a central emblem to which we, the semi-circle of waiting people, had been assigned. But this was changed—all those eyes raised themselves to the door, and there, long after the workman had passed through, they remained.

Presently the workman came out, his eyes watering. He walked slowly to his seat, felt for the arms and sat down again to wait. The small woman in the knitted cap was called—the door reopened. Within the room the figure with its bowed head had never moved.

Presently the door again opened, the small lady came out—her eyes weeping—and the nurse's finger pointed to me.

I had just time to see the Eye Man's head bowed in exactly the same position. And suddenly to recollect, as I placed my hat on my chair, a phrase from some literature on the eye: '. . . the two eyelids form a little recess called the internal canthus, occupied by a small red eminence, just external to which a vertical fold of conjunctiva may often be seen representing the third eyelid of birds . . .' It was possible, they said, now to remove the live eye, to let it dangle on its tendons against the cheek, while something inside the socket was scraped—and then the eye was returned—blep!—to its rightful place. Were the tendons elastic? Was there cutting and bleeding? The small old lady with the watering eyes sat down in a dazed, slow way, feeling with her hands for the chair. I walked through the door into the specialist's room.

He raised his head and half-smiled. His face with its heavy cheek bones and finely-chiselled mouth and eyes called for a

wig and three-cornered hat; there was, too, a triangular
impression—the broad high brow graduating to a slim and
pointed chin—and some sort of cravat and high collar; his
hand that gestured me to the chair performed a highly-
tailored motion; his suit was thick and rich, of a grey that
gleamed; there were things that glittered on the desk before
him, lenses and gold instruments; and the smile ended gravely
against his eyes, so that for a moment among that elegant
accoutrement such gravity appeared as a sneer, until one saw
the pale experience in his eyes and something of suffering in
his thin lips that now courteously said: "Sit down."

I explained my symptoms, the aching, the hours of reading,
the sharp plaster-dust in which one had to work—but all the
time my voice grew distant to me, a comforting hypnosis
seemed lightly to be drugging my defences. The glitter? The
sudden warmth of gold light? The Sister standing behind me,
exerting her nurse's mother-force? The suavity of the Eye Man
himself? Somehow the air was charged, my head became
light and small, I felt grow to an intense degree that sensation
which often possesses the patient waiting in a hospital, the
sense of nakedness, the stripping of the defences.

Then abruptly the Eye Man moved. He crossed his legs,
leaned back easily, extended a hand. A little door became
open, a light was switched on—and there appeared on a
stand a plaster cone inscribed with an abracadabra of black
letters: inset in its own bare recess, isolated on the iron stand,
this surprising object had the significance of a tall cone-
shaped cap covered with cabalistic figures—an object of
geometric mystery, occupied, alone in its recess, existing on
its own.

I read out the lines indicated and then the light switched off,
the door closed. The specialist nodded, digesting me. His very
action suggested the prologue of powers to come—but now
without pausing he flourished his arm again and this time
said: "Sister, those drops, please, cocaine and . . ." The last
words were Latin, and lost after the impact of 'cocaine.'
Already the Sister was behind me, mixing something for a
syringe. Cocaine! Forbidden, dangerous, impelling cocaine

. . . she was pulling my head back, lifting an eyelid, pouring in the glare from the light above and now a more intimate glitter of pointed glass as the syringe inclined nearer . . . suddenly the cold shock of the drops, washing over the glare that swam far off behind so much liquid. A smarting, but only a slight smarting. . . . And as the Sister lifted the second eyelid I heard the specialist say—it seemed from far away beyond the dazing intimacy of eyes and water and syringe and the Sister's huge face—I heard him say: "When the pupils open we can look inside."

I was told to wait in the dentist's room until the drug should have had its effect. Soon I was on my old chair, others were called in, and with watering dazed eyes I waited, faced again by the shrouded dental chair and its yellow-haired occupant still plunged backwards in expectation.

Such an air, indeed, of expectation among all of us. An air that is intrinsically part of the hospital waiting-room, of all the waiting-rooms of surgeries, when people lose some of their responsibility, when they are prepared to deliver themselves into the hands of others, with foreboding perhaps but little real restraint. In these waiting-rooms one is denuded, it is even difficult to direct one's mind, to read the magazines rather than turn the pages. And on that morning, surrounded by patients who seemed not to be of the passing ill, but rather to belong to some infirm circle that had made this room for many years their valetudinarian home—there was in their settling down and informal chat some aspect of the tea party —surrounded thus, the sensation of waiting became extreme. A strange emphasis seemed to be distorting us. I blinked, and looked more closely. . . .

Then what had happened became clearer. Each of us, by now, had received the cocaine drops—even the lady on the dental chair. The drops were beginning to have their effect. It was simply that the pupil expanded to an abnormal size. The eye became bulbous, full of a dark pulpy flower, of the texture of a sea-anemone, luxuriant like a grape. Now a circle of glaucous old frogs nodded drowsily towards the door of their keeper . . . they goggled, they lolled, their huge dull eyes stared listlessly waiting. No blind stare, but a gaze of slow, ruminative motion, as though the blood had run fishily slow and cold—the stare, in fact, of those goggling giants that leer, incredibly human yet monstrous and uneasily ancient, above the carnival. Nor was there any respite, nor was this any momentary illusion that a shake of the head would put right. In the first place I saw them with eyes already dazed, any scene would have appeared out of its exact proportion, distorted, vaguely unreal—as the world appears after swimming under water. But now the drug was growing on us, asserting itself more strongly every moment, so that soon one felt alarmed that the process would perhaps extend beyond the newly-fleshy eyes and creep down over a face of grizzled toadskin.

From then on it was magic all the way . . . surprise on surprise had crowded upon each other throughout the morning, confusing the sensibilities, providing each object and incident with its own obsessive independence. Such feelings could, of course, have been resisted. It would have been possible to have lit a cigarette, to have sniffed and been alienated—by the taking up of a hat and simply walking out, or by a composure towards a clinical regard of such phenomena, resisting the participation of blood and the senses. But . . . a magic was at work, and the nurse again beckoned and I went through the door to the Eye Man.

This time he was standing. Instantly he indicated the chair. The nurse was already drawing the curtains. A lamp, a powerful lamp with reflectors, glared down from the ceiling. It cast a precise circle of light, bright and of solid refulgence, cutting off the rest of the room into shadow. The shadow was black, the curtains beyond, black. Now the specialist was fingering adroitly those glittering optical engines on his desk. I saw them—ranged in a box, preciously set in their velvet slots, row upon row of lenses, fine precise lenses each with a thin golden rim, spectral jewels, ground and polished glass of nightmare acumen. These he fingered lovingly, as a connoisseur, and then with that right hand reached beyond the tray and drew forth another thing, black and shining and intricate. He placed this across his own eye and stepped back into the shadow.

He could be seen vaguely from inside my cone of light—now wearing over his right eye the stupendous black optical contrivance, a monocle built up of a geometric progression of polished black boxes that served some dark central lens, a malicious pygmy camera of unpredicted capability.

Kreeeep! He shot out his hand and brandished before my eyes a glittering gold and diamond jewel, a sheaf of bright flashes infusing the light with sharp irridescence, glittering knives of light radiating from the jewel, each knife defined as a diamond rod, each cutting a coloured brilliance against the shadow tenting the cone of light—a jeweller's shop was being bunched up and smashed into my face with the force of an arclight. My head jolted.

That man's hand, that man's foot! With his hand he presented the jewel as a conjurer presents his ultimate fable, as the mephistopheles sweeps from beneath his cloak his last alchemy, with diabolic grace, with the cruel smile of the trump. And beneath this hand, somewhere through the glittering rays, a foot performed its dance, pointed its toe outwards, leant its ankle elegantly in, performed the pantomime of the dancer-courtier's bow. No longer was this a hospital, was the man a doctor, was the process a refraction. . . No longer was there a relation to fact, it was a mystery, a marvel, a montage of impressions that held the perceptions in drug, and in remarkable free wonder. The black-masked figure of Venice, the chain of gold on the black doublet, the darting sureties of Harlequin, the grand jeweller ensconced over his flashing trays, the elegant pointing of the mazurka-dancers rounding their corner in file, the mystique of all presentation—all that lies in the funnelling cloak, the diamond-coloured limb, the gold rapier, the high black curtain of penetrable velvet, masks and furnaces . . . the alembic of minerals concentrated and chiselled too finely for the spirit's endurance, the dark murder that lies in the rich night behind them.

The light faded, the Sister was drawing back the curtains

and the old daylight washed in like grey-soaked cloth. The specialist stood by his desk, monocle in hand, and he was saying: "Glasses for reading . . . in three weeks. . . ."

But I sat still dazed, only just feeling the daylight beginning to creep through me like blood awakening a numbed limb. It was not yet possible to move . . . and as if he sensed that too, as if he also resented an anti-climax about this daily light, the Eye Man switched on again a fierce yellow globe—the colour thrilled like the lesser dose of a disintoxication—and gave a last flourish to the Sister: "Close his pupils. . . ."

From the Water Junction

I

HOW did the three boys ever come to spend their lives in the water-main junction?

That is a question indeed, although not of the first importance.

Who could really tell how they first arrived there? Perhaps on some ramble through the countryside above, they once ventured into the weed-grown opening of the old sewer. Thence they would have wandered through ancient brick tunnels until by chance they arrived at a point of connection with the modern water-main. Such a connection exists far underground. Perhaps the boys were afterwards unable to find their way out. Or could they have dropped through an open manhole in the road, down some shaft left carelessly uncapped —yet inexorably closed after the error had been made? Not all three of them—surely? Perhaps, then, they were the unwanted sons of wives or sisters of waterboard employees, women who had bribed the employees to carry their tragic sons far from a world which would only reject them, far underground into a forgetful obscurity? Or even—but there is no end to these possibilities and no means by which their validity can be measured. Let it suffice that, for as long as they remembered, the three pale long-legged boys had made their home on the subterranean quays of the water-junction.

These water-junctions occur at all multiple confluences of the great mains. The mains—endless tubular tiled tunnels each as high as a train—gush their water at pressure from pumping stations far away in the hills, so that many thick, fast-moving streams come tearing and bubbling down to converge in one large transparent whirlpool at the junction. With redoubling speed, as though on a helter-skelter, the water comes slipping through the smooth-tiled channels, making no sound at all, slipping silently—until the moment at which it reaches the check of the junction. But then from the wheels, gates, weirs and locks at the junction there is heard a deep submerged rumble, a thunderous churning of heavy water that echoes wetly, like the presage of some mighty rainstorm, up to the tiled dome of the junction ceiling. Above this greatly moving mass of water are raised quays and jetties. These, too, are constructed from the same white-glazed tiles. Here and there are dotted brass turncocks, little bubbling glass cisterns, levers that control and measure the work of all the complex underwater machinery. Such is the water junction, lit by dull electricity, smelling of dried water.

The boys had some difficulty in finding sufficient food. They lived on the mosses which grew in corners, on iron scraped off the rusting pipes, and sometimes on a few crumbs scattered from the luncheon baskets of passing water officials. In addition, they were able to catch a few of the sightless fish and white-backed crustacea that inhabited the slime·of a subterranean river lying nearby. There were passages connecting both the underground river and the ancient sewer with the junction. Thus one can picture the three separate tunnellings really as one—the immaculate water junction, the darkly oozing river, and the dry gravel and brickbed of the disused sewer. It was along the sewer that the boys made their famous excursion.

Do not imagine that they lived an idle life. Far from that— for by some tacit understanding with the waterboard employees, the boys were expected to perform definite tasks at the junction. They were not recognized as employees themselves, they were not granted this security, although they had each been presented with an old uniform and boots. Their tasks were simple manual tasks, but endless, so that finally in some way or another the boys were kept toiling throughout the long underground days. For instance, they were expected to swab away the persistent fungi and moulds that accumulated on the passage doorways. And it was their responsibility to keep the copper pipes painted and innocent of rust. And there were certain turncock duties, certain daily openings and closings of the great lock-gates, or of the underwater teeth of the weir. The wheel-hubs to be oiled, the tiles to be washed with rubber brooms.

It was therefore a long day, a life of days of uncomprehending labour. The boys acted mechanically. Occasional water-board employees came wandering from time to time along the quays that led from distant stations. Their supervision was strict, although infrequent. They were empowered to punish the boys if any of the set tasks had been neglected. And yet, for all the boys knew, these employees might have been as insecure in their positions as themselves! Facing each other in their similar uniforms, it was difficult to distinguish one from the other, employees or boys. Nevertheless, the boys had no means of discovering whether the employees were really superior to them. They dared not even question this fact. They continued to work in their uncomprehending fashion, making no effort to improve their circumstances, although deep within them they were conscious of a great inequality. This sense of injustice derived in no way from a dissatisfaction with their personal conditions, which they scarcely bothered to query: but it was prompted instead by a function of their minds that required all things in the world to be equivalent. They felt a persistent embarrassment that the employees differed at all from them, lived under different conditions, acquired different possessions. They used the employees purely as a measure for their sense of inequality, which was, of course, heightened by the impact of quite small matters—perhaps a badge, a number, or a peak on the caps of the employees, some little thing denied to the boys. For instance, they considered the moustaches of the employees to be an unfair advantage over them. Why should they, the boys, not be able to grow moustaches? And who knew what other greater moustaches might not be enjoyed in the far world of the pumping stations? Perhaps there were men at the pumping stations who wore great footlong moustaches above their lips, and epaulettes of glittering gold on their shoulders!

So the boys thought and envied. They envied every inequality. They felt that all matters should be precisely equal.

Yet without the measure presented by the appearance of the employees, they would probably have been content with their lives. They never bothered to question defects inherent in their nature. They were like men who are deeply affronted by the size of the next man's garden, yet never think to complain of deeper injustices, heaven sent disparities—like the intrinsic sadness of their souls. The one—man-made, unequal, unjust, inadmissible; the other—natural, fatal, acceptable.

Nevertheless the boys worked on until at length a time arrived when they were advanced ahead of their schedule; then they decided to leave the water junction and enjoy an excursion. They were prompted by curiosity, natural boyish ambition, and not a little of the dissatisfaction that invited them to investigate other worlds.

So one day, early in the electrically-lit morning, they set off down the passage that led to the ancient sewer. They chose that way not because it was old, but because it was a tried way, it had been used before, it was an accepted route that must lead somewhere.

Dark in the sewer way. Cold damp, the crumbling damp of old brick walls, the draughty damp of growing soil and powdering mortar. It was as well the boys were well wrapped. They wore thick black sweaters beneath their dark uniform coats. Egon, their leader—for of the three there was necessarily one whose personal force thrust him forward—Egon carried their only lamp, a spluttering oil lantern that cast swinging shadows on the brick walls and the beaten earth. They walked in single file, slowly, for the way was uncertain. No one talked much. Occasionally Egon would warn those behind of a crevass, or of a sudden brick promontory. Or he would summon a hasty conference to decide which turning of a fork should be taken. Several times the tunnel branched into two or three separate passage-ways each running in a different direction: but it was really unnecessary even to confer on their direction, for each tunnel was either indistinguishable from the other, or so sharply distinguished that one could tell at a glance which was the main sewer and which the tributaries. Since the object of the excursion itself was almost indefinable, since what propelled the boys was vaguely a desire to find something else that only they believed existed— then roughly this something would be most likely to occur along the main tunnelling, rather than among the tributaries.

So they clumped forward slowly in their square-footed boots, their white faces showing little expression, their eyes, nearly blind from so long a divorce from the daylight, scarcely flickering with any interest. They were not concerned to see a curious iron ring jutting from the brick, or a giant cluster of white fungus, or even the hoop of a rotted barrel thrusting from a patch of weed. Such things, of interest to other travellers, could not concern them, for the interest that moved them was too deep, a profound yearning that superseded all sensations purely of the moment. Inside each of them was the picture of a waterboard employee's golden badge, glittering with its light of inequality. How could such a light illumine a face? No, the three boys strode on set in their faces, with eyes dulled by years of colourless labour, with premature lines graining their white foreheads, with thin mouths lipless from lack of anything to savour. Only—their chins were set, their heads bent forward, and in the methodical clumping of their boots was a leaden determination to progress. That was their only expression. They were marching forward. To what, they scarcely guessed. But forward they moved.

At seven o'clock that evening one of the boys—the second in the line—cried out suddenly with pain. The others stopped. In the dark he sobbed, and Egon swung the lantern over him.

The third boy looked up at Egon, who stood frowning in the wan light of the lantern. He looked at the bowed head of the boy on the ground, and then glanced quickly along the tunnel. Egon suddenly raised the lantern high and peered also in the direction in which they were bound. The tunnel was dark, there was nothing to be seen except the rounded brick roofing, a few thin weeds, the gloom beyond. Yet that very gloom, that deepening dark circle, contained somewhere their aspirations. For a second, in the terrible quiet of the tunnel, the two boys stared forward. In each heart there still glittered the idea of those golden badges—in each heart separately. For although the boys worked and lived together, their hearts were still separate organs, each heart contrived its own desire, each considered the possibility of a golden badge quite separately and personally. Why would the hearts have worked together? True, their aim was the same, a similar idea propelled the emotions of each boy—but each heart in each boy remained, nevertheless, an entirely separate organism, each an individual. Each individual boy's heart beat for its own boy—and not for an idea that controlled all boys. Indeed, the idea was there, but could it ever propel anything but individuals?

So each boy's heart beat in the silent tunnel. One boy on the chilled earth, sobbing, and for the moment lost to all other desire but freedom from the pain that tore at his foot. And the other two boys staring into the darkness that beckoned so forcibly, Egon with his lantern high, the third boy gripping his satchel of food, each with his boot poised for the journey. For hours now they had walked that way. For hours the deepest yearning in each personal heart had drawn them on through the darkness. Yet suddenly Egon lowered the lantern, and without a word exchanged, he and his comrade tenderly lifted the wounded boy and laid him out straight.

Quietly they put down their food satchels. They massaged the twisted tendon. They lay down beside him for the night. They stayed there for perhaps three or four days—time was barely distinguishable in that desolate place—without complaining, scarcely commenting on their delay, only nursing the wounded limb to health. Miraculously two strong personal ambitions, those that are said to be the motors of all individual hearts, without which, in fact, the individual simply does not exist—two famous inalienable human egoisms had been discarded. Two hearts had automatically sacrificed their desires, bending suddenly their pulsing towards another without whom they could well have walked forward. There was no sentimental cause. Though their lives had been led together at the water junction, the boys had no love for each other beyond their common association with the quays. That closeness, indeed, had established a contact between them—but a common interest does not necessarily beget more profound obligations than those of the moment.

No, it seemed that suddenly the boys threw aside their selfish desires and worked for the common good. And yet—could that have been so? Could three hearts have been beating as one? It is unlikely. One would imagine rather that the hearts still continued to beat separately, yet acted in unison. Then—were the separate hearts still beating each its own secret anthem of personal desire? For instance, one heart might have recognised in the wounded sobbing a cry, a piti-fully slow pulsing that could have been its own : this heart had hastened to the side of its mirrored self. Or another heart had leapt at the thrust of some mathematical instinct that had said, 'Three hearts are stronger than one! I must not lose this valuable aid.' And, again, one lonely heart might simply have cried out for companionship, simply for the echo of other heartbeats in that very lonely tunnel. There are cer-tainly deeper instincts, instincts of the herd itself, that quicken the ventricles beyond all purely human endeavour.

Although the mosses and fish in their satchels had begun to dwindle, the boys never considered returning to the safety of the water junction. When the twisted ankle was healed, and Egon was sure that the boy could walk again, they simply gathered together their satchels and waterbottles, drew on their boots, hitched at their waists, and again in file began to plod away into the waiting tunnel. Each pale aged boy's face peered forward into the lantern's swinging light, each neck bowed itself again to the oppressive darkness. Yet—for four days they had been walking away from the water junction. Their satchels were already light. In the dried sewer, water was scarce. Occasionally, a greenish patch of damp smeared the roof and from these dripped a stale dew. The boys could hope for no more than this.

On the fifth day their food was exhausted. They plucked at the bitter weeds and chewed them as they marched. No thought of the unattended water junction disturbed them. They had already outstayed their leave. They should have been working at the levers a full four days before. By now, for all they knew, the huge weight of accumulated waters might be bursting the sides of the main passages. Now the domed junction itself might be a solid globe of churning water, the machinery smashed and sunk, girders and pipes and gates crushed and splintered. And the water, where would that break to? Into the subterranean river? Into the sewer? Perhaps even at this moment the great water they had left unattended might be crashing along the dried sewer to swallow their retreating footsteps in a furious tidal wave. Yet—the boys plodded on, careless of these dangers. Perhaps they never thought of them. Perhaps their cold eagerness for a different future obliterated all other obligations. Or, if the water junction did, in fact, from time to time occur to them, then they said: "Let it work itself! We're on our way out of that old affair!" For they extended their dissatisfaction with the waterboard employees to the whole system, which must for them have somehow symbolized the inequality they detested, although, nevertheless, the water system was at the same time their only source of food, their only real roof, and, more important, their habitual way of life. But it would have been difficult for boys of that age to have realized the importance of custom, clothed as it was in grey water and endless tile, badgeless.

So they murdered their chance of survival. They trusted entirely to revolt. Hungry, parched, they stumbled on after Egon's lantern. Their boots weighed heavily. Soon their wearied legs could no longer lift the boots on them. They limped. The ground sucked at them like a bog, the ground that was really so dry. On the seventh day—Egon saw before him the lowest rungs of an iron ladder.

II

At Seegram's Folly, the Countess of Reval was entertaining. The weird old house glowed with light. Set among trees, in its own valley, its glade, with the yellow chandeliers sending tall light streaming from each ornamented window on to the terrace, across the glittering mosaic terrace and its guardian stone menagerie, out into the dark shrubberies and the speckled willows and the frowning forest behind. Nailed among the trees themselves were gleaming white antler-heads, on which had been strung chains of streamers and little coloured lanterns. Beneath these, two great mirrors placed in the shrubbery reflected the shuddering light of torches that were held on the terrace staircase by goddesses and dolphins of writhed iron. Music seemed to swell the immense carved wood façade of the house, its baroque balconies, its embattle-ment of tufted savage spears. A roman captain strode out onto the terrace, followed by a faun. They embraced, yet were interrupted by a footman in velvet wearing an ass's head, who then served them with glasses and wine.

Inside, Henry Pinip and the Countess were having fun. Henry cowled as a monk with a painted face, the Countess nearly naked to represent a convenient New World. They sat close together on a raised divan: but that was not the fun. The fun was Cardinal Equort, in his own full robes, eyeing Henry's licentious cowl with a glassy severity—yet reeling drunk himself, so that one could not decide whether the glass of his eyes was properly severity or in fact the wine itself. From beneath the hem of his flowing scarlet robe there stuck out a white webbed thing of whalebone and lace that was plainly not his foot—but apparently his stays, broken and fallen in the rout. The Cardinal stared at Henry and swallowed another glass of wine.

Back through the mirrored hall that reflected a thousand other mirrored halls the guests thronged and danced and sat. These were the generals, ballerinas, stock-brokers, women aviators, duchesses—all the cosmopolitan, highly-monied and sensitised acquaintanceship of the Countess. The masquerade was in full progress. The time was four o'clock on the second morning. Music supplied by a quintet in knee breeches and powdered wigs, specialists in swing mazurka. White-clothed buffets still piled high with delicacies, champagne in silver tureens, gleaming aspics, cresses, pink sliced fish, pedestals of rolling purple grapes. Liveried servants in their milk-white asses' masks. Occasionally, grotesque masqueraders would approach these requesting food, drink, bedrooms.

The Countess shook her naked shoulders and dropped a sugared cherry into her glass, lowering her lids towards Henry.

"Look!" said Henry suddenly. He pointed across the hall to the terrace doorway. "Rather good, don't you think? Queer how a doorway isolates a group. Don't they look isolated?"

The Countess spiked another cherry with her lacquered fingernail.

"Isn't it rather the colour that does it? You see, they're dressed in such dark clothes. There's so much colour everywhere else. What are they meant to be, anyway?" She looked into the cowled harlot's face beside her. It peered with its thin nose towards the terrace.

"Highwaymen? Something from Charles, with those top-boots?"

"In those hats, dear?"

Henry arched his thin lips. "Roundheads then? Whoever they are, they don't seem to be moving much. Shall we get them over?"

"Let's. And give them to the Cardinal." She poked another cherry into a mouth, this time Henry's.

"But who are they?" he said.

The Countess shrugged her shoulders and beckoned to one of the footmen. "My dear, don't ask me. What a bore if only one's friends came."

In the doorway the three boys blinked their weak eyes at the dazzling light of the hall. Behind them, the blue shadows of the night, the false greenery. Their boots stood awkwardly on the smooth mosaic floor. But isolated, removed from their background of slimes and dust, they appeared on the smooth floor like artificial boots, like showboots crusted with false plaster mud. And in the rich light, their torn uniforms were again so inconsonant with their surroundings that they too appeared torn, by artifice fastidiously shined and worn.

The boys never realized that they were taking part in an old joke. How could they? They were quite unaccustomed to manners above ground. And none of the guests, nor any of the servants were to realise this either. For at Seegram's Folly a joke of that nature would never have been thought of. This fabulous society had advanced far beyond such banality: so that even if the joke had been pointed out to them, by some outside observer, they would never have been affronted, nor bored. They would have been charmed afresh, so far had they risen, so long ago was it that they had first forgotten even their scorn of the platitudes. They would have welcomed such a phenomenon at the Folly as enchantingly fresh: but in the first place they would never have noticed it.

It had taken the boys some time to gather sufficient strength to climb the ladder. But finally they had reached the summit, to find that the ladder ended in a long brick cellar, apparently part of a honeycomb of foundation works. Then, observing a curious strong blue light above them, they had climbed some stairs, they had stepped out into the moonlight. To them, sub-terranean creatures, there had never been a light so strong, never a country so varied and strange. For a while they stood in bewilderment. Even a pumping station had not occurred to their imaginations in such grotesque terms as this. Their eyes never grew accustomed to the moonlight, so that objects and atmosphere were still blurred to them—yet beyond this they were impressed by a stronger patch of light that appeared a small way along the valley, the lights of Seegram's Folly. They walked towards this blurred radiance.

They had emerged from the basement works of an ancient mill. This lay at the end of the glade in which the Folly had been built. Now they walked along the side of a brook, between the frowning cliffs of dark tree-shapes, until they reached a dyke where the first lawns of the Folly were greeted by a white wooden bridge. Later, at the steps to the terrace, servants had approached and handed them masks. The asses' heads had whispered that the Countess desired the hour to be masked. The boys had made no protest, believing in fact that this was some engine that would improve their sight. One of the wandering waterboard employees had once appeared with a similar strange contrivance, like two small cistern globes, yet of glass, suspended by steel wire on either side of his nose. But the masks gave them no help, except perhaps that now they experienced less bewilderment. They felt that they were being helped. All right, let these strange creatures with the hairy heads help them. It was now easier to see.

The servants had led them to the threshold of the ballroom and there left them.

All these glittering people, this unearthly gleaming radiance, these flecks and clusters of brilliant gold that decorated their clothes! Why, this magnificent pumping station glowed within as if it were one immense dazzling badge of gold! This gilded pumping station, these gold-flecked rotating crowds of proud employees! Was it possible that they, three pale boys, meagre pale underlings, should be permitted to cross the effulgent threshold? Was this possible? Apparently, for the queer creatures with hairy faces had invited them, wonderful creatures with hair, with moustaches quite covering all of their faces! Or—perhaps this was a trick, a torture of hope, so that the cruel employees were in reality merely tantalising the boys with a sight of such superior splendour, so that in perhaps one or two minutes strong armed subordinates would drag them inexorably from the very threshold and cast them back into their tiled prison.

One of the boys—it was Egon again, his lantern now paled by the munificent chandeliers—took a pace forward. Nothing happened! No subordinates rushed forward to prevent them! No—and this, could it be? yes, this was the incontrovertible truth—nobody even noticed them. Tentatively, toe-stepping even in their boots, all three took another pace forward. Still no one turned a head towards them . . . but yes! That is incorrect! Somebody has at last turned a head! They have been noticed! Here indeed comes the first subordinate, a man also with gold on his suit and moustaches covering his face! See how certain they are! They send only one subordinate, they realize their terrible potency, they know that one muscle alone is sufficient to erase these meagre boys.

But we—oh Egon!—we will stand our ground! So near to this badge we cannot retreat! The perils and the fatigue endured, the hope that burns within us, the very forward tendency that aggregates our natures—these will egg us to prevail! But—to strike first, or to talk first? Egon! Make up our minds! The subordinate approaches, crossing the great floor on mincing silken legs, ever nearer, Egon, ever nearer! How will we strike him? Will he understand if we talk? Is it in the capacity of these people to understand the wishes of others, wishes that might cross their own wishes? Can such people ever understand? In silken legs, Egon, he approaches.

III

He grasped the handle of his lantern tighter. He swung it slightly behind him, to bring it forward with the whole smashing force of its iron weight into the ass's face that approached. And this milk-white snout of hair came bobbing towards him, stupidly decorous, with no hint of aggression, a peaceful face riding on velvet and silk and over the serene polished floor.

It drew within distance of the sweep of Egon's arm, and Egon was already bringing the lantern forward when suddenly it bowed itself, as though in deference to the very blow half-struck, and a quiet, firm voice spoke, "The Countess of Reval's compliments, gentlemen . . ."

Somehow Egon controlled the lantern. He kept it from swinging its full arc, so that it circled up well short of the bowed ears and paused then high in the air, as if Egon were in fact raising the lantern high to see the servant better.

". . . but would the gentlemen kindly step over to her ladyship and Mr. Pinip?" Without waiting for an answer, as though everything were prearranged, the creature turned, bowed, indicated the direction of the dais, and began to lead the way. The three boys were astounded. At first timorously, yet strengthening as they proceeded, they trooped across the polished floor. No attack was made. Surely there must be a trick? Surely they were not immediately to be accepted into this fabulous society? But it seemed as if they were even expected!

By the time they reached the dais, all their fears had left them. They walked upright, with no fearful glances to the side, staring straight before them with erect heads into the eyes of the Countess and the painted, cowled Pinip. They noticed that both the naked-looking lady and the gentleman in the peculiar hood were quite hairless, and perhaps this absence of moustaches betokened to the boys a lack of superiority. These were not such fabulous creatures after all! They, too, had their short-comings! The boys were vaguely disappointed to see that even here in the magnificence of surely the greatest of all pumping-stations there were people who suffered the same defects as they themselves, in all their underling humility.

The Countess said: "My dears, I don't know who on earth you are,"—motioning the boys to sit by her on the divan— "but Henry and I—this is Henry, if you don't know him— Henry and I did want to ask you what you are. I mean, what are you? Look Henry, isn't it realistic? Mud, and everything. My dear boy, what are you dressed as?"

Egon looked down at his boots. "You mean—our clothes?"

"Clothes and everything—what a clever white make-up, Henry dear . . . do you see?"

Egon said: "We're waterboard employees, of course." He spoke seriously, perplexed by the Countess' ignorance. None of the boys had smiled yet. They sat blinking behind their masks, straining to see with their weak whitish eyes.

The Countess wriggled her shoulders in appreciation. "Oh, but how exquisite! Henry, I think they're lovely! Water-board Employees—little hairless white old men waterboard employees . . . they remind me of fish, very old fish. . . ."

Henry giggled in rapture beneath his cowl. He ordered some wine. Food was brought, such delicatessen as the boys had never tasted before: and yellow bubbling wine in tall-stemmed glasses. Water had never bubbled so delicately in any cistern, no such fine pink fish as these had hovered in the underground ooze! They sat, the three of them, in a row on the divan, between the Countess and Henry Pinip, and while Henry and the Countess talked and laughed, they ate and drank their fill of the marvellous and profuse new foods. Footmen kept arriving with new plates, fresh glasses. The Countess seldom stopped talking, and then only to lavish upon one or other of the boys a quieter coquetry, her lowered lids, her gleaming shoulder. Henry Pinip maintained a dry witticism, now and again thrusting his painted face from his cowl in emphasis, like a tortoise.

The boys ate and drank. They understood little of the conversation, and certainly none of its implications. They never smiled, their faces remained fixed in the form moulded by their toil. Yet gradually, as the hours passed, their eyes began to function more truly, and they were able to observe closely their surroundings. Sitting on the plush in their rough uniforms, they had felt at first awkward. But as the food fuelled their initiative, they grew more sure of themselves, although they never quite discarded a sensation of being lost.

The morning proceeded. The carnival night greyed into dawn, the dawn grew golden with sunlight. Cardinal Equort was introduced to the boys. Several games were played. The boys danced, ate more, drank more, and joined in generally with the various pleasures offered. In themselves they were a success for their very silence, which was perhaps understood as a sign of wisdom, of dry criticism, even of wit. Their costumes were admired. Received everywhere, fawned upon, feasted, they were refused no delight of the Folly. They were steeped in gold, they kissed the long hair they had coveted.

But towards the end of the second morning—watch Egon's hand!

Instead of reaching for the glass, instead of shading his eye the better to admire the luxuriously curving substance around him, instead of these—his hand descends to his knee. And there on the harsh rubber five dirt-grained fingernails begin quietly to clutch, to scratch, to search for something they cannot feel. They revolve sleepily at first, like slow insect legs. Then, as though accelerated by a growing awareness of the instinct that moves them, like a sleeper awakening, they move faster— until all the fingers are drumming on the rubber, clutching and clawing as if Egon's whole spirit is troubled. And the other boys—one is looking now over his left shoulder and now his right, jerking his head in a startled fashion, as though he, too, is searching for something; the other stares still at his plate of cherries and fish, but with at last an expression dawning on his face, a bewildered opening of his white eyes, as though he expects to see more on his plate than lies there, as though at any moment he might raise the plate and look underneath.

The Countess stands before them, one knee bent, a shoulder raised, and with her face inclined towards them, peering into their masks with her dark, inviting eyes. Standing on her left is the Cardinal Equort, who still drags his webbed foot beneath him, and who glances appealingly to the boys, one plump hand outstretched. Henry Pinip sniggers from his cowl on the other side of the Countess. He sways from side to side, a mobile tempter, while his rouged lips repeat in soft tones an exquisite sonnet. But above this the Countess speaks. "Yes, my dears, this little show is nearly over." She leans even closer to them, the Cardinal's hand reaches nearer, Henry Pinip's voice intones louder—and these three presences seem to enfold the boys in a deepening mist of invitation that looms above them and on all sides. "But the masquerade," continues the Countess, "is only one of many. You must promise me—you must promise you will come to the others. And more than that I would dearly like to extend my invitation, I would like to ask all of you to remain here with me at Seegram's Folly. Perhaps you cannot stay, perhaps there is somewhere else for you—but even so, I implore you, think of staying here with us. The Folly is yours, treat it as your home. Live here, and with all our other friends, we can rest and taste for ever the beauties."

Egon's fingers are clutching nervously at his boots. He raises his face to hers. Now is the time that he must answer. He sits bewildered. In his slow mind great instincts are pulling. Gradually he is realizing the immensity of the future. He thinks, "We three, we three underlings, we have been asked to live on in the pumping station for ever! From now on we can live as great officials! Certainly, it was marvellous to be feasted, to have been allowed even to taste this life for a few hours. But now to be invited into it for ever! Ever since we arrived—it has seemed so easy. Certainly we endured a long and irregular journey to attain this place. But now we're here, we've been accepted. We're offered a life of brilliance, and soon the hairs will sprout on our cheeks. And with the gold badge all the things that accompany it—the coloured foods, the music, beautiful words, all the fabulous sensations that lie in this radiance. This is for us—for we three—for us!" Such thoughts rotate thunderously in Egon's mind as more and more clearly he realizes what is offered. A fever seems to be swelling inside him. Suddenly he feels that so much excitement, such magnificent thoughts will kill him. Yet he forces his lips to speak. He must answer now! They are bending over him. The Countess's eyelids, the Cardinal's hand, Pinip's voice hover across his eyes and hum through his ears. An aroma of delicatessen clouds his nostrils, a silken garment brushes his cheek. His lips stretch to voice what must be the choked beginning of the final affirmative. . . .

But there the lips froze. Two cold hands have grasped his wrists! From each side the other two boys have touched him, hesitatingly, timorously distracting him. But just as the hands have touched him, perhaps even before—for this was a slow minute of imperceptible fractions—a new thought has fused in his mind. Suddenly he has imagined that the tremendous burden swelling within his forehead is not only joy. No, joy alone could not cause this pain. There must be something else. A conflict! Some other wish is fighting mightily against what he thought he wanted.

Egon looks down at his hands. Now they are tearing at the knees of his boots. He watches them. They are moving in such a peculiar way. Those hands are not scratching, not really clutching at the rubber! They are searching for—suddenly he realizes—a lever, a wheel, a broom-handle, some solid stanchion to grasp and work. His nostrils fill with an old smell—the smell of dried water. He hears the churning beneath the lock-gates, the bubbling of little cisterns, the rushing of water. He tastes the sharp rust, the bitter mosses. And a tenderness, perhaps the first he has ever felt, begins to weep in his heart. His throat swells and chokes him, he stands up. The two boys on either side rise with him. They face the Countess, hand in hand, and for a second their hairless eyes cease blinking.

"So—you will stay?" screams the Countess in shrill delight.

Egon can see her no longer. In place of her naked shoulders lies the intolerable vista of white tiles, instead of her voice he hears the thunder of endless waters. These are things that he understands. He began his life with them, his subtlest perceptions are attuned to their song. Although the Countess glitters, although Pinip sings—he will never understand these two. A deep difference of interests, deeper than his reasoned desires, will separate them for ever. His hands itch to feel the textures they first felt. The move of the rhythm of the labour they lack. For deep in all the boys is the instinct to labour. Perhaps their hands are inspired by virgin feeling, the desire to touch the things they first touched? Perhaps an ancient need to strive for each other rises in them afresh? Perhaps instilled in their bones is a sense of retribution, the ancient guilt that if they do not work, they will from somewhere be punished, by human hand, by starvation, by even greater forces?

The three boys turn and begin clumping away across the polished floor. The light from the chandeliers shines for the last time on their worn uniforms, and then the new night takes them. Presently they will be entering the dark foundations of the ruined mill. And then the journey back through the sewer. But this time not a long journey—instead a swift one, a sure journey, until once more they reach the water-junction and the work without which they can never be able even to begin their search for a contentment they may never find.

THE END